THE CELESTIAL GUARDIAN

VATICAN SECRET ARCHIVE THRILLERS
BOOK EIGHT

GARY MCAVOY

LITERATI
EDITIONS.

Hardcover ISBN: 978-1-954123-43-4
Paperback ISBN: 978-1-954123-44-1
eBook ISBN: 978-1-954123-45-8
Large Print Edition ISBN: 978-1-954123-46-5

Library of Congress Control Number: 2024902178

Published by:
Literati Editions
PO Box 5987
Bremerton, WA 98312-5987
Email: info@LiteratiEditions.com
Visit the author's website: GaryMcAvoy.com
R0001

This is a work of fiction. Names, characters, businesses, places, long-standing institutions, agencies, public offices, events, locales and incidents are either the products of the author's imagination or have been used in a fictitious manner. Apart from historical references, any resemblance to actual persons, living or dead, or actual events is purely coincidental.

All trademarks are property of their respective owners. Neither Gary McAvoy nor Literati Editions is associated with any product or vendor mentioned in this book.

This book contains original and copyrighted material that is not intended to be used for the purpose of training Artificial Intelligence (AI) systems. The author and publisher of this book prohibit the use of any part of this book for AI training, machine learning, or any other similar purpose without prior written permission.

BOOKS BY GARY MCAVOY

FICTION

The Celestial Guardian

The Confessions of Pope Joan

The Galileo Gambit

The Jerusalem Scrolls

The Avignon Affair

The Petrus Prophecy

The Opus Dictum

The Vivaldi Cipher

The Magdalene Veil

The Magdalene Reliquary

The Magdalene Deception

NONFICTION

And Every Word Is True

PROLOGUE

FLORENCE, ITALY – 1511 CE

As dawn began to break over a labyrinth of winding cobbled streets and rustic, ocher buildings in the vibrant heart of the Italian Renaissance, the first golden rays of the day pierced the stained glass windows of a particular workshop. In their ethereal glow, Leonardo da Vinci, a genius far ahead of his time, hunched over a wooden desk of ancient oak, its surface worn down by countless hours in the relentless pursuit of knowledge and innovation.

The desk was littered with sketches, quills, and splotches of ink—testaments to a mind that never rested, that dared to dream and transform those dreams into tangible realities. The drawings scattered across the desk contained designs that most could only comprehend in their wildest dreams— bizarre yet intriguingly intricate models and prototypes of machinery unlike any other.

Encompassing him was a dazzling array of his imaginative creations, each a testament to his unyielding curiosity. There were skeletal constructs of flying machines, their vast wings crafted with immaculate precision, mimicking birds in flight. The design was so advanced that

1

one could almost imagine them taking off, soaring above the city, unhindered by the earthbound shackles that limited mere mortals.

To one side lay an innovative design for underwater diving gear, with rudimentary yet ingenious breathing apparatuses, designed to conquer the depths of the unknown sea. Tubes, flippers, and helmets, all of leather and glass, promised a new realm of exploration, an escape from the solid ground into the endless blue.

In another corner of the room, paper plans for advanced fortifications lay scattered across the table. Fortresses with curved walls, designed to divert and dissipate the energy of oncoming projectiles, blending aesthetics with practicality. It was the blueprint of a stronghold, capable of withstanding time and war, its durability etched in the strength of its unique architecture.

Leonardo's haven—his fortress of solitude—wove an enchanting world from the threads of science, art, and an unquenchable thirst for knowledge. It was a microcosm of his mind itself, teetering on the thin line between genius and madness, order and chaos. In this place, the future was conceived in the present, dreams became plans, and plans became prototypes. The air within this workshop hung heavy with possibility, punctuated by the scent of ink, the dust of wooden models, and the metallic tang of his various contrivances.

Everything within that room was a piece of a grand puzzle—pieces of Leonardo's vast, intricate mind, made tangible in wood, metal, and parchment. The bewildering tangle of ideas and inventions stood as a testament to the spirit of the Renaissance and the man who dared to look beyond the horizon. The only constant in this organized chaos was Leonardo himself, a tireless architect of dreams, forever lost in the pursuit of the unattainable.

Set amid the clutter of inventive genius, Leonardo's latest marvel, *Il Guardiano Celestiale*, held a place of distinction. A harmony of intricate clockwork and expert craftsmanship, the device was a magnum opus of science, a physical representation of Leonardo's groundbreaking understanding of the celestial heavens.

Il Guardiano Celestiale, the Celestial Guardian, wasn't just an ordinary mechanical instrument; it was a prodigious orrery, a microcosm of the universe, built from the finest bronze and rich, walnut wood. At its core was a complex network of gears, each precisely cut and meshed with the others in an orchestration of metallic teeth. These gears drove the larger components of the instrument, an array of rotating spheres and dials that gracefully mimicked the heavenly bodies' ballet.

Each dial represented a constellation, exquisitely etched with the most minute detail and gilded with gold leaf, shimmering with a resemblance of the night sky. The rotating spheres represented the planets, their moons, and other celestial objects, like comets, each set in motion with a calculated rotation speed. Every twirl, every rotation, every tiny movement on *Il Guardiano Celestiale* corresponded to an actual celestial event, both past and future.

This intricate device was a remarkable testament to Leonardo's multifaceted brilliance. It combined his in-depth knowledge of astronomy, which he had painstakingly gleaned from countless hours of stargazing and meticulous observation, with his profound understanding of mechanics and mathematics. It was as if he had woven the mysteries of the cosmos into a comprehensible piece of earthly machinery.

One of the most staggering feats of *Il Guardiano Celestiale* was its precision in predicting celestial events. In the year 1504, it had accurately indicated the impending alignment of Mars, Venus, and Saturn, an event that left the astronomical community of the time astounded. Not long after, it had foretold the spectacular reappearance of the Comet C/1506 Y1 (named retrospectively). This was a comet of such incredible luminosity that it was clearly visible in broad daylight, a breathtaking spectacle for all of Florence to witness.

Every celestial event predicted by the device only further validated its astonishing accuracy, cementing its—and by extension, Leonardo's—reputation among his contemporaries. Leonardo himself was in awe of what he had created, a tangible embodiment of his thirst for knowledge and understanding of the universe. *Il Guardiano Celestiale* was more than a machine to him; it was a looking glass into the intricate dance of the cosmos, a testament to the timeless orbit of celestial bodies, and a reflection of man's eternal quest to understand his place in the universe.

As he watched the delicate ballet unfold, however, a chill swept over him. His skilled, albeit aging, eyes noted a troubling future pattern. According to *Il Guardiano Celestiale*, a celestial event of catastrophic proportions was fated to occur in just over five hundred years.

The monumental significance of this forecast struck Leonardo like a thunderbolt, its sheer gravity threatening to pull him into a vortex of despair. His heart seemed to weigh heavily in his chest, the rhythmic beat echoing the dread that coursed through him.

His gaze swept around the familiar surroundings of his workshop, his personal sanctuary where his dreams took physical form, where metal and wood were molded under his fingertips to give birth to future realities. This was a space that had once given him the power of a god, where his imagination could reach the farthest corners of the universe and bring back knowledge yet unknown to man.

Yet, standing before the intricate movement of gears and

spheres of *Il Guardiano Celestiale*, he was painfully aware of his mortality—and his inability to mold the universe's overriding future events. The usually comforting walls of his sanctuary seemed to close in, and the familiar sounds of the workshop—the *tick-tick* of mechanical creations, the gentle rustle of parchment—were drowned out by the echoing silence of the cosmos. He sensed humanity's insignificance and fragility under the vast, indifferent dome of the universe. Each spin and rotation of the spheres was a stark reminder of the celestial bodies' unyielding dance, oblivious to the fate of the mortals below.

A deafening silence descended upon the workshop, shattering its usual tranquility like a fragile pane of glass. The whispers of inspiration, the melodious symphony of creativity that usually filled the air were replaced with an ominous hush, a haunting stillness that spoke volumes as he comprehended the prediction of the world's inevitable end.

Despite the consuming dread, Leonardo found himself unable to look away from *Il Guardiano Celestiale*. His heart swelled with a strange cocktail of emotions—less pride in his achievement than an acute, gnawing fear, a profound awe for the fateful instrument he had unwittingly brought to life. Once a beacon of human ingenuity, tracing the heavens with breathtaking precision, the Guardian had become an omen of inevitable ruin, its gleaming orbs and intricate dials a grim mirror to the approaching apocalypse.

Yet, as Leonardo stared at the Guardian, his mind teetered on the precipice of another revelation. His gaze fell on the meticulous detailing of the celestial bodies, the precise and intricate mechanisms that not only mapped the sky but suggested an intimacy with the stars beyond mere observation. The instrument's depth and complexity whispered of potentialities beyond its original design, beyond what he had initially dared to imagine—a promise of something more, something far greater...

And as he stood there, a new dawn illuminating the dust-speckled air, an even greater chilling weight of realization pressed upon him.

CHAPTER
ONE
ROME, ITALY – PRESENT DAY

The week following the passing of Pope Ignatius had been one of mourning and prayer, an outpouring of grief for the lost spiritual leader. But as the rituals of remembrance were completed, the Vatican transitioned into a period of anticipation, of preparation. A new pope was to be chosen, and the Conclave, the centuries-old process to elect the next Bishop of Rome, was about to commence.

St. Peter's Square, normally bustling with tourists and pilgrims, was eerily quiet. The grand basilica stood solemn against the evening sky, its imposing dome casting long shadows across the piazza. The Swiss Guards patrolled the perimeter, their colorful uniforms a stark contrast against the gray cobblestones, their presence a silent testament to the important event taking place within the holy enclave.

Inside the Apostolic Palace, the atmosphere was a mix of somber reflection and high-strung tension. The cardinals, one hundred twenty in number, gathered in the Sala Regia, a grand room adorned with frescoes depicting significant moments in the Church's history. They stood in silent prayer, each aware of the monumental decision they were about to make.

In the small, well-lit chamber adjacent to the Sistine Chapel, six men sat in quiet contemplation. These were the *papabile*—the cardinals considered most likely to be elected as the next pope. Each brought a different perspective, a different strength, but all shared a deep faith and a lifetime of service to the Church.

Cardinal Eduardo Sanchez from Brazil was considered a strong contender, particularly given his work in championing the rights of the poor and the marginalized. His pastoral approach, deeply rooted in liberation theology, had endeared him to many within the Church and beyond. Sanchez was admired for his humility and dedication to social justice.

From Uganda in the heart of Africa, Cardinal Thomas Akot had earned a reputation as a vocal advocate for the environment, leading the Church's efforts in promoting ecological stewardship. Akot's leadership in interfaith dialogue was also noteworthy, encouraging a sense of shared responsibility and mutual respect among different religious communities.

Cardinal Lorenzo Ricci, a native of Italy, was an influential figure within the Curia known for his administrative acumen. Having reformed several key Vatican departments, he was respected for his ability to enact change while observing Church traditions, though his narcissism and imperiousness made him less popular to many cardinals.

Representing the United States, Cardinal James O'Brien was a prominent theologian who had made significant contributions to the Church's understanding of modern bioethical issues. He was seen as someone who could navigate the Church's path through the increasingly complex landscape of medical and technological advancements.

From India, Cardinal Aniket Patel was renowned for his

efforts in promoting inter-religious understanding and harmony. A scholar of comparative religion, his deep respect for diversity and his advocacy for peaceful coexistence had earned him respect both within the Church and in interfaith circles.

And lastly, there was Cardinal Bennett Dreyfus, who hailed from Canada. A linguist and philosopher by training, his powerful oratory and insightful homilies had earned him admiration worldwide. Known for his diplomatic skills, he had successfully navigated several complex negotiations within the Church, preserving unity in times of potential discord. His approach to theology, blending tradition with select reforms of the modern world, appealed to the more conservative factions within the Church.

However, the potential of Dreyfus's papal robes casting their shadow over St. Peter's Square signified more than a mere changing of the guard; it promised the dawning of a formidable era steered by a man well-versed in the game of survival. His anticipated reign hinted at an era of transformation and progression, yet the exact price of these advancements remained shrouded in the unknown.

Dreyfus had played his hand well in the recent and treacherous interactions with England's Lord Lucius Pelham —head of the mysterious Order of Papal Guardians—but Dreyfus was a chameleon, a master of adaptation. Since that episode with Pelham and the Pope Joan affair, he had quietly blended back into the heart of the Vatican, biding his time within its hallowed halls. Since then, he had donned the cloak of humility, of penance, his actions shrouded under the veneer of servitude to the Church.

Dreyfus had long remained a patient man, his underlying aspirations tucked away within the tangled depths of his psyche, poised for such an opportune moment as this to surface. The extent of his true intentions was yet to unfold, with only time to reveal the intricacies of his veiled ambitions.

EACH OF THESE men had the potential to lead the Church, to navigate the challenges of the present while honoring the teachings of the past. As the last echoes of prayer faded, a procession was formed. Led by the Dean of the College of Cardinals, the cardinals made their way toward the Sistine Chapel, the site of the papal election. The doors of the Chapel swung open, revealing the grand interior, Michelangelo's magnificent frescoes looking down upon them. One by one, the cardinals entered, their red cassocks a bright stream against the marbled floor.

As the doors of the Chapel closed behind the last cardinal, the Conclave officially commenced. With the world's eyes on the Vatican, the cardinals were sequestered, cut off from the world until a new pope was chosen. The signal everyone awaited was the smoke from the Chapel's chimney—black for an inconclusive vote, white to signal the election of the new pope.

Outside, in St. Peter's Square, thousands of faithful began gathering, their eyes glued to the small chimney atop the Sistine Chapel, their prayers a collective whisper in the cool Roman air. And within the hallowed halls of the Vatican, history was about to be made, the legacy of Pope Ignatius about to find its successor in an age-old ritual steeped in secrecy and sacred tradition.

Beneath a cerulean sky, the lush expanse of the Villa Borghese gardens bloomed, a verdant jewel nestled in the heart of Rome. Located on the Pincian Hill, not far from the Spanish Steps and Piazza del Popolo, the Borghese Gardens, covering an area of eighty hectares, were developed in 1606 by Cardinal Scipione Borghese, who wanted to turn his former vineyard into the most extensive gardens built in Rome.

The afternoon sunlight dappled through the canopy of towering trees, casting a latticework of light and shadow on the gravel paths below. In the distance, the echoing laughter of children playing near the fountains mingled with the sweet song of the cicadas, a symphony of life reverberating through the park.

Walking hand in hand along the serpentine paths, Father Michael Dominic and Hana Sinclair enjoyed the beauty around them. Yet inside, each considered their future, its possible winding path, and the life's adventure now before them.

An athletic figure with a scholarly demeanor, Michael bore

the weight of responsibility that his position commanded. As prefect of the Vatican Secret Archives, he was the guardian of the immense trove of knowledge contained within the Church's historical annals—a position that required an extraordinary dedication to the preservation of history and an unquenchable thirst for knowledge. And it demanded he be a priest with all the marital restrictions that had been required for centuries. Until now.

Hana Sinclair, an investigative journalist for Paris's *Le Monde*, had been stationed in that newspaper's Rome bureau for the past several months.

Hana, as a reporter, and Michael, as a scholar of the Church, shared an enthusiasm for history and knowledge that had led them on many adventures in the past. Between their joint interests and close encounters with death in their pursuits, they had grown to be more than friends, yet the strictures of the Church had held them back from the physical passion their hearts desired. Now Hana glanced at Michael. Had time finally brought them an answer to their future together?

On a day off from his duties, clad in light blue jeans, a black polo shirt and a rugged pair of Doc Martens Chelsea boots, Michael was almost unrecognizable from the solemn, priestly figure known to his colleagues in the Vatican. His usual countenance was softened, the weight of his collar replaced with the gentle touch of Hana's hand in his. Hana, with her radiant smile and the warmth in her green eyes, was the perfect counterpoint to the recent melancholy that had enveloped him on the passing of his father, Enrico Petrini, who the world knew in his final years as Pope Ignatius.

As their conversation continued, Michael and Hana slowly waded into the realm of Pope Ignatius's enduring legacy—his transformative reforms that had rippled through the very fabric of the Catholic Church. During his papacy,

Pope Ignatius had exhibited a progressive mindset that was a rarity among the traditional clergy. With a vision far beyond his time, he had sought to adapt the Church to the changing societal norms, to keep it relevant in an ever-evolving world.

Under Pope Ignatius's leadership, one of the most groundbreaking changes had been the dispensation for priests to marry. This decision had caused tremors throughout the rigid foundation of the Church, challenging the long-held vows of celibacy. Pope Ignatius had argued with compelling passion, backed by thorough theological reasoning, that love and devotion to a partner didn't undermine the commitment to the Church or its people. Rather, he believed it could bring priests closer to their congregations, understanding their familial experiences and struggles better.

Michael and Hana, bound by a love that had blossomed amid faith in each other and similarly shared ideals, were living proof of his father's conviction. The decision had been controversial, met with resistance from conservative factions, but Pope Ignatius had stood steadfast, guided by his belief in a more humane and inclusive Church. The fact that Michael had sprung from a decades-earlier liaison with a woman, something held secret until Michael was, himself, in the priesthood, created an undercurrent of unspoken contempt from conservative Church members. Indeed, the pope's decision to sanctify marriages in the priesthood was viewed by many as his way of legitimatizing his own past sin.

In another pioneering—and now always appreciated—stride, Ignatius had also championed for women to assume greater roles within the Church. For centuries, women had been sidelined, their contributions confined to the humble shadows of convents and nunneries. However, recognizing the untapped potential and the need for a feminine perspective in the Church's functioning, the pope had taken steps to rectify this historical oversight.

He had not only encouraged but created pathways for women to ascend to leadership positions within the Church. They were now able to serve as deacons, offering the sacraments of baptism and marriage. Moreover, their voices were included in matters of theological debates and decision-making, providing a broader perspective and enabling a more balanced approach to serving the faithful.

As Michael and Hana strolled through the Villa Borghese gardens, they couldn't help but feel the impact of Pope Ignatius's transformative vision. These monumental changes had altered the trajectory of their lives and countless others, opening doors to possibilities previously unimagined. The world was changing, and under Pope Ignatius's leadership, so had the Church. Even in his absence, his legacy of love, inclusivity, and progress echoed, shaping the path forward.

Amid the tranquil beauty of the gardens, they spoke of Michael's father, each anecdote and memory a bittersweet balm for their shared loss. Hana listened, offering her quiet support, occasionally squeezing his hand as if to remind him of her steadfast presence.

Their steps slowed as the topic veered toward the sea of changes in the Church's doctrines—in particular, the decision that now allowed priests to marry. This significant shift had stirred the stagnant waters of tradition, presenting them with possibilities they had scarcely dared to dream of. Yet the choice wasn't simple.

Hana broached the subject first. "Michael, have you thought more about... the changes? I mean, within the Church?"

Michael glanced at her, sensing the weight of the question. "Ah, you mean the marriage doctrine?"

"Yes." She nodded. "It's a shift of tectonic proportions,

and I can't help but wonder how it affects us. You, especially."

Michael sighed deeply, weighing his words. "It's strange, Hana. For so long, the path was clearly laid out. The Church, the priesthood—these were absolutes. Unchanging. And now, this shift in doctrine has upended all that. It's like someone has redrawn the map, and I'm not sure where I stand anymore."

Hana looked at him intently. "Do you see it as a bad thing? This change?"

"No, not necessarily bad," Michael clarified. "Just different. And different can be disorienting, especially when you've spent a lifetime adhering to a certain set of beliefs."

Hana nodded, understanding the depth of his sentiment. "I get that. We've been swimming in a pool with defined edges, and suddenly someone has removed the walls. We're not sure where to go, or even if we should go anywhere at all."

"Exactly," Michael agreed. "That's why I think we need to be careful, take our time. Understand what this change means, not just for the Church, but for us as individuals. The waves of change are still cresting; we need to let them settle."

Hana smiled softly, though her eyes conveyed something different. "Well... I agree. I suppose we don't have to make any decisions now. The world around us may be changing, but there's nothing compelling us to rush into changing with it. We can be two constants in a sea of variables, at least for now."

Michael felt a warmth spread through him at her words, comforted by the understanding they shared. "You're right, of course. We can be constants, at least for a while. Let the world adapt to its changes; we'll figure out ours in due course."

As they resumed their walk, each felt a silent agreement settle between them—a pact to navigate the changing tides of their lives hand in hand, but only when the time was right. For now, the existing path, however uncertain, was enough.

Despite the conservative nature of their decision, their affection for one another was no longer veiled behind the façade of mere friendship. Their hands remained entwined, their shoulders brushing lightly, as they walked under the Roman sun. Their affection was evident in their lingering glances and the tender warmth in their smiles—a stark contrast to the private reserve they had once been compelled to maintain.

Looming ahead was the result of the Conclave, the assembly to elect the successor to Pope Ignatius. The weight of the responsibility, the inherent complexities of the process weighed heavily on Michael's mind, yet he found solace in Hana's presence.

THEY STROLLED THROUGH THE GARDENS, the sunlight stippling the path before them. The silence between them was a comfortable one, filled with unspoken understanding. Michael broke it, his voice thoughtful. "Do you remember the moment my father announced the changes in the Church?"

Hana's fingers tightened around his in response. "Yes," she said softly. "Even as someone not particularly religious, it felt significant. Like the world was shifting beneath us."

"He had a vision for a more inclusive Church," Michael added, his eyes tracing the pattern of sunlight and shadow on the gravel. "A Church that valued the input of women as much as men. A balance that seemed necessary to him."

She turned to look at him, her gaze steady. "He wanted to create space for voices like mine in a world he cherished. That's a rare kind of courage."

"He also fought to redefine the Church's perspective on love and commitment," Michael added, his voice growing softer. "In a way, he paved the way for *our* relationship, even though we come from different faith backgrounds."

Hana's smile was warm as she nodded. "He gave you the freedom to choose to share your life with someone else. That's a powerful legacy."

"And now"—Michael sighed, his smile tinged with a bittersweet note—"we find ourselves in the wake of his changes, with choices of our own to make."

"And we'll make them," Hana responded, her voice steady. "In our own time, together."

As they continued to walk, their voices softened amid the ancient trees, a quiet testament to the lasting impact of Pope Ignatius. His legacy, while primarily rooted in faith, had reached beyond, touching even those like Hana, who existed outside the sphere of organized religion.

THREE

I n the sprawling, subterranean labyrinth of the Vatican Secret Archives, a vast collection of centuries-old knowledge, Michael Dominic, prefect and guardian of this treasure, stood amid towering shelves lined with dusty parchments and ancient texts. The musty scent of age-old paper filled his nostrils, mingling with the faint smell of the thousands of extinguished beeswax candles that had lit the path to knowledge over the centuries.

This particular morning, while the ancient city of Rome stirred and hummed with life under the golden embrace of the rising sun, Michael found himself submersed in the still, hushed serenity beneath the Vatican's vast Pinecone Courtyard. Most often, his days began before the rest of the world had roused from slumber, when he took long runs through the streets of Rome. But having recently lost his father, he found himself waking even earlier, an unsettled restlessness feeding his wakefulness. Instead of running through the waking city, he now sought silence and meditation, something he would surely find deep in the belly of the underground storehouse that held the Secret Archives, far removed from the hustle and bustle above.

Navigating the shadow-draped, endless corridors, Michael moved with the reverence and familiarity borne of countless hours spent amid the parchment-scented aisles. The dimly lit paths lined with teetering stacks of ancient manuscripts, their leather spines worn from centuries of learned hands, whispered tales of forgotten wisdom. They were his silent companions, his guides in this journey through mankind's spiritual and intellectual legacy. On this day, his morning lauds, besides his usual prayers for others in need, included an aching plea for his personal guidance, a balm to soothe the grief of losing both his earthly father and spiritual mentor in a single death. With faith that his plea had been heard, he had calmed his mind and now wandered the halls of the archives, looking for no more than peace.

On this particular day, his methodical inspection of the Archives' stacks took him down a rarely trodden path. His keen eyes, so attuned to the usual order of things, were instinctively drawn to an oft-ignored corner, a seemingly neglected alcove that lay swathed in dense shadow and veiled in a delicate shroud of cobwebs that glittered in the sparse light like silver thread.

A faint ray of light, slipping through an old, begrimed window—a tiny portal to the world above—illuminated this solitary corner with an ethereal glow. It cast a dance of shadows and light on the towering shelves and painted a soft, luminescent pathway that fell upon a sliver of space between two gargantuan volumes of ancient texts. As beautiful as it was symbolic of history itself, he thought. These books, the forgotten titans of knowledge, stood as weathered sentinels guarding this narrow crevice, the last vestiges of their former grandeur barely visible under layers of accumulated dust.

He gently moved aside the silken cobwebs, considering

the proper cleaning of this alcove, and peered through the narrow gap. His gaze fell upon an anomaly—a small manuscript, its edges peeking out from the shadows. The sight was unexpected, a deviation from the Archives' meticulously maintained order.

With great care, Michael retrieved the manuscript. As he dusted off the cover, he frowned. *Was this…?* Yes, he realized, his familiarity with ancient manuscripts clearly revealed the unmistakable hand of Leonardo da Vinci. His breath hitched at the sight of the sprawling diagrams and the distinctive mirror writing—the secret language of da Vinci himself.

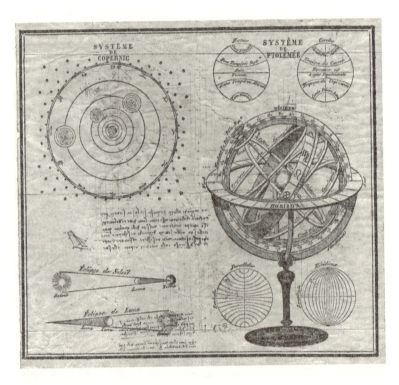

The parchment, despite its age, was in remarkable condition, its surface filled with intricate diagrams, notes, and drawings that showcased Leonardo's unique blend of art and science. The manuscript seemed to contain a series of designs, some recognizable as his earlier works, while others were completely unfamiliar. The centerpiece of the manuscript, however, was a large, detailed diagram that bore an uncanny resemblance to *Il Guardiano Celestiale*. On the reverse were what appeared to be instructions on how to assemble the machine.

Intrigued by this mysterious artifact, Michael slowly traced the diagram's lines with his finger, carefully following the whirl of gears and spheres, the mathematical notations, and the astronomical symbols that adorned the parchment. His mind spun as he tried to make sense of the notes and the detailed diagram.

Could this be a hitherto undiscovered design of da Vinci's famed Celestial Guardian? Historians had found allusions to such an arcane device in previously discovered documents, but only in partial form, nothing to be certain of its actual existence.

Or was this something else entirely—a relic of Leonardo's genius lost to time, now waiting to reveal its secrets?

Michael moved the parchment slightly in the faint light from above. The only lighting, a sliver of morning light that seeped in through the tiny window, caressed the fading ink and cast an ethereal glow on the meticulously detailed diagrams it held.

His heart hammered with a mix of exhilaration and apprehension.

With the precious document safely cradled against his chest, Michael made his way toward his office, his footsteps echoing softly in the hallowed silence of the labyrinthine Archives. The office was a haven of sorts, a sanctuary within the larger sanctuary, where he had spent countless hours lost in the intriguing maze of historical mysteries.

The thick, oak door closed behind him with a resounding

thud, a solid sound that held a comforting familiarity. It sealed him off from the rest of the Archives, from the rest of the world, leaving him alone with the enigma he held in his hands. The room, dimly lit by the antique desk lamp, felt cozier, more intimate than the sprawling Archives beyond that door. And this treasure in his hands might be the perfect answer to his prayers—a validation of his purpose in life while a distraction from the pressures of the outside world.

For Michael, the thrill of the chase was about to begin anew, and the intoxicating rush of being on the brink of a potentially world-altering discovery was an adrenaline spike like no other. The hours ahead promised a riveting journey through time, a voyage of the mind that would span centuries. His future could be set aside as he plunged into this relic's past. He was ready to decipher, ready to unlock the celestial secrets held in Leonardo's manuscript.

CHAPTER
FOUR

T he city of Rome lay bathed in the soft glow of twilight when Michael led Hana to his office near the entrance to the Apostolic Archives, an air of palpable excitement surrounding him. Spread across his polished mahogany desk was the object of his exhilaration: the long-lost manuscript describing Leonardo da Vinci's Celestial Guardian.

Hana's heart quickened as she leaned over the spread of parchment, her eyes drawn to the elegant swirls of mirror writing and painstakingly crafted diagrams. They danced across the paper in a dizzying array of scientific complexity, the marks of the great polymath, Leonardo da Vinci, unmistakable. She had always been captivated by the intrigue of the Renaissance period, but to witness the work of the maestro himself stirred a new level of awe within her.

"Where did you find this, Michael?" Hana asked, her voice hushed. Her gaze remained on the document, taking in the elegant, aged curves of da Vinci's handwriting, the etchings of the celestial device seeming almost alive on the yellowed parchment.

Michael's eyes gleamed in the soft lamplight as he spoke with an air of reverence and a touch of disbelief, marveling at his own good fortune. "It was tucked away in a dusty corner of the Archives."

He moved closer, his hand hovering just above the document, tracing the journey he had taken in the elaborate archives. "I'd wandered deep into the vaults, farther than I'd ever ventured before. That's when I saw it, nestled between two mammoth texts. It's remarkable, isn't it? To think that something of this magnitude was lying there, untouched, unnoticed for maybe centuries..."

His words echoed in the stillness of the room, as if they had been transported back in time, pulled into the currents of a bygone era, into the workshop of Leonardo da Vinci himself. Each line of mirror script, each detailed drawing and complex equations, were whispered secrets from the past, offering a tantalizing glimpse into the mind of the genius that was da Vinci. And now, they had become the fortunate guardians of this priceless legacy, handed the extraordinary opportunity to unravel its story.

As Hana peered closer at the ancient parchment, her journalist's instinct began to assemble a vivid narrative around the artifact. The parchment bore signs of travel and careful preservation. The faint marks of distress on the edges, the slightly blurred ink in certain areas, all pointed to an object that had seen multiple hands and places.

"During the Napoleonic invasions," she began, her fingers hovering just above the document as though she could sense its past, "many valuable artifacts were seized from private collections, from noble homes, and from universities. Napoleon had a deep appreciation for art and knowledge, and his troops were instructed to collect anything of value."

Her eyes were fixed on the diagrams, seeing beyond the lines and shapes to the historical narrative they represented.

"I suspect this was one such artifact, saved from being lost to the ravages of war. Scholars or clergymen of the time must have recognized its value and decided to keep it safe."

She turned to Michael. "They might have smuggled it into the Vatican, considered a sanctuary for knowledge and culture during those tumultuous times. And as the years went by, as wars raged and peace returned, the manuscript was likely forgotten, left to gather dust in the depths of the Archives."

She paused, taking a moment to absorb the enormity of their discovery. This was more than just a piece of parchment with da Vinci's scribbles on it. It was a testament to the enduring journey of knowledge, of the human spirit's desire to protect and cherish our collective past. Lost and forgotten for centuries, it had now been given a new lease on life, ready to share its secrets with those willing to listen.

As her eyes traced the lines of da Vinci's sketches, the details of the blueprint began to unfurl. It wasn't merely an astronomical device. The sophistication of the design was unparalleled, even by today's standards. The device was a mesh of gears and rotating spheres, each representing a celestial body, their movements mimicking the very dance of the cosmos.

Hana's gaze remained anchored on the ancient manuscript, as she gestured to the enigmatic diagrams spread out before them, the dense clusters of intersecting lines, the precise swirls of mirror writing, all bearing the telltale strokes of da Vinci's hand. "Just look at the precision in these diagrams, the intricacy of the construction—it speaks of a purpose far beyond mere idle doodling. Leonardo, despite being an artist at heart, was known for his penchant for engineering and natural sciences. His notebooks are teeming with mechanical wonders, inspired by the rhythms of the natural world."

Pausing momentarily, Hana collected her thoughts before continuing. "What we have here appears to be an intricate blend of astronomy and mechanics. See these rotating spheres?" She pointed to the delicate shapes meticulously etched on the parchment. "They appear to correlate to the celestial bodies. And the network of gears that links them, it mimics the synchronized movements of the planets in the cosmos."

She cocked her head as her gaze settled on one figure, then she frowned. Her pause prompted Michael to ask, "What? What is it you see?"

"I can't say what it is," she cautioned, leaning back to regard the entire document, "but this isn't your typical orrery. These additional components here"—her fingers traced the complex network of levers and pivots—"they resemble early calculating devices. My guess is that they were designed to account for gravitational pulls, orbital eccentricities, and a myriad of other cosmic variables."

"Which we would expect of any orrery, right?"

Meeting Michael's gaze with earnest clarity, she continued, "I'm an investigative reporter, not an astronomer, but based on the evidence at hand, the historical context, and the known facts about da Vinci's inclinations, it's plausible that he intended to construct a predictive device. A mechanism capable of anticipating specific celestial alignments and, just possibly, their effects on Earth."

Now it was Michael's turn to frown. "Like astrology? Assuming the movement in the heavens have a bearing on our human lives? Or you mean like predicting incoming meteors or other direct and physical impacts on human life?"

Hana gazed once more at the parchment. She let the weight of her silence linger in the air between them before explaining, "It appears to me that Leonardo da Vinci, the Renaissance polymath, may have been devising a tool to forecast potential earthly events caused by heavenly movements. Maybe more than meteors or asteroid collisions. And now, centuries later, it's in our hands."

A profound silence fell over the room as they grappled with their discovery. This was more than just a forgotten artifact from a long-lost past; it was a testament to human innovation, a bridge between the past and the future, bearing a message that still resonated centuries later. Had the inveterate logician and mathematician da Vinci fallen prey to an unfounded occult science? Or had he determined the fate of future astronomical events? Amid the dusty manuscripts of the Vatican Secret Archives, they had stumbled upon a piece of history that had the potential to shape their future.

CHAPTER
FIVE

A rmed with the relentless determination of an investigative reporter, Hana threw herself headlong into the mystery. Her laptop became a tool as vital as da Vinci's quill had been centuries prior, the modern echo of his inventive spirit. She began by plumbing the depths of public and private databases, scouring them for any hint or whisper of the manuscript's past. She was hunting for a phantom manuscript that had seemingly slipped through the cracks of history.

Her eyes, hardened by countless late nights spent unraveling enigmatic leads, sifted through a vast sea of data. She delved into antique booksellers' catalogues, obscure academic dissertations, private auction records, and even underground collectors' forums, her digital quest leaving no stone unturned.

It was during one such late-night hunt that she stumbled upon a forgotten auction catalogue from the late eighteenth century. A single listing within the tome caught her eye: *"Complicated Astronomical Manuscript With Unusual Mirror Writing."* Her heart pounded with excitement as she read the vague yet tantalizing description. The listed item's location and timing seemed to dovetail perfectly with their own manuscript's presumed journey, but frustratingly, after this solitary reference, all trace of it vanished like smoke in the wind.

This sudden disappearance, this historical void, gnawed at Hana. She found her mind circling back to her extensive knowledge of history, probing for potential events that could explain the manuscript's abrupt disappearance. Her thoughts collided with a significant disruption that rippled across Europe in that era—the Napoleonic invasions.

Hana recalled how Napoleon's marauding armies had often looted art and rare artifacts from conquered territories, most notably Vatican City itself in 1809. The idea that many such private collections were seized or misplaced during this tumultuous period wasn't far-fetched. In fact, it seemed likely that in the chaos, a document of this nature could have been misappropriated, lost, or hidden away quite easily.

Could it be that the manuscript was seized during these invasions, only to end up lost and forgotten among the complex order of the Vatican Secret Archives? If so, she and Michael weren't just uncovering a historical relic, but also retracing a path through the tumult of history.

To validate her hypothesis, she plunged into the tumultuous epoch of the Napoleonic Wars, hunting for corroborative evidence within a labyrinth of historic records. The trail was a cryptic one, a delicate tapestry of art and literature, interwoven with military maneuvers and societal upheavals.

Her first breakthrough came in the form of a soldier's diary, an obscure relic tucked away within the dust-laden folds of military archives. His candid entries painted a vivid portrait of his life, his experiences, and his encounters.

Pierre Moreau was a rank-and-file footman hailing from

the small town of Blois in the heartland of France. Driven by the stirring rhetoric of nationalism and the promise of glory, Pierre had joined the ranks of Napoleon's Grand Army, eagerly embracing his role in the shaping of a new world order.

Deployed in Italy, he was ordered to seize none other than the illustrious Villa d'Este, a renowned architectural marvel perched on the picturesque shores of Lake Como, the summer residence for Cardinal Tolomeo Gallio, brandishing all the grandeur of the Renaissance era, complete with terraced gardens, ornate fountains, and a majestic view of the lake.

Pierre's orders to seize Villa d'Este weren't random. It was believed that the villa housed invaluable artifacts, works of art, and documents from the Renaissance period, including a secret collection of Leonardo da Vinci's works, discreetly amassed by its previous owners. Napoleon, a fervent admirer of da Vinci and a relentless hoarder of art and artifacts, had directed his soldiers to secure the villa, intent on claiming its rumored treasures for France.

Pierre's diary entries described the villa, its opulence, and the treasures it held, inadvertently offering Hana Sinclair a previously unknown window into Leonardo da Vinci's life and works.

One entry stood out—a note about a *"strange manuscript filled with complex diagrams and mirror writing."* This description was eerily akin to their da Vinci illustration. Could this be the same one? The thought sent a thrill of excitement coursing through her. It was as if a ghost had stepped out of the past, bringing with it a crucial piece of the puzzle.

Intrigued, she probed further into the soldier's life, scouring muster rolls and troop assignments, delving into the details of his service, discovering that after the fall of Napoleon, the soldier was reassigned to Rome and put in charge of a substantial shipment of confiscated items. These treasures, their provenance tainted by conquest and looting, were to be sent to the Vatican, an attempt to safeguard them amid the upheaval of the post-Napoleonic period.

As the pieces began to fall into place, a compelling narrative emerged. The da Vinci manuscript was most likely a part of this art-laden shipment, its importance unrecognized or perhaps just ignored amid the chaotic shuffle of the era. Hana pictured the manuscript, bundled unceremoniously with countless other confiscated treasures, journeying to the Vatican. There, within the hallowed walls of the Secret Archives, it was inadvertently placed, forgotten, its relevance and origins swallowed by the inexorable march of time and vast abundance of other materials competing for precious space.

The manuscript lay hidden in the shadowy recesses of the Archives, buried beneath the weight of history, until Father Michael Dominic, guided perhaps by providence or sheer chance, stumbled upon it. The journey of this historic artifact from a prominent patron's villa to the Vatican Archives, its hibernation through centuries, and its eventual rediscovery was an epic tale in itself—a tale that Hana was uncovering, one thread at a time.

～

WITH THE NEWFOUND knowledge of the manuscript's history and its creator, Michael and Hana were drawn toward an inevitable path, one that da Vinci had walked upon centuries ago.

In Rome, they first journeyed to the Vatican Museums, the custodian of many of da Vinci's works. The bustle of the city fell away as they entered the hallowed galleries, their attention drawn toward *Saint Jerome in the Wilderness*, one of da Vinci's unfinished paintings.

"I remember reading about *Jerome*," Hana said, her gaze fixed on the solitary figure of the saint. "He's often depicted with a lion because of the legend that he removed a thorn from a lion's paw."

Michael followed her gaze, noting the intensity of the lion's focus. "Yes, but look at its gaze. It seems directed toward that rocky outcrop."

Guided by the lion's contemplation, they noticed an unusual, barely perceptible constellation sketched into the rocky background, too distinct to be a mere artistic flourish. From her research, Hana recognized it as an actual celestial alignment that occurred in 1511, concurrent with the "Extreme" intensity-rated Idrija earthquake in what is now Slovenia and Croatia.

"But"—Hana frowned after explaining that to Michael— "da Vinci painted this in 1483, twenty-eight years *before* that earthquake." The two of them stared back at the painting, further entranced by da Vinci's need to display his predictive prowess, even if only to be hidden in a painting.

THE QUEST that began in the Vatican took them through the windswept fields of Tuscany and now brought them across the border to France, to the grand edifice of the Louvre in Paris. Within the halls of this hallowed museum resided a trove of artistic marvels that chronicled the tale of human civilization, from antiquity to the contemporary era. Amid this collection of irreplaceable masterpieces, they found one of da Vinci's most revered works: *The Virgin and Child with Saint Anne*, painted in 1510.

Their gaze was drawn toward another oddly shaped rock formation sketched subtly in the background of this painting.

It was a detail that could have easily been dismissed as an artistic abstraction, but to their now discerning eyes, it was another breadcrumb in their trail.

"Look, Michael," Hana said, her voice hushed yet threaded with excitement, "That formation... it's strikingly similar to the one in *Saint Jerome in the Wilderness*... and the celestial alignment up there... it mirrors the one we discovered."

The connections were becoming evident. The alignment of celestial bodies across da Vinci's paintings wasn't a mere representation of his fascination with the cosmos. It was an encoded message, a celestial cipher that held the key to comprehending the nature and timing of an impending event.

As for the rock formations, their resemblance across the paintings pointed them toward a singular location—Florence. Known as the cradle of the Renaissance, Florence wasn't just a city but a canvas where great minds like da Vinci had painted the strokes of an intellectual revolution. It was there, to the City of Lilies, that their path took them next.

In the meandering halls of the Uffizi Gallery, Michael mused, "Leonardo was telling us something. He was aware of the event... and he left us a trail to follow."

As Hana nodded in agreement, they knew their quest was far from over. The celestial alignment, the recurring motif of the rock formations, were all pieces of a puzzle—a riddle set by Leonardo himself, a warning hidden within the strokes of his brush, waiting to be deciphered.

Stopping in the gallery's gift shop, they purchased a copy of *The Last Supper*, since they weren't going to Milan to see the original. While there, as with other museums, they also purchased copies of Leonardo's other works for easier reference.

"Incredible," Michael murmured, tracing his fingers over

the copied artwork. "Leonardo hid these details in plain sight."

The quest for answers continued, with each subsequent revelation leading them closer to the truth hidden in da Vinci's art. In the faded fresco of *The Last Supper*, an ingenious tableau of Apostles and earthly objects, they found a celestial map cleverly encoded. The precise placement of the Apostles, the very arrangement of bread, goblets, and hands upon the table—all seemed to reflect a cosmic dance. The spatial configuration, when compared to a star chart, seemed to mirror the night sky's unique alignment during a certain celestial event.

Hana carefully mapped out the positions and drew connections, her fingers tracing over the image as if weaving an intricate cosmic tapestry. The thirteen figures around the table—Jesus and the twelve Apostles—suddenly took on a new meaning. Each one, it seemed, stood as a symbol for celestial bodies, their placement a cryptic record of a future celestial alignment.

In another corner of the Uffizi Gallery, they found themselves engrossed in the delicate hues of *The Annunciation*. The angelic encounter, traditionally depicted with celestial overtones, took on a more profound significance. Hidden in the angel Gabriel's outspread wings and the Virgin Mary's submissive posture were echoes of lunar cycles. The crescent-shaped arc formed by Gabriel's wings, the circular halo around Mary's head—everything pointed toward the moon's movements and phases.

The deeper they delved, the clearer the picture became. da Vinci's oeuvre, in all its grandeur and subtlety, was more than just a collection of religious commissions or studies of nature. They were also pages from Leonardo's secret diary, scribed not in ink but in oil and canvas. The maestro had cleverly intertwined his observations and predictions of celestial events with his art, effectively making his paintings a timeless chronicle of catastrophes yet to come.

Leonardo da Vinci wasn't just a visionary artist and scientist, but a harbinger of celestial disasters, his prophecies encrypted within the strokes of his brush. He had left behind a legacy of foresight, a warning deftly woven into the fabric of his artistry, awaiting the discerning eyes of future generations to decipher. They had become the unlikely heirs to this legacy, the decipherers of Leonardo's prophecy. And with each revelation, they moved a step closer to understanding the true gravity of any impending disasters that awaited the world.

Driven by their findings, Michael and Hana pored over da Vinci's art and writings, working against the ticking clock. The weight of the knowledge they possessed was a heavy burden to bear. But they found comfort in the quest, a sense of purpose guided by Leonardo's genius, hoping to decipher the full extent of the prophecy before it was too late.

Their journey into the heart of Leonardo's world had only just begun.

CHAPTER
SIX

As the Tuscan countryside sped past them in a blur of sun-drenched vineyards and ancient hill towns, Michael and Hana sat in the first-class compartment of Trenitalia's Frecciarossa, immersed in conversation.

Scattered around them were copies of Leonardo's paintings they had acquired from various museums: *The Last Supper*, *The Vitruvian Man*, *Saint Jerome in the Wilderness*, and of course, the enigmatic *Mona Lisa*. Each was riddled with symbols, a testament to Leonardo's genius of seamlessly merging art and science.

Hana studied the images intensely. "We've been so focused on the Celestial Guardian manuscript," she began, "but Leonardo's work was never one dimensional. He communicated through layers of meaning. His paintings, his inventions, they're all interconnected."

"True." Michael nodded, his gaze drifting to *The Last Supper*. "The positioning of the hands, the glances... they're all intentional. He was using this painting as a medium to tell a larger story."

"And *Vitruvian Man* too," Hana added, pointing to the figure inscribed within the circle and the square. "It was more than just a study of human proportions. Leonardo was linking the workings of the human body to the workings of the universe."

They fell silent, each lost in their thoughts. The train rocked gently as it sped down the tracks and on toward Rome, the rhythm mirroring the ticking clock in their minds.

Michael finally broke the silence. "We need to build the Guardian," he said, meeting Hana's gaze. "If we're right, if these are all pieces of a puzzle Leonardo left for us, then the Guardian is the key. It's the culmination of his work, the tool to decode his message."

With that, they plunged back into their work, a renewed sense of urgency spurring them on. The puzzle that Leonardo da Vinci had left behind was slowly coming together, piece by piece.

Under the hum of the train and the intermittent *click-clack* of the wheels over the tracks, Michael and Hana's compartment transformed into a makeshift research lab. They cleared their tiny table, making space for copies of da Vinci's paintings, a copy of the blueprint of the Guardian, and their growing set of notes.

Michael, leaning forward, traced the lines of *The Last Supper* with a pensive look. "Do you notice the positioning of Christ's hands?" he asked, pointing at the painting. "Leonardo never does anything without reason."

Hana squinted at the print, her fingers subconsciously tapping the edge of her notebook. "He's gesturing toward the heavens with one hand, while the other seems to point toward the earth," she noted.

"It's as if he's indicating a connection between the heavens and the earth," Michael mused aloud, his eyes gleaming. "And what if that connection... is the Guardian?"

Hana looked thoughtful. "An earthly mechanism to interpret the heavens... it's plausible. Leonardo was deeply interested in the correlation between macrocosm and microcosm."

With a quick look through their notes, she picked out another example. "See here..." She pointed to a detailed sketch of the Guardian. "This gear arrangement mirrors the Golden Ratio. And this principle also appears in the *Vitruvian Man*. He was replicating universal principles in his device."

"The same principles he believed governed the celestial bodies," Michael mused, his eyes transfixed on the elaborate sketch spread before them. His finger delicately traced the intricate outlines of the Guardian's blueprint, following the neatly penned annotations scrawled in mirror writing—a telltale sign of the maestro's hand.

"We know he was deeply invested in astronomy, almost as if he was attuned to the cosmic rhythm," Michael continued, his voice filled with admiration for the Renaissance master. "He, like those of his era, also believed in astrology—how heavenly movements could predict seemingly unrelated earthly events." His gaze was firmly fixed on the layered wheels and cogged mechanisms depicted in the blueprint, an echo of the celestial bodies they were meant to represent.

"Da Vinci was, after all, a polymath. He never limited his intellectual pursuits to one field or another," Hana chimed in, her brows furrowed in concentration as she examined the diagrams. "He blurred the lines between disciplines, seeing connections where others only saw separations."

"To him, astrology wasn't some arcane superstition. It wasn't separate from his scientific pursuits; it was a parallel discipline," Michael expanded on Hana's thoughts. He imagined Leonardo in his workshop, surrounded by a myriad of tools and papers, star charts overlapping with anatomical sketches, botanical studies juxtaposed with mechanical designs.

"He saw the universe as a grand design, complex machinery where everything was interconnected," Hana added. "The stars, the planets, the earth—all moving parts in a vast cosmic dance."

"And so he crafted the Celestial Guardian," Michael concluded, his fingers gently caressing the blueprint. "To capture this dance, this intricate choreography of celestial bodies. To find meaning in their movements, to predict their paths and understand the impact of their alignments."

His eyes reflected the awe-inspiring realization of da Vinci's genius and the burden of his prophecy. Michael and Hana weren't merely observers, but entwined in this interplay of art and science, of astrology and astronomy, just as Leonardo had intended.

Their conversation ebbed and flowed as the kilometers sped by. With each passing landscape, they found more similarities, more points of connection. da Vinci's grand design was emerging, a centuries-old puzzle slowly being pieced together by two eager minds on a train racing through the Italian countryside.

By the time the outskirts of Rome came into view, they had made up their minds. Building the Celestial Guardian was no longer just an academic exercise. It was a necessity. They had a window into da Vinci's genius and, potentially, a warning for mankind. They needed to bring his device to life. It was a race against time, and they couldn't afford to lose.

CHAPTER
SEVEN

There was a newfound sense of urgency that seemed to charge the air within the hallowed halls of the Vatican as Hana and Michael took on the daunting task of breathing life into da Vinci's celestial vision: recreating the genius's masterpiece—*Il Guardiano Celestiale.*

To aid them in this Herculean task, they assembled a team of scholars well-versed in ancient scripts and Renaissance history, along with engineers who had honed their skills on the bleeding edge of technology. Each brought their expertise, contributing to a synergy of old and new, history and future, imbued with the spirit of da Vinci himself.

Underneath the Vatican's serene façade, the underground workshop buzzed with an energy uncharacteristic of its typical somber quiet. Here, within these stone walls imbued with history, a corner was being transformed, replicating a Renaissance workshop reminiscent of da Vinci's own.

A mixture of scents wafted through the air: the earthy zest of freshly sawed timber, the metallic tang of newly machined parts, and the timeless smell of parchment thick with ink. The workshop hummed, alive with the rhythmic heartbeat of machinery, the clatter of tools, and the rustle of ancient manuscripts.

In the center, a table served as the meeting point for minds and hands working in unison. Scholars with eyes squinting behind spectacles pored over the mirror-script blueprint. They gestured animatedly, their fingers tracing the meticulously drawn gears and celestial spheres while engineers, smeared with grease and glowing with enthusiasm, nodded along, their eyes darting between the scholars and the nascent device taking form.

"Look here!" Dr. Giorgio Parisi, a renowned historian and paleographer, pointed to a section of the manuscript, his voice filled with excitement. "Leonardo's notes indicate a unique arrangement of gears to represent the lunar cycle."

Silvano Bianchi, a seasoned engineer with a reputation for bringing life to age-old designs, leaned in closer. His gaze swept over the intricate notes, then drifted to the half-assembled device. "An irregular gear... Ingenious. We'd need to fashion it specially."

The workshop rang with the sound of shared ideas, the confluence of the old and new. Every line of Leonardo's handwriting, every diagram was scrutinized, translated, debated over. The academics, with their understanding of da Vinci's world, conversed in a language of theories and historical context, while the engineers responded in a vocabulary of materials and mechanisms.

"Here," said Bianchi, pointing at another section of the manuscript, "Leonardo indicates the use of a primitive spring mechanism. We could update this with a modern torsion spring for better accuracy."

Parisi looked thoughtful. "Would it not alter the authenticity of Leonardo's design?"

Bianchi smiled, a glint in his eye. "Leonardo was a man ahead of his time. I believe he would appreciate the improvement."

AS EACH DAY bled into the next, the workshop's silence was continuously broken by the sound of progress, the voice of the past merging seamlessly with the language of the present. Every conversation, every solved riddle brought them closer to understanding the genius of Leonardo da Vinci and, through him, the secrets of the cosmos.

The building of the device was a study in patience and precision. The design called for an intricate mesh of gears, their teeth cut to an accuracy that challenged the dexterity of the Vatican's finest craftsmen. These gears, when set in motion, would breathe life into the spheres that represented the celestial bodies, creating a mechanical dance that mirrored the symphony of the cosmos.

Glass lenses, painstakingly ground and polished, were positioned to project the device's indications onto a surface. It was a delicate balance of science and artistry, demonstrating da Vinci's keen understanding of optics.

The calibrated dials, ornate with engravings, provided the human interface to the cosmic mechanism. With each turn, they would engage with the underlying gears, setting the celestial ballet in motion, each rotation, each alignment predicting potential celestial events.

As the days turned into weeks, the silhouette of the Celestial Guardian began to take form. There was a sense of awe among the team, a silent reverence for the genius of Leonardo da Vinci. Each gear that meshed seamlessly, each dial that turned smoothly, and each lens that focused perfectly felt like a salute to the polymath whose spirit had guided them in their task.

The completion of the device wasn't an end, but a beginning—the first step into uncharted territories. The Celestial Guardian, a bridge spanning five centuries, stood as a testament to humanity's endless pursuit of knowledge, bearing the weight of a warning from the past and the hopes of the future.

THE MONUMENTAL TASK of assembling da Vinci's *Il Guardiano Celestiale* was nearing its conclusion. As scholars and engineers added the final components, the device stood resplendent and enigmatic, a tangible testament to Leonardo's genius. Intricate clockwork gears meshed with calibrated dials, creating a network of precise movements beneath a celestial canopy of bronze and glass.

The builders watched with fascination as the miniature planets moved in their orbits, replicating the celestial motions of the cosmos. Their paths were traced out across the polished bronze sky of the device, each revolution a testament to da Vinci's deep understanding of celestial mechanics.

The scholars observed the orchestrated movements with a reverence that was palpable. The clicking and whirring of gears filled the room, punctuating the silence like a cosmic metronome. It was as though they were witnessing the universe in motion, its mysteries unfurling before them within this microcosm.

Each celestial body moved with delicate precision, tracing arcs that mirrored their heavenly counterparts. The scholars meticulously tracked these orbits, the rhythm of the cosmos transposed into the language of notes and numbers.

The dazzling spectacle was more than just a feast for the eyes, however. It was a cryptograph, a window into the future. The alignments, timings, and revolutions were not random but held profound implications. Every orbital rotation, every alignment, was a piece of a jigsaw puzzle that, when put together, painted a haunting picture of an impending disaster.

The breathtaking beauty of the cosmic dance was, therefore, tinged with a chilling sense of dread. The scholars, captivated by the celestial choreography, were also acutely aware of the gravity of the message it held. As they continued to decipher the celestial code, the room hummed with a quiet intensity, for within this awe-inspiring movement of miniature planets lay the potential to predict—and perhaps avert—a catastrophe of, literally, astronomical proportions.

As the celestial mechanism aligned, the scholars consulted their astronomical charts and calendars, anxious to see how close its predictions of the heavenly movements would be to the scientifically produced predictions made from extrapolating known movements witnessed by such scientific instruments as the James Webb Space Telescope. One point after another, their smiles grew and amazement increased. da Vinci's device continued to mirror the known events—minor asteroid hits and flooding caused by king tides—over recent centuries, then over current decades.

Then their fervent discussions stopped as they witnessed yet one more—this time future—event predicted by the device. Their stunned silence as the implications of the alignments began to sink in made Michael ask, "What? What are you interpreting here?"

The device was mapping celestial movements and predicting a future configuration—a celestial event of a magnitude seldom seen. One which didn't correspond to any of their scientific counterpart predictions. Within this awe-inspiring mechanical representation of movement of miniature planets lay the prediction of an event unexpected by today's astronomers.

Dr. Parisi, his hands trembling slightly, broke the silence. "This alignment," he said, his voice thick with dread, "it indicates an imminent event. An event of extraordinary scale."

The air in the room was electric, fraught with a tension that was both palpable and daunting. Years of meticulous research and arduous study had led them to this pivotal moment, yet the nature of their discovery made the triumph bittersweet. Was da Vinci's device fallible? Certainly, modern science would have noted such an impending event... wouldn't it? Yet every past instance of an astronomical event impacting earth had been clearly predicted by the device. So why wouldn't this future one also be accurate? Amid the grandeur of their findings was the specter of impending catastrophe, turning their excitement into a heavy sense of dread.

"What sort of event?" asked Bianchi, his voice barely more than a whisper, his brows knitting together as he braced for the answer he suspected was forthcoming. There was a tightness around his eyes, an apprehension that had begun to creep into his demeanor since they first deciphered the initial cryptic clues of the Celestial Guardian.

Parisi cleared his throat, his normally jovial demeanor replaced by a solemnity that underscored the gravity of their situation. "The data doesn't lie, Silvano," he began, his voice a hushed echo in the room, reverberating off the walls and filling the space with an ominous resonance.

"*Il Guardiano Celestiale,*" he continued, uttering the name with a reverence that was laced with unease, "is pointing us toward a celestial event. And not just any event—one of cataclysmic proportions."

As the implications of his words hung in the air, Bianchi raised his gaze, his eyes widening behind the lenses of his glasses. His hand moved unconsciously to push his glasses up his nose, a habitual gesture that belied his increasing anxiety. His face was etched with disbelief, his mind attempting to reconcile the implications of the revelation.

"You're suggesting..." he started, his voice hesitant, "an asteroid collision?"

Parisi simply nodded, his face a grim mask of reality. "That's the most plausible explanation, given the data we have." His voice was quiet, resigned. He reached out to touch the intricate mechanism of the Guardian, tracing the orbits and alignments with a fingertip. "A massive asteroid on a direct collision course with Earth. And, according to the alignment data we've extracted, it's due to hit sooner than we'd like to think."

Dr. Bianchi, a distinguished scholar in geophysics, had seen simulations of asteroid impacts, understood the theories, knew the science. But to confront the reality of an impending catastrophe... That was a bitter pill to swallow.

He pushed his chair away from the Celestial Guardian and ran a hand through his silvering hair, his mind grappling with the apocalyptic scenario.

"The impact would be unimaginable," he said, his normally steady voice wavering. He gestured to the celestial blueprint laid out before them. "It's not just the strike itself, though that alone would have the power to wipe out entire cities, cause massive tsunamis, and trigger fires on an unprecedented scale."

Pausing to draw in a deep breath, he looked around the room at the assembly of scholars and engineers who had followed the celestial breadcrumb trail to this moment. Their faces reflected his own dread, the weight of knowledge pressing down on them.

"But the ripple effects..." Bianchi continued, his fingers drawing invisible patterns on the table, as if he could physically illustrate the gravity of their predicament. "The dust and debris hurled into the atmosphere would block out sunlight, drastically lower global temperatures. It could potentially lead to what scientists refer to as an 'impact winter.'"

His eyes, haunted by the realization, swept over the room again, resting briefly on each face. "Crop failures, widespread famine, species extinction… a potential ecological collapse."

He let his words hang in the air, the echo of their implications shuddering through the silence. The enormity of the situation weighed heavily on them, the scientists and engineers united in their newfound understanding of the ominous path of the celestial bodies on da Vinci's ingenious device. They had decoded more than just an enigma from the past; they had uncovered a prophetic warning for the future.

"Yes," Parisi agreed, moving toward a large whiteboard. Picking up a marker, he started sketching a crude diagram. "On impact, the asteroid would release energy equivalent to thousands of nuclear weapons. The initial blast would cause widespread destruction, but that's just the beginning.

"Assuming it hit in the Tyrrhenian Sea—say, somewhere between the western coast of Italy and the islands of Corsica, Sardinia, and Sicily—it would be the epicenter of an unimaginable disaster. The asteroid would vaporize a significant portion of the sea, creating a blast wave that would annihilate everything within hundreds of kilometers. Coastal cities, such as Rome, Naples, and Palermo, would be completely destroyed.

"The impact would create enormous tsunamis, possibly hundreds of meters high. These tsunamis would radiate out from the impact site and strike all the surrounding coasts. The waves would penetrate far inland, especially in low-lying areas. Coastal regions around the Mediterranean would suffer devastating damage. The impact would likely cause significant seismic activity, possibly triggering earthquakes throughout Italy and surrounding regions. This could lead to further destruction and destabilization of infrastructure.

"The heat generated by the impact would cause fires to break out across the region. Combined with the shockwave, this could result in firestorms that consume entire cities and forests. And the amount of material ejected into the atmosphere would lead to the nuclear winter scenario I mentioned. Dust, ash, and sulfur compounds would block sunlight, leading to a dramatic drop in temperatures worldwide. This could last for months or even years, leading to the failure of crops and widespread famine. The changes in climate, along with the immediate destruction and contamination, would have long-term effects on the environment. Ecosystems would be disrupted, and recovery would take decades if not centuries.

"The loss of life would be in the tens of millions, possibly more. The destruction of major cities and infrastructure, combined with long-term climate effects, would have profound consequences for the entire world. The scale of destruction would be unlike anything humanity has experienced in recorded history, and the global community would have to work together to address the immediate disaster and its long-term implications."

Parisi dropped the marker onto the table, his gaze meeting Bianchi's. "And if da Vinci's device is accurate... well, we need to prepare. Now. We need to warn the world. It may already be too late."

The room filled with an eerie silence as the hard realities of the prediction washed over them. The device had served its purpose, but the message it conveyed was a chilling prophecy of destruction. An event that had the potential to wipe cities off the map, claim countless lives, and disrupt the balance of global power was looming in the not-so-distant future. Leonardo da Vinci's Celestial Guardian, once a fascinating relic of the past, was now a harbinger of potential devastation, thrusting the team into a race against time to decipher any possible clues that could help avert the impending catastrophe.

CHAPTER
EIGHT

Within the intricate social and political web that constituted the Vatican, few threads of information ever slipped past the attention of one Cardinal Lorenzo Ricci. A seasoned cleric, his role within the Church had granted him a deep understanding of the inner workings of the institution.

In the regal halls of the Apostolic Palace, where the decisions affecting the vast expanse of the Catholic world were made, Cardinal Ricci was a man of some standing. Since the passing of Pope Ignatius, Ricci's influence had subtly grown, his ambitious nature seizing upon the *sede vacante* period—that vacuum of regnal power between the death or retirement and election of popes—to extend his reach within the Vatican's intricate power structure.

The day after the pope's passing, before the Conclave began, Ricci had convened a special meeting of the senior cardinals, pitching an idea that had long occupied his thoughts but had lacked the opportune moment to propose. The proposition was for the creation of a new congregation, an arm of the formidable Congregation for the Doctrine of the

Faith but devoted to the preservation and understanding of the Church's vast collection of historical and religious artifacts.

And as it happened, more than just a man of faith, Ricci was also a connoisseur of antiquities, his passion for the Church's rich history and relics well-known among his peers and underlings. His office in the Apostolic Palace was a testament to his obsessions: walls lined with ancient theological texts, relics carefully preserved under glass, and centuries-old paintings hand selected from the Vatican's own collection. His keen intellect and hawk-eyed attention to detail had won him admiration and fear in equal measures. For Ricci, the annals of history were more than mere records of the past; they were tools to shape the present and future.

There was resistance initially to his proposal for a new congregation, questions about the need for a separate body, about its jurisdiction, about the cost. But Ricci, a seasoned diplomat, had been prepared for these objections. He spoke passionately about the untapped wealth of knowledge hidden in their vaults, the potential understanding they could glean from the artifacts that lay, untouched and unstudied, in the deep recesses of the Vatican. He promised transparency, collaboration, a new dawn of ecclesiastical research and preservation.

In the absence of a pontifical authority, the decision fell to the collective assembly of the cardinals. A vote was called and, by a narrow margin, the creation of the Congregation for the Preservation and Understanding of Ecclesiastical Artifacts was approved, tasked with preserving, cataloging, and studying significant historical and religious artifacts within the Church's possession.

Ricci, of course, was elected the congregation's prefect. The speed with which the decision was made and the haste with which Ricci assumed control raised whispers of empire-building, but in the void left by Pope Ignatius's death, they remained just that—whispers.

The CPUEA—or more simply, the Congregation for Artifacts—would provide Ricci with extensive access to a variety of sacred and historical objects and relics, including items stored within the Vatican Secret Archives which would be pertinent to the department's remit. This position would also afford him a degree of power and influence within the Curia, given the cultural, historical, and religious significance of the items under his department's care. Additionally, his role would involve liaison with various other congregations and offices within the Roman Curia, potentially increasing his sphere of influence.

It would also give him supervisory powers over not only the Vatican Secret Archives, but over Father Michael Dominic himself.

∾

WITHIN DAYS, the new congregation was operational. To Michael's consternation, a dedicated wing of the Vatican Secret Archives was earmarked for their use. Scholars were brought in, tasks assigned, and the gears of the new congregation began to turn.

So, when hushed whispers of a remarkable discovery within the confines of the Vatican Secret Archives reached his ears, Ricci was intrigued. The words "manuscript" and "da Vinci" reverberated in his mind, setting off a symphony of curiosity. A discovery of this magnitude could potentially reshape historical narratives and could even hold significant implications for the Church.

Acting upon his instincts, Cardinal Ricci sent a missive through his extensive network of aides. The note, scribed with a request for a meeting, was addressed to Father Michael

Dominic and Ms. Hana Sinclair. The nature of their joint efforts had caught his attention, and he expressed an eagerness to understand more about their project. Under the guise of academic interest, Ricci prepared to delve into their findings, oblivious to the Pandora's box he was about to pry open.

Unbeknownst to nearly everyone, Ricci's new domain had set the stage for a looming power struggle, one that held the fate of an ancient prophecy in its hands.

CHAPTER

NINE

T he frescoed walls of the Sistine Chapel reverberated with the echoes of whispered prayers and the rustle of heavy robes. The Conclave had been in session for weeks, and the air in the room had grown thick with weariness. The crimson-clad cardinals sat on rows of wooden benches, their faces etched with fatigue and anxiety under their red zucchettos. An unspoken question hung in the air: when would the white smoke finally billow from the chimney of the Sistine Chapel, signaling the election of the new pope?

Bishop Mario Mancini, the Camerlengo, stood at the front of the chapel, his eyes sweeping over the sea of red before him. He was reminded of the longest conclaves in history; the conclave of 1268-1271 had lasted a staggering two years and nine months, leading to the adoption of new rules for papal elections to avoid such lengthy deadlocks. More recently, in the eighteenth century, the conclave of 1740 had lasted six months, the longest of the modern era.

"Brothers," he began, his voice filled with the solemnity of the occasion, "we have been here for weeks, praying and deliberating, seeking the guidance of the Holy Spirit. Let us remember that our task is of utmost importance—we are choosing the Vicar of Christ on Earth."

The cardinals responded with a murmur of assent, each man acutely aware of the weight of responsibility on his shoulders. They knew they couldn't rush this decision, yet they also understood the urgency of their situation. The Church needed a leader, especially in these trying times, but the question remained: who among them was ready to assume the mantle?

Several previous votes had leaned heavily in favor of two of the *papabile* in particular: Cardinal Bennett Dreyfus and Cardinal Lorenzo Ricci. But neither had achieved the required two-thirds majority of votes. As it happened, the two men were, while not bitter enemies, far less inclined to favor the other as their Church's spiritual leader. Over time, Dreyfus had attained a formidable loyalty among many of the electors, while those supporting Ricci did so largely due to favors he had bestowed upon them in his Curial duties over recent months, as Pope Ignatius's failing health made it clear that a new pope would soon be needed. Ricci was a scheming predator, and even his closest supporters knew that.

As the voting continued, it soon became clear that this Conclave had now become a showdown between just these two men. It remained a simple matter of time before the holdouts from one of the two cardinals would jump ship and elect his opposite. It was yet to be determined if loyalty could hold out over the appeal of promised future special favors.

Thus, in the hallowed silence of the Sistine Chapel, the voting resumed, each cardinal casting his vote in the hope of ending the impasse. With every ballot cast, the prayer was the same: "May the Lord, who sees all, grant us a shepherd who will guide His flock with wisdom and love." The wait was long and tedious, but the cardinals understood that their duty was to the Church and God's people. And so, they prayed and waited, hopeful that the next ballot would bring them their new pope.

CHAPTER

TEN

Karl Dengler and Lukas Bischoff, two of the Swiss Guard's most dedicated members, stood resolute at their posts outside the entrance to the Sistine Chapel. Clad in their traditional uniforms, resplendent with the vibrant hues of blue, red, and yellow, they were a vivid contrast to the austere marble corridors of the Vatican. Their polished halberds glistened under the hallway's ambient light, casting long, ominous shadows that seemed to symbolize the weighty task at hand.

The Conclave was in session, and their duty was clear and inviolate: to ensure the sanctity of the voting process, and to maintain the strict isolation of the voting cardinals from the outside world. It was an ancient practice steeped in tradition, and they were the stewards of its integrity.

Karl, a seasoned guard with a distinguished military background, scanned the corridor, his sharp senses missing nothing. His experience made him a figure of quiet authority. His hands, though steady and firm around his halberd, were more accustomed to the tactile feel of modern firearms. But in the Swiss Guard, it was as much about the tradition as it was about security.

Beside him, Lukas was the younger of the two. His tenure with the Swiss Guard wasn't as lengthy as Karl's, but his dedication was no less. He was a quiet man, his eyes always watching and learning. His attention to detail and heightened alertness was a product of his upbringing in the Swiss Alps, where vigilance was a way of life.

As the cardinals filtered into the chapel, each man in his crimson robes carrying the heavy burden of the decision they were about to make, Karl and Lukas stood their ground on either side of the great wooden doors. Each nod of recognition from the cardinals was met with a stoic nod from the guards in return, their faces impassive masks of professionalism.

The silence of the hallway was broken only by the soft rustle of robes, the whispered prayers, and the somber tolling of the distant bells. There was a palpable tension in the air, an electrifying anticipation. History was being made beyond the chapel doors, and they were its silent sentinels.

Once the last of the cardinals had entered, Karl stepped forward, his boots echoing on the stone floor. With a formal, practiced movement, he closed the heavy wooden doors of the Sistine Chapel. The muffled click of the lock reverberated through the corridor as the Camerlengo turned the great iron key to secure the only door to the room. The Conclave was now in seclusion. The world outside would wait with bated breath until the white smoke rose from the chimney.

Karl and Lukas resumed their stoic vigil, the silent guardians of a centuries-old tradition, their duty a testament to the trust bestowed upon them. As the hours rolled into days, their steadfast presence was a symbol of the unwavering commitment to their charge. The world outside waited, and they stood guard, bound by duty and honor, until the bells of St. Peter's tolled again to announce the new pontiff.

CHAPTER
ELEVEN

S t. Peter's Square was a seething mass of anticipation. Despite the leaden skies, thousands huddled beneath a patchwork of umbrellas, their collective gaze fixed on the slender stovepipe protruding from the hallowed roof of the Sistine Chapel. The prolonged Conclave had stretched nerves to breaking point, but the faithful masses remained, waiting, hoping.

Suddenly, a ripple of excitement surged through the sea of people. Smoke began to curl from the chimney, murky and dark. Disappointment whispered across the square. But then, the color began to shift, lightening until it was irrefutably white. A collective gasp echoed around the square. "Habemus Papam!" The cry rippled through the crowd, their earlier impatience dissolved in a wash of jubilation. "We have a pope!"

The chimes of the city's many churches began to peal, declaring to Rome and the world beyond—a new pope had ascended. The trepidation of the past several weeks was replaced with an electric current of anticipation.

As the gloaming fell, the immensity of St. Peter's Basilica

was bathed in a celestial glow. The towering balcony doors creaked open, revealing a figure swathed in fresh, gleaming vestments. Pope Clement XV, a name chosen to echo power and authority, emerged, silhouetted against the grand edifice. The world watched, breathless.

He was a commanding figure, his new title settling on his shoulders like a mantle he was born to wear. His face was stern, his eyes sparkling not with the gentleness of a pastor but with a resolute determination that sent a shiver of awe through the crowd. This was a man prepared to shoulder the responsibilities of the papacy, willing to guide the ship of St. Peter through both tranquil waters and the wildest storms.

The throng fell silent as the Cardinal Protodeacon intoned the ancient formula, *"Annuntio vobis gaudium magnum; habemus Papam."* The hallowed Latin words rang across the square, a declaration to the world that a new era had dawned. *"I bring you tidings of great joy; we have a pope."*

As Pope Clement XV raised his hands, a hush fell. His inaugural blessing as pope, *"Urbi et Orbi,"* was delivered with an iron-clad resolve, a proclamation of his intent to wield the power of the Church as he saw fit. The crowd erupted in applause, their cheers echoing through the night air, as a new era under Pope Clement XV began. For better or worse, only time would reveal.

As the applause subsided and the echo of the papal name, Clement XV, faded, the announcement of the birth name of the newly elected pope sent a murmur through the crowd. "Cardinale Bennett Dreyfus," the Cardinal Protodeacon proclaimed. The square fell silent, the murmurs replaced by a tangible sense of realization. The world wasn't just welcoming a new pope; it was bearing witness to the ascension of Cardinal Dreyfus—a man renowned for his cunning and calculated moves, a chess player who had reached the ultimate checkmate.

The newly minted Pope Clement XV turned, his crimson cape swirling behind him, and retreated into the shadowy recesses of the palace. As the balcony doors closed behind him, the crowd began to disperse. Whispers of trepidation rolled across the square, the seeds of unease sown.

Inside the Vatican, relief at the conclusion of the Conclave was tinged with apprehension. The long, grueling process was over, but it had given rise to a reign of uncertainty. The Church was now in the hands of a man whose ambitions were as vast as they were opaque.

Over the following days, bishops and other clergy from around the globe converged on Rome, their ecclesiastical vestments lending vibrant hues to the ancient city. The ornate halls of the Vatican thrummed with Latin prayers and the rustle of holy scripture, an undercurrent of unease threading through the litany of voices.

Throughout the frenzied preparations for the inauguration ceremony, Pope Clement XV, formerly Bennett Dreyfus, remained a figure cloaked in enigma. His public appearances were sparse and measured, his expressions inscrutable, his words poised and deliberate. The man who had emerged from the white smoke of the Sistine Chapel was a master of the art of survival. The shepherd of the flock was more a wolf in sheep's clothing.

And when Clement delivered his first Papal Mass, his voice rang out through the vaulted nave with an authority that commanded obedience. His sermon, focused on unity and strong leadership, was laced with a clear reminder of the power he now wielded. The basilica, illuminated under the candlelight, was more a theater, and the world, his audience.

As the days passed, Pope Clement began to reveal his vision for the Church, with subtle yet significant changes. New appointments were made, old traditions subtly reinterpreted, a clear indication of his intention to mold the Church according to his design.

The dawn of Clement XV's reign had come, promising to leave an indelible mark on the history of the Church. With a chess master at its helm, the world watched, an uneasy anticipation settling over the faithful and the skeptics alike. As the winds of change began to blow through the ancient halls of the Vatican, the Church began its journey into uncharted territory, guided or manipulated by a man whose intentions remained as cryptic as the man himself, far removed from the world of his predecessor, Pope Ignatius.

CHAPTER
TWELVE

I
n the somber seclusion of the Secret Archives' offices, away from the ceremonial opulence of the Vatican, three figures huddled over a worn wooden table. Father Michael Dominic, his assistant Ian Duffy, and the unassuming Sister Teresa Drinkwater, Vatican City's switchboard manager and network administrator, were engrossed in quiet conversation. The room was filled with a sense of restrained tension, the air almost heavy with their collective thoughts about the new leadership.

Ian, a lean Irishman in his early thirties with a mop of red hair cresting a fair, freckled face, was the first to break the silence. "Of all people, Cardinal Dreyfus as the new pope..." He trailed off, shaking his head slightly. His usual joviality was replaced with a distinct note of apprehension. The elevation of a man with a reputation for craft and calculation to the highest rank in the Church wasn't a development that came without concern.

Sister Teresa, or Teri, a whip-smart young woman with the confidence of someone wise beyond her years, added, "I was there when he visited the switchboard one day. The way he carried himself..." She shook her head, her eyes distant. "There was always an air about him, a certain... hardness."

Michael sat quietly, absorbing their words, his fingers tracing the worn grooves in the table. He had known Bennett Dreyfus before he became Clement XV. He had seen the man beneath the cardinal's robes—the ambition, the will to power, the unyielding determination. He too shared Ian's and Sister Teri's unease, yet he had to remind himself that God worked in mysterious ways, that He had a plan even if its workings were obscured from mortal view.

"God does not play dice with the universe, nor does He with His Church," Michael finally said, his voice measured. He met their worried gazes, a calm determination in his eyes. "Clement is our pope now. It's not our place to question God's wisdom."

"But Father, you know as well as we do the whispers about Dreyfus... I mean, Pope Clement." Ian's voice was strained, reflecting his struggle between the obedience demanded by his faith and the apprehension in his heart. "What if...?"

Michael raised his hand, cutting him off. "*What ifs* will not help us, Ian. We must keep faith. We pray, we watch, and we continue our work." His gaze was steady, his enforced conviction shining through his words, even if he didn't entirely believe them himself.

"However..." Michael's eyes took on a far-off look as his mind wandered back to his years of study, to a time in history that was marked by tension within the Church. "In view of his taking the regnal name of Clement..." he mused, and Ian and Teri looked at him, waiting for him to share his thoughts.

"In 1773," he began, "Pope Clement XIV issued a papal bull known as '*Dominus ac Redemptor.*' It was a significant decree... one that led to the suppression of the Society of Jesus."

Sister Teri, familiar with the historical undercurrents that shaped the Church, nodded solemnly. Ian looked puzzled. "The Society of Jesus... you mean the Jesuits, Father?"

Michael affirmed with a nod. "Yes, Ian. The Jesuits. *My* order. Back then it was a time of intense political pressure. The Catholic monarchs of Europe were threatened by the Jesuits' independent spirit and their influence. They had a certain sway... a power that even kings and rulers felt uneasy about.

"Up until then, as a religious order, the Jesuits had emerged during the Counter-Reformation, a time when the Catholic Church was pushing back against the Protestant Reformation's widespread challenge to its authority.

"The Jesuits quickly became the spearhead of this Catholic revival. They were renowned for their intellectual rigor, discipline, and absolute obedience to the pope, earning them both acclaim and suspicion. They started schools, universities, and seminaries across the world, contributing to a well-educated clergy and an enlightened laity. They were also paramount in missionary work, expanding Catholicism to far-flung corners of the globe like China, Japan, and the Americas.

"However, their influence wasn't appreciated by everyone. Jesuits often faced opposition from local clergy and other religious orders who saw them as overly ambitious. Their activities also brought them into conflict with secular authorities. Kings and queens of Europe, particularly in France, Spain, and Portugal, felt threatened by the Society's transnational allegiance to the pope and its extensive power and influence.

"By the mid-eighteenth century, these monarchies began to exert pressure on the papacy to suppress the Jesuits. King Louis XV of France, King Charles III of Spain, and the Marquis of Pombal, the de facto ruler of Portugal, were all instrumental in this movement. They saw the Jesuits as an obstacle to their vision of a modern nation-state with a controlled church.

"Clement XIV, who became pope in 1769 after a contentious conclave, was left to navigate this explosive situation. Although initially resistant, a few years later, Pope Clement fell under the constant strain of political pressure and the threat of a schism in the Church. His resultant decree suppressing the Jesuits was an act that rocked the Church and had far-reaching implications."

Ian leaned forward, his curiosity piqued. "So, Pope Clement XIV gave in to the political pressure?"

"In a way," Michael admitted. "The papal bull ordered the dissolution of the Jesuit order. They were driven out from Catholic countries, their properties confiscated. It was a devastating blow. Clement himself was said to have been distressed by the decision, but he saw it as a necessary sacrifice for the preservation of the Church.

"The suppression seemed to be a victory for the European monarchs and many perceived it painting the papacy as weak and susceptible to outside influence.

"But," Michael continued, "the act was seen by many within the Church as a grave injustice to a religious order that had served the Church devotedly. The suppression disrupted the Jesuits' educational, pastoral, and missionary work. The decision was so controversial that it was ultimately reversed. In 1814, Pope Pius VII issued a papal bull restoring the Society of Jesus. This reinstatement, however, couldn't erase the memory of the unprecedented suppression, which remains one of the most dramatic events in the history of the Catholic Church."

There was a silence as the trio considered this piece of history, the interplay of power, faith, and politics... the fraught line the Church had to tread in a world where its spiritual authority often clashed with temporal powers.

Teri broke the silence, "And now we have Pope Clement XV. Do you think there's a significance to his choosing that name, Father?"

Michael rubbed his chin thoughtfully. "Names chosen by popes often reflect their aspirations, their visions for their pontificate," he explained. "Perhaps it's a coincidence... Or perhaps our new pope is sending a message, aligning himself with a past marked by decisive, even controversial, action. One thing I feel certain about: this is not a Clement who will capitulate to outside forces but could potentially bring his own ambitions to bear on others instead."

His voice faded into the quiet, leaving them all to only hope and pray for wisdom to decipher the path ahead.

At the distant tolling of St. Peter's Basilica bells, a sense of resolve settled over them. They were servants of the Church, bound by their faith and duty. And so they would serve, keeping watch and praying for wisdom in the face of the uncertain future.

But until proven otherwise, each of them would always remain vigilant, suspicious.

CHAPTER

THIRTEEN

As the descending sun marked the end of the day for most, the Renaissance workshop hummed with a palpable intensity. As scholars and engineers bent over the Celestial Guardian, lost in concentration, the workshop door creaked open. A tall figure silhouetted against the fading light stepped in—Cardinal Lorenzo Ricci.

The room fell into a reverential silence as he entered, his scarlet cassock lending an air of authority that was hard to ignore. As eyes turned to him, Ricci smiled, the corners of his eyes crinkling in what appeared to be genuine delight.

"Father Dominic, Ms. Sinclair," he greeted, his voice echoing in the quiet workshop. His eyes roved across the room, lingering on the device and the scattered copies of Leonardo's manuscript. "I've heard of your fascinating discovery. Might I have a closer look?"

While Hana and Michael found his interest marginally flattering, they couldn't shake off a sense of unease. Ricci's reputation preceded him—his ambition and knack for bending the rules were infamous within the Vatican. And with the future of humanity potentially in their hands, they knew they had to tread carefully. "Of course, Your Eminence," Michael said, leading Ricci toward the manuscript.

The cardinal examined the blueprint with rapt attention, the furrow on his brow betraying his intrigue. "Remarkable," he muttered, more to himself than anyone else in the room. His fingers traced the mirror script, a faint, knowing smile playing on his lips. "To think that da Vinci, in all his brilliance, may have left us a roadmap to the workings of the heavens…"

He looked up, locking eyes with Michael and Hana. "Tell me, how does it work?"

His question hung in the air, the underlying curiosity hinting at more than just academic interest. Hana and Michael exchanged a glance, aware that they were on the precipice of revealing something potentially powerful, which in the hands of someone ambitious could become dangerous.

Michael cleared his throat, breaking the silence that had gripped the room. He gestured toward the mechanism. "The device predicts celestial alignments," he began, glancing at Hana, who picked up the tenor of their explanation.

"It interprets those alignments and their potential impacts on Earth," she added, her journalist's instincts noting the keen interest in Ricci's eyes. "Comparing those predictive results to past actual events, like asteroids colliding on Earth, it appears his device was exceptionally accurate."

Ricci stepped closer to the device, his fingers tracing the edges of the intricate gears, a thoughtful frown etched onto his face. "Appears to be?"

Hana hesitated. "Actually, they were quite accurate in the past."

Ricci frowned, obviously gathering more from Hana's words than she had intended. "And in the future? What do these predictions mean, Father Dominic?"

The room grew quiet once more, the significance of the impending prediction weighing heavily on all present. Michael hesitated, then spoke, his voice barely a whisper. "An imminent catastrophe, Eminence. The alignments indicate an event, due to occur in the next few months. An event that has not yet been noted by scientific observations."

A shock passed through Ricci's eyes, but it was quickly replaced by a calculating look, his mind racing through the potential implications. He glanced once more at the manuscript and the device, a newfound determination hardening his features.

"Well, Father Dominic, Ms. Sinclair," he said, his voice steady, "it seems we have a duty to protect this… and use it, for the greater good."

But as he departed, leaving Michael and Hana in the bustling workshop, the echo of his words rang hollow. The hint of greed in his eyes, the brief flash of power-lust, didn't go unnoticed. They knew then the danger their discovery was in and the lengths they might have to go to protect it.

Unwittingly, they had set a dangerous game in motion. Their challenge now was not just to decipher Leonardo's prophecy, but also to safeguard it from those who would use it for personal gain.

～

EVENING HAD FALLEN OVER ROME, and in the elegant quarters of Cardinal Lorenzo Ricci, the soft glow of an antique desk lamp cast long shadows across a room steeped in history. Classical portraits of popes past watched silently from their gilded frames, the air heavy with the weight of centuries.

Ricci sat at his mahogany desk, a rare moment of solitude in a day otherwise dictated by endless meetings and obligations. In his hands, he held a report on the Celestial

Guardian prepared for him by Hana Sinclair. As he read, his brow furrowed in concentration, his mind racing with possibilities.

A smile tugged at the corners of Ricci's mouth as he began to imagine the scenario. Governments, organizations, even superpowers bowing to the wisdom of the Church. He could see himself standing before them, not just as a representative of the Vatican, but as their savior. Since for the time being he couldn't be pope, he would settle for what might otherwise be available to him given this extraordinary opportunity.

Ricci's eyes moved from the report to a copy of the Guardian blueprint on his desk, the miniature gears and cogs seemingly glinting in the lamplight. As he traced the intricate mechanisms with his fingers, his mind echoed with possibilities. With the Guardian under his control, he would hold the power to shape the world's response to the impending catastrophe.

Suddenly, the room didn't feel as small, the Vatican's influence didn't seem as limited, and the path to the power he had always sought seemed much clearer. The thought sent a shiver of anticipation through him. It was a dangerous game he was contemplating, but the potential rewards were too enticing to ignore.

Ricci allowed his gaze to wander across the room, finally coming to rest on an antique crucifix hanging on the wall. The figure of Christ, eyes upturned and arms outstretched, seemed to challenge him, to question his motives. But Ricci was unfazed. He was a pragmatist, a man of the world, and he knew the power of symbols.

Just as that crucifix symbolized hope and redemption for millions, the Celestial Guardian could become a symbol of a new era. An era where the Church wouldn't just preach about the divine but would harness the knowledge of the cosmos. Ricci imagined a world where the Church's words carried weight beyond the spiritual, a world where the Vatican's authority was unquestionable, as it once was centuries before. Where science over the last decades had undermined much of the Church's ability to hold sway over the masses, it would take but one observable victory over science for those same masses to swarm back to the arms of faith. And in the face of a catastrophe? They would beg to be let into the fold.

His mind then began to wander to his peers. How would they react? Dreyfus, the newly elected Pope Clement XV, with his calculated charisma and strategic cunning, would undoubtedly pose a challenge. But Ricci was no stranger to the intricacies of Vatican politics. He knew the art of manipulation, the power of alliances, and the importance of maintaining a façade. He would have to tread carefully, keep his intentions veiled until the right moment.

His heart began to quicken at the thought of the confrontation to come. He could almost hear the gasps in the Vatican's halls when he would reveal the existence of the Guardian, could see the stunned faces of the cardinals as they realized the magnitude of the threat looming over humanity. And through it all, Ricci would stand, a beacon of hope and leadership amid the chaos, eclipsing the feckless new Pope Clement.

A sense of purpose washed over him as he let the scenario play out in his mind. He was certain now, more than ever, that the Guardian was the key to not only the Church's future but his own. No longer would he be just another cardinal in the shadow of the papacy, passed over again as he just was in the election for pope. With the Guardian, he could become the very embodiment of the Church's power, its unquestionable authority.

As the night wore on, Cardinal Ricci sat alone amid the opulence of his lavish apartment, his mind abuzz with plans and possibilities. The once daunting challenge now appeared to him as an unprecedented opportunity. His path was clear, his resolve unshakeable. The Celestial Guardian would be his. It wasn't just a desire now; it was a necessity. The future of the Church, and indeed his own future, depended on it.

In the quiet of his quarters, as the rest of Rome lay unaware, a plan began to take shape in Lorenzo Ricci's mind. A plan that had the potential to change the very course of the Church, and indeed, the world. As the night deepened, the cardinal leaned back in his chair, a steely resolve setting into his features. The game, it seemed, was far from over.

CHAPTER
FOURTEEN

Inside the opulent papal offices of the Apostolic Palace, Pope Clement sat behind his ornate desk, still adjusting to the weight of his new title. The air was heavy with the scent of old books and polished mahogany, and the faint echo of choral hymns wafted in from the distant corners of the Vatican.

The tall office door creaked open, revealing the familiar figure of Lorenzo Ricci being escorted by a papal aide. The cardinal's face bore the austere, solemn expression Clement had come to know over their years of service together, but today there was an undercurrent of anticipation in his gaze.

"Your Holiness," Ricci greeted, his voice steady and as respectful as he could muster. He genuflected, rising to meet the pope's gaze, then kissed the Ring of the Fisherman. "My heartfelt congratulations on your divine appointment."

"Thank you, Lorenzo," Pope Clement responded, acknowledging the man he had known long before they had ascended to their respective ranks. And before they both vied for the same ultimate position.

"There is a crucial matter I wish to discuss," Ricci said, his voice echoing off the marble in the expansive room. "Something that might significantly influence the future of our Church. It is a device called the Celestial Guardian."

A curious frown creased Pope Clement's forehead. He leaned forward, intrigued. "The Celestial Guardian? I have not heard of such a thing. Please, enlighten me."

"Of course, Your Holiness," Ricci replied, obliging the pope's curiosity. He took a moment to gather his thoughts, well aware of the gravity his next words carried. "*Il Guardiano Celestiale*, as it is known, was designed by none other than Leonardo da Vinci himself."

Clement blinked in surprise at this revelation. da Vinci, the master of the Renaissance, the man who bridged the realms of art, science, and imagination like no other.

"Da Vinci's genius, as we know, was far-reaching. The Celestial Guardian, however, is perhaps one of his most profound creations," Ricci continued, his voice steady, yet hinting at the overpowering implications of such a device. "It is said to predict the movements of celestial bodies, and more importantly, their impact on Earth."

He allowed a moment for the pope to process this before continuing. "Moreover, Vatican craftsmen have been working tirelessly under the direction of Father Dominic, prefect of your Apostolic Archives, to replicate such a device based on da Vinci's blueprints. The dedication and commitment of our scientists and consultants have resulted in a working prototype of this Guardian."

Clement leaned back, his mind a whirlwind of questions, implications, and wonder. An artifact of such potential influence, designed by a genius—and now within reach of the Church—could be a historic discovery.

"Da Vinci's creation in the hands of the Church... it's an immense responsibility, Lorenzo," Pope Clement murmured, his voice barely above a whisper, as his gaze wandered through the distant stained-glass window, the colorful rays fracturing into a kaleidoscope of possibilities and dilemmas.

His mind spun with the enormity of the revelation. The Church had been the steward of many sacred relics, each holding its place in the heart of the faith. But this Guardian was different; it held not only spiritual but also scientific implications, blurring the boundaries between faith and reason, theology, and astronomy.

"Imagine," he continued, his voice regaining its strength, "the influence it holds, the shifts it could cause within our doctrine. The predictions it makes could be interpreted as divine signs, guiding us and our followers on the path of righteousness."

His gaze turned back to Ricci, his eyes sharp, probing. "Yet it also brings forth its own trials. How do we reconcile these predictions with our faith, our teachings? What if it foresees events that contradict our understandings? The Church will have to tread cautiously, interpreting these signs without causing dissent or confusion."

Clement's fingers drummed on the desktop, a quiet rhythm in the silence of the office. "And then there's the matter of its protection. If this Guardian is as powerful as you say, it is bound to draw attention, perhaps unwanted. We'll need to safeguard it not only physically but also intellectually, ensuring its use and interpretation remain within the Church."

Ricci looked deeply into Pope Clement's eyes, an unspoken understanding passing between the two old adversaries. "This is not just about having da Vinci's creation, Your Holiness. It's about understanding its power, its implications. It's about guiding the Church through a new era of enlightenment and challenges."

The pope's gaze returned to the window, the fractured sunlight casting a myriad of colors across his face. The

Celestial Guardian, a creation of the past, could now hold the keys to their future. The journey they were about to embark upon was fraught with unknowns, and the responsibility weighed heavily on Clement's shoulders.

"An intriguing object, indeed," he said thoughtfully. "And why do you bring this to me, Lorenzo?"

"Your Holiness," Ricci continued, his voice steady and insistent, "given the Guardian's potential, it is, as you say, imperative that it be safeguarded and properly understood. I believe the Congregation for Artifacts is best equipped to manage this responsibly. The Holy Father's Archives is no place for such a device."

Pope Clement studied Lorenzo Ricci carefully, seeing beyond the veneer of the dutiful cardinal. There was a particular gleam in his old rival's eye, a fervor that whispered of personal desires tucked away beneath layers of ecclesiastical decorum. Ricci coveted the Celestial Guardian, not just for the Church, but for himself—this much was unmistakably clear to the discerning pope.

The years they had spent serving the Church together had fostered a deep understanding between them. Clement had observed Ricci navigating the sacred halls of the Vatican, his ambition often concealed behind a façade of humility and servitude. But Clement knew, beneath the cardinal's restrained exterior, dwelled a fierce hunger for influence and authority. Not unlike Clement's own.

Ricci's enthusiasm for the Celestial Guardian wasn't simply about spiritual enlightenment or preserving a historical artifact. No, it was an outright bid for power, an opportunity to imprint his own legacy within the Church's annals. This majestic creation of da Vinci's could elevate him in ways few other things could. As it could well do the same for Clement.

The Celestial Guardian was more than a divine artifact to

Ricci; it was a celestial chess piece in the intricate game of power and influence he so subtly played. But as pope, it was Clement's role to see beyond personal desires, to discern what would serve the Church and its vast congregation best. Not to mention to reinforce his own standing among history's popes.

The layers of their shared history and the complex dance of their current roles painted a multifaceted portrait of intrigue and anticipation. The Celestial Guardian was set to become a pivotal entity in their personal narratives and the broader canvas of the Church's destiny.

The Church at the crossroads of science and faith was a compelling but complex prospect. The pope nodded slowly, his gaze steady on Ricci.

"Thank you for bringing this to my attention, Lorenzo," he said solemnly. "I need to pray on this and seek God's guidance. We shall continue this discussion soon."

Ricci bowed in acknowledgement, his face revealing nothing of his disappointment that the pope didn't immediately take him up on the idea of securing the device within his own Congregation for Artifacts. As he left the pope's office, the magnitude of their conversation hung heavy in the air. The Celestial Guardian was now a part of their narrative, promising to shape not just their future, but that of the entire Church, if not the world.

CHAPTER
FIFTEEN

Under an early evening sky filled with stars and the neon glow of the European Space Agency's (ESA) Near-Earth Object Coordination Center (NEOCC) in Frascati, Italy, just outside of Rome, Father Michael Dominic and Hana Sinclair entered NEOCC's glass-and-steel operations building. The ultra-modern edifice was a stark contrast to the centuries-old architecture they were accustomed to in Vatican City, but it was here they hoped to find validation for their extraordinary artifact.

Greeted at the entrance by Dr. Sofia Neri, a distinguished astrophysicist and the director of NEOCC, and her associate, Dr. Lars Henriksson, a leading expert on asteroid prediction and a jovial man with a passion for celestial mechanics, they were led through a maze of corridors to a high-tech conference room where a large projector displayed real-time images of outer space from NASA's James Webb Space Telescope.

Once seated, Michael unclasped a case he had been carrying, revealing the Celestial Guardian prototype. The machine, a mesh of orbs, cogs and gears, ancient design and new craftsmanship, glinted under the artificial lighting, an artifact that seemed almost surreal amid the futuristic setting.

Hana took the lead, her articulate voice narrating the Guardian's capabilities, while Michael handled the delicate machine, revealing its intricate inner workings. The air in the room grew dense as they shared what little they knew about the forthcoming catastrophe predicted by the device, their words etching a stark picture of the future.

Dr. Neri, usually composed, blinked at the revelations, her analytical mind racing to process the information. Dr. Henriksson, on the other hand, seemed more intrigued than shocked, his gaze never leaving the Guardian, his mind making rapid connections.

The room was bathed in the soft glow of computer screens, the constant hum of the central processing unit providing an underscore to their intense examination. The Guardian sat in quiet anticipation, an enigmatic guest amid this meeting of minds.

Hour by hour, the scientists engaged with the Guardian's now active readings. Charts of celestial movement, graphs of orbital paths, and projections of near-Earth trajectories filled their monitors. With each passing moment, the analog design of da Vinci's creation was transformed into digital correlations and simulations, blurring the lines between the past and the present.

Dr. Neri, her brows furrowed in deep concentration, moved between the Guardian and her own data. Her fingers danced over the keys of her laptop, inputting the Guardian's projections into their advanced software. Simultaneously, Dr. Henriksson studied the charts, his gaze intense as he traced the potential pathways of celestial bodies, mapping out their future in the tapestry of the cosmos.

There was no idle chatter, no superfluous conversation, just a steady exchange of theories and ideas. The room was filled with a symphony of soft clicks, whispers, and the rustle of papers as the scientists pored over the information, cross-referencing, verifying, and comparing.

As the second hour marked its departure, a silence fell over the room, broken only by the soft hum of the machines. The scientists had retreated into their own realms of thoughts, their eyes focused on the screens before them, their minds grappling with the monumental reality being unfurled by the Guardian.

Dr. Neri was the first to break the silence, her voice cutting through the heavy anticipation that had enveloped the room. She looked up from her monitor, the blue light reflecting in her wide eyes. "It's remarkable..." she murmured, her tone bearing a hint of disbelief intertwined with awe.

Dr. Henriksson, having moved to stand beside her, looked at the same data, his face etched with solemn understanding. "Indeed," he agreed, his voice deep and somber. "Our data corroborates the Guardian's projections. The alignment of celestial bodies, their impending proximity to Earth, the potential impact... it's all there.

"Nobody saw this coming, because when an asteroid is positioned between Earth and the Sun, it's said to be in 'superior conjunction.' In this position, the sun's overwhelming brightness tends to wash out or hide the object, making it difficult to detect with telescopes. This is similar to trying to find a small light in front of a very bright spotlight. Moreover, solar radiation and solar flares can interfere with the detection and observation of asteroids. They can lead to an increase in the noise in the data that astronomers collect, making it harder to identify a relatively small and faint object like an asteroid. As it comes closer, these factors would have had a less cloaking influence. But of course, early detection is the key to planning effective counter measures—if there are any that can be employed."

In the face of the ancient Guardian's revelations, the scientists found an intersection of time, a communion of ancient wisdom and modern science, and it held in its cradle a future that was both fascinating and terrifying.

"Now, as for the cold, hard truths," Dr. Neri added, "if an object like this, six kilometers in diameter, collides with Earth at a speed of roughly 72,000 kilometers per hour, the immediate consequences would be... well, catastrophic would be too gentle a word."

Henriksson nodded, his face reflecting the same unease his colleague felt. He gestured for her to continue.

"The impact would vaporize the ground instantly, creating an immense shockwave that would devastate anything within hundreds of kilometers," Neri explained. "Then there's the impact crater, which would be approximately twenty times the size of the asteroid itself."

Hana drew in a sharp breath, "And the debris from the impact?"

Dr. Neri nodded, her tone grim. "It would be ejected into the atmosphere at high speeds, even reaching space. But what goes up must come down, right? This debris would reenter Earth's atmosphere, igniting due to friction. This could result in numerous fireballs raining across the globe, causing wildfires and significantly increasing global temperatures."

"But those initial effects, the shockwave, the heat, where would they hit first?" Michael questioned, his brow furrowed.

Neri shook her head. "Well, it depends on where the asteroid lands. Those effects would be more localized. But the real issue is the dust and soot. It would block out sunlight, causing what's described as an 'impact winter,' one that could last for years. Without sunlight, photosynthesis would stop. That would lead to a collapse of the food chain. We could be looking at a mass extinction event similar to what happened to the dinosaurs."

∽

EARLIER, in the bustling, open-plan office bay just outside the conference room, Ari Finelli, a young astronomical engineer with an insatiable curiosity, had been sitting hunched over his desk, his eyes darting from the classified documents spread out before him to the glass-enclosed conference room across the office.

He didn't recognize the two visitors who had just entered the room with Dr. Neri and Dr. Henriksson, though one was clearly a Catholic priest. *Why would a priest be here at the ESA?* he wondered.

The object of their discussion appeared to be a strange, intricate model that the priest had placed on the conference table, a contraption that looked as if it had stepped out of a steampunk film. It was unlike anything Ari had ever seen, and his curiosity was piqued.

Feigning nonchalance, Ari rose from his chair, clutching a sheaf of papers, and made his way toward the conference room. As he approached the room, he affected a slightly harried expression and knocked politely on the door.

Dr. Neri looked up from her conversation, offered a small smile, and beckoned him in. As Ari entered the room, he offered a quick apology. "Sorry to disturb, Dr. Neri. I just need to grab the Hubble project files."

Dr. Neri waved him toward the cabinet. "Of course, Ari. Help yourself."

Ari thanked her and made his way to the cabinet. As he shuffled through the files, he casually turned toward the conference table. On the pretext of straightening the files he had retrieved on the top of the cabinet, he subtly flicked on the intercom switch of the landline phone setting there, knowing that it linked directly to his desk phone outside.

Ari excused himself and exited the room. Back at his desk, he positioned himself so he could continue watching the meeting and, after tapping the Mute button, picked up his receiver, his heart racing as he began to listen in on their conversation.

His innocent curiosity was about to lead him into a mystery of celestial proportions.

CHAPTER
SIXTEEN

L ate the next afternoon, Michael was once again poring over da Vinci's blueprint of the Celestial Guardian. His gaze traced over the familiar lines, the genius of Leonardo's mind manifest in every meticulous detail. Yet, despite the familiarity, something niggled at the back of his mind, a sense that there was something he was still missing.

In the quiet of the Archives, surrounded by stacks of parchment and the faint scent of aged ink, a small detail caught his eye—a sequence of dots at the corner of the blueprint. He had seen them before but dismissed them as a simple decorative element, a product of Leonardo's artistic flair. Today, however, they struck him as purposeful, intentional. It was as if Leonardo was trying to communicate something.

Motivated by this hunch, Michael decided to dig deeper. He retrieved an infrared lamp from his assortment of tools —a device commonly used to reveal faded or hidden ink that becomes visible under infrared light. As a historian and an archivist, he knew that messages hidden in plain sight were a common tactic among the scholars and thinkers of the past, especially someone as enigmatic as Leonardo da Vinci.

The infrared light cast an eerie scarlet glow over the ancient blueprint as Michael carefully scanned it. He held his breath as the luminescent dots seemed to multiply, revealing a dense pattern of symbols and diagrams that had been invisible under normal light, likely written using lemon juice, a historically proven way of embedding secret messages onto paper documents. Lemon juice, as a form of invisible or sympathetic ink, traditionally became visible when heat was applied to the paper or parchment, since heat causes the sugars in the juice to caramelize, revealing the hidden message.

His heart pounded in his chest as he leaned closer, his eyes wide with discovery. Hidden within the main blueprint of the Celestial Guardian was an entirely different design, invisible to the naked eye but glowing under the infrared light. A secret message from Leonardo, preserved through centuries, waited to be deciphered.

"*Impossible...*" Michael murmured, but there it was, hidden in plain sight. The Guardian wasn't just meant to forecast celestial movements; it was designed to *influence* them!

He ran over the intricate diagrams with his fingers, his mind reeling at the revelations the hidden notes contained. It was like peering into the past, catching a glimpse of a genius at work, pushing the boundaries of his time. Leonardo's hypotheses seemed to echo the later theories of Einstein, suggesting an intertwined relationship between gravity and time. His drawings, formerly believed to be simple representations of celestial bodies, now suggested a vision of these bodies warping the fabric of space around them.

With a growing sense of awe, Michael's gaze returned to the blueprint of the Guardian, revealing an intricate network of energy pulses, guided by complex mathematical models. According to Leonardo's notes, the Guardian could resonate with the gravitational pull of celestial bodies, altering their movement through subtle manipulations of the space-time fabric—not unlike a conductor directing an orchestra.

As Michael delved deeper into the cryptic notes, he uncovered a complex mathematical model intertwined with elements of astrological lore. It became clear to him that da Vinci was conceptualizing not just an object of prediction but of interaction—a sort of celestial instrument.

Through some unexplained Renaissance fusion of science and mysticism, da Vinci seemed to believe that the harmonies of the universe could be "played" in a sense, manipulated like notes on a sheet of music. It was a concept far ahead of its time and even challenging to the modern mind. However, Michael began to wonder if Leonardo had stumbled upon a universal truth that modern science was only beginning to comprehend: the potential interconnectedness of all things in the universe.

This secondary function of the Celestial Guardian—its ability to influence celestial movements—might involve subtle manipulations of gravity or space-time, or some undiscovered science that Leonardo could only hint at through his own understanding. It could work as a sort of "gravity conductor" capable of pulling or nudging celestial objects along different paths. It was, however, speculative and based on theories far from being proven.

If so, the implications were staggering. In the wrong hands, such a device could become a weapon of unimaginable power—capable of diverting asteroids, yes, but also of causing untold havoc. Michael realized that this knowledge made the Guardian even more dangerous, raising the stakes in the silent battle with Cardinal Ricci for its control.

This revelation sparked a new urgency in Michael. He must now find a way to ensure the Guardian was used responsibly, for the good of humanity, and not as a tool for power or control. It wasn't just about saving the world by an early prediction of an asteroid impact anymore; it was about preserving the balance of power on Earth and in the heavens.

~

LATER THAT EVENING, Michael was joined by Hana. Under the soft glow of the table lamp, they sat huddled over the complex blueprint of the Celestial Guardian, their eyes darting over Leonardo da Vinci's ornate handwriting and meticulously detailed diagrams. The quiet of the Vatican Archives wrapped around them like a shroud, lending an air of solemnity to their late-night study.

"Look at this, Hana." Michael traced a gloved finger over the faint lines of an additional layer beneath the main blueprint, revealed only after careful examination under infrared light. "It's as if Leonardo concealed an entirely different design within the primary one."

Hana squinted at the papers, her eyes widening as realization dawned. "Are you suggesting...?" She left her sentence hanging, the implications vast and startling.

He nodded slowly. "This isn't just a Guardian, Hana. Leonardo designed it to be more—a manipulator of moving celestial bodies. He was imagining a device that could interact with the cosmic dance, not just predict it."

She took a moment to absorb this, her gaze drifting over the intricate illustrations. "So, are we talking about some form of gravity manipulation? But that's..." She trailed off, grappling with the enormity of the claim.

"Extraordinary, I know," Michael picked up on her unfinished thought. "And it's also uncharted territory. The science behind it is only theoretical, even in our time. But here"—he tapped the blueprint—"Leonardo seems to be hinting at an understanding of the universe that aligns with what we've only recently come to appreciate: the entanglement of space and time."

Silence fell between them as they both contemplated what this could mean. The Guardian wasn't just a shield against potential threats, but also, potentially, a conductor of cosmic events.

"But how could this work, Michael?" Hana asked, breaking the silence. "How could Leonardo conceive something this advanced? Let alone how could he power such a thing?"

Michael leaned back in his chair, his gaze fixed on the blueprint. "I think da Vinci had a sense of the interconnectedness of all things. Maybe he couldn't explain it in the way we can now, but he perceived it. And in that perception, he theorized a device that could manipulate those connections. As for the power it would take for it to work, well, likely that is why he never went further with this. No such power source existed at the time."

The implications hung heavy in the air. This knowledge could save the world or, in the wrong hands, wield devastating power.

"We really need to proceed with caution here. The ability to manipulate the path of space objects could be utilized for noble or evil intentions," Michael said, his voice low but firm. "This could be the key to saving the Earth from the approaching asteroid, but if this information falls into the wrong hands, it could also turn the Guardian into a weapon of unprecedented proportions."

Hana met his gaze, determination lighting her eyes. "Then we must ensure it doesn't find its way to those with nefarious intent. This discovery, it's not just a step toward averting a global disaster, but a leap in our understanding of the universe. And that... that's worth protecting."

Michael nodded. "We need to visit with the folks at the NEOCC again. They must hear about this."

As the magnitude of their task settled over them, Michael and Hana turned back to the blueprint, continuing to decipher Leonardo's design. But as they reached the end, a growing sense of confusion and dread set in. The invisible writing simply stopped, mid-sentence, as though there were pages missing.

"There's something odd here," Michael said, his voice thick with worry. "The writing just... stops."

Hana leaned closer, her eyes narrowing as she studied the manuscript. "You're right. It's as if he was interrupted. Or..."

"Or there's more to this manuscript. We might be missing pages," Michael finished, his heart pounding.

They exchanged a worried glance. "I wonder if I missed one or more parchments when I first discovered it."

He glanced at his watch. "It's too late to start searching now, and I'm beat as it is. Let's come back another time."

"Agreed," Hana replied, standing up and stretching. "It's not like it's going anywhere in the meantime."

CHAPTER

SEVENTEEN

The European Space Agency's NEOCC conference room buzzed with an unspoken tension as Michael Dominic and Hana Sinclair took their seats across from Dr. Neri and Dr. Henriksson.

In the office bay outside, Ari Finelli watched through the glass wall as the four settled in. He had arrived at work early that day, his curiosity piqued by the cryptic discussions of the previous meeting he had overheard. Recognizing the priest and his colleague as they entered the building, he had quickly made his way to the conference room under the guise of checking equipment and had again stealthily activated the intercom on the conference room phone. Now back at his desk, he observed the four faces, each etched with a seriousness that made him lean closer to the muted phone receiver, pretending he was on a call.

Inside the conference room, Dr. Neri was the first to break the silence. "You seem anxious, Father Dominic, Ms. Sinclair. Has something happened with the Guardian?" she inquired, her eyes flicking between the two. Little did they know that their answer would echo not just within the four walls of the room but would also reach an eavesdropping engineer, ratcheting up the wheels of intrigue a notch higher.

Michael looked at Hana briefly before responding. "We have discovered something... new," he said, his voice steady despite the tumult of thoughts within him. "Something hidden within the blueprint."

Hana carefully pulled out the original Guardian parchment from her valise, and they all leaned in as she spread it across the table. "Using infrared light, we found notes, hidden layers within da Vinci's designs," she said, using an infrared pen light as she pointed to the areas where they had found the hidden text. "They suggest a secondary function of the Guardian, beyond its predictive capabilities."

Dr. Henriksson furrowed his brow. "What kind of secondary function?"

Michael met his gaze squarely. "Influence. As in, influencing celestial movements."

The scientists exchanged a glance before Dr. Neri asked, "But how?"

Michael began to explain, "Da Vinci's hidden notes seem to hint at a concept of using focused gravitational waves, almost as if he were suggesting a way to shape the fabric of space-time."

Dr. Henriksson looked at the blueprint, visibly intrigued. "And to generate these waves, what sort of power source would be needed?"

Hana answered, "Something on the scale of a nuclear reactor."

Dr. Henriksson blinked, absorbing the implications. "That's... extraordinary. And potentially catastrophic if misused!"

Michael nodded. "Indeed, that's why we're here. We need your help."

Understanding dawned on Dr. Neri's face as she leaned

back in her chair. "So, you're not just *predicting* the celestial movements anymore... You're planning to *change* them?"

The room fell into a tense silence as the scientists digested the weight of Michael's revelation. Dr. Neri, her gaze distant, chewed lightly on the end of a pen in her hand. After a moment, she met Michael's eyes and nodded.

"I think I understand what you're proposing," she began, "but let me clarify to be sure. You're suggesting that the Guardian, powered by a nuclear reactor, could generate focused gravitational waves to subtly manipulate the fabric of space-time around the asteroid, effectively nudging it onto a different trajectory?"

Michael nodded, but the doctor had already gone on, eyes squinted, speaking aloud the methods implied by this idea as it came clear to her. "Gravitational resonators, following the Guardian's calculations, might generate a complex pattern of gravitational waves. Each resonator creates waves of a specific frequency, amplitude, and phase, together creating a composite wavefront that effectively 'sculpts' the fabric of space-time in a localized area.

"This composite wavefront is then focused and directed toward the asteroid. Then, as these modulated gravitational waves reach the asteroid, they could create subtle distortions in the space-time fabric around the object. The asteroid, naturally following the path of least resistance in space-time, is nudged onto a different trajectory. Is that right?"

Michael nodded, impressed with her clear grasp of the situation. "Yes, Dr. Neri. That's precisely it. But you explain it so much better than I could. This would effectively mitigate the need for using spacecraft to alter the course of the asteroid, which would be a much more challenging project, I assume."

"Oh, indeed," Dr. Henriksson said. "NASA's ATLAS survey—that's the Asteroid Terrestrial-impact Last Alert

System—currently searches the dark sky every twenty-four hours to locate and identify near-Earth objects that might pose high risk to our planet—and they've found at least one. In 2022, NASA actually used an automobile-sized object to impact the Dimorphos asteroid moon in their Double Asteroid Redirection Test, or DART, mission. It was a huge success. But you're right. Those missions are phenomenally expensive and require long-term planning. So you're saying the principles guiding this kind of effort, they're all encoded within Leonardo's blueprint?"

"They are," Hana replied, nodding. "His theories seem to prefigure a concept of space-time similar to Einstein's. The manipulation of space-time, it's similar to… to a conductor leading a symphony. It's not a direct push or pull on the celestial bodies. It's more like leading a dance with the subtle baton of gravity and space-time."

Dr. Neri let out a low whistle. "That's nothing short of astonishing. And terrifying."

"You're telling us that this device, based on a design from the fifteenth century, might have the potential to save Earth from a catastrophic asteroid collision?" Dr. Henriksson said, a hint of awe lacing his words. "This needs to be made open to every—"

Michael cut him off with a wave. "Doctor, think about this before you finish that sentence. Any device that could move objects in the heavens away from Earth could also…" He paused.

"Ah, yes." He sighed. "Human nature at its worst could use it as a weapon, bringing foreign objects toward its targets. So, if it falls into the wrong hands…"

He didn't need to finish the sentence. The room was thick with the unspoken danger.

"We're racing against time here," Michael concluded, his gaze steady on the two scientists. "We need to work together to understand this device thoroughly and ensure that it's used wisely. The fate of the world could quite literally depend on it."

His mind spinning with possibilities, Ari Finelli leaned back in his chair after quietly setting the phone receiver back onto its cradle, completely removed from the reality around him. His normally meticulously organized desk was a mess of half-drunk cups of coffee and scattered notes. His co-workers chattered away, oblivious to the monumental secret he had just stumbled upon. His fingers hovered over his keyboard, his work forgotten, as the implications of what he had heard slowly settled in his mind.

Hidden away in the shadowy corner of the room, the small red light of the intercom device blinked innocently. From that device, a conversation, one Ari was never meant to hear, had emerged. The discussion replayed in his mind, each word sending a new wave of disbelief crashing over him.

The Guardian, a device crafted by the genius of Leonardo da Vinci, held the key to manipulating celestial bodies? It was an idea as audacious as it was worrying. It promised a new frontier for humanity, but it also held the potential for unimaginable disaster. Ari was an engineer, a man of facts and figures, but this... this was beyond anything he had ever encountered or even conceived.

He glanced around the room, anxiety knotting in his stomach. His co-workers were engrossed in their tasks, their minds filled with computations and observations, blissfully ignorant of the knowledge he now held.

His mind raced. What should he do with this information? He was an engineer, not a diplomat or a strategist. He had no experience with political machinations or ecclesiastical maneuverings. He needed advice.

Suddenly, a thought struck him. His brother, a Catholic priest named Father Benito Finelli, would know what to do. Benito was his opposite, a man who had chosen the path of faith and was now working in the Vatican. Ari didn't always understand his brother's world, but right now, he needed someone who did.

Pulling out his phone, Ari dialed Benito's number, his fingers trembling. This was bigger than any comet trajectory or star chart, this was about the fate of the world.

His call went straight to voicemail. "Benito," he began, voice trembling, "I need to talk to you about something… something big." As he uttered those words and more, even identifying a priest from the Vatican as being involved, he looked back at the red light on the intercom, its innocuous blink hiding the incredible secret it had revealed.

CHAPTER
EIGHTEEN

Deep within the fortress-like complex of the National Security Agency in Fort Meade, Maryland, was an immense surveillance center—a top secret hub of global information gathering. Signals Intelligence Analyst Helen Leeds was a cornerstone of this intricate operation, a seasoned veteran who had spent years weaving through the digital webs of countless high-value targets. One such subject was an astronomical engineer employed by the European Space Agency named Ari Finelli.

The NSA's interest in Finelli wasn't personal; it was a matter of national security. Finelli was part of a team coordinating a satellite payload for the rogue nation of Carpathia, a young Moldovan breakaway state located in the turbulent Balkan region. As far as Leeds and the NSA were concerned, this particular payload held the potential to shift the balance of power within the region, thereby demanding their utmost attention.

Inside the NSA's rambling complex, Leeds sat at her station, the glow of the massive monitor in front of her illuminating her focused features. A new batch of intercepted communications had arrived, ready for her expert analysis. As she began sifting through the latest unencrypted trove of information, her routine task took an unexpected turn.

Ari Finelli wasn't discussing the Carpathian project. Instead, the audio she was monitoring suggested he was eavesdropping on a conversation occurring in a conference room at the European Space Agency's NEOCC in Frascati, Italy. Finelli's colleagues—a Dr. Neri, Dr. Henriksson, and two others in the room apparently from the Vatican—were engaged in a discussion that was entirely foreign to her.

They were talking about something they referred to as a "Celestial Guardian." The conversation was dense with scientific jargon and cryptic references. Terms like "manipulation of celestial bodies," "gravity influence," "cosmic positioning," and "weapon" weaved an intriguing and confusing picture, made more captivating by the apparent involvement of the Vatican and even an asteroid approaching Earth. Leeds found herself leaning in, drawn to the mystery unfolding in her headphones.

For a moment, she forgot about Carpathia and the satellite payload. This was something else, something potentially much bigger. She scrambled to keep up with the conversation, to make sense of the breadcrumbs of information.

Feeling a rush of adrenaline, she realized she wasn't just dealing with a routine surveillance operation anymore. This Celestial Guardian, whatever it might be, seemed to possess significant importance and potentially even pose grave concerns. This was something that the upper echelons needed to know about.

With a newfound sense of urgency, Leeds began crafting an encrypted report, summarizing the intercepted conversation and its potential implications. As she forwarded the report up the chain of command, she couldn't help but feel a shiver course through her body. This wasn't just about a satellite payload for some tangential rogue nation anymore. This was about a mysterious object called the Celestial Guardian. And something told her that things were about to get very complicated very quickly.

The gears of the intelligence machine had been set in motion. An unsuspecting Ari Finelli had inadvertently revealed a secret of cosmic proportions, and now, not only the Vatican or potentially the black market, but powerful governments around the world were being drawn into the unfolding drama of the Celestial Guardian.

CHAPTER
NINETEEN

As former chaplain for the European Space Agency, Father Benito Finelli was no stranger to the mysteries of the cosmos. He had recently left his position at the ESA to serve the Church more directly, becoming the trusted assistant of one of the most powerful princes of the Church: Cardinal Lorenzo Ricci, head of the Vatican's Congregation for the Preservation and Understanding of Ecclesiastical Artifacts. Although he enjoyed his work for the cardinal, a part of him still longed for the thrill of scholarship and scientific correlations he had known in his previous life, though his second love—biblical archeology and ancient religious artifacts—was being well served in his current role.

As evening fell over Rome, Benito Finelli moved with familiar ease around Cardinal Ricci's office, attending to the customary after-hours tidy up. Always meticulous, he ensured that everything was organized for the following day. It was an act of service, almost meditative in its routine.

A low buzz from his pocket disturbed his rhythm. Checking his phone, he found a voice message from his younger brother Ari, an astronomical engineer at the ESA's NEOCC facility. The message was jumbled with jargon but clear about this being a revelation of something momentous. Something about a *celestial guardian*.

With a newfound sense of purpose, Benito continued his task. As he emptied the trash bin, a torn piece of paper caught his eye. It was Ricci's handwriting, and even though it was half torn, he could make out the words "Celestial Guardian" and "Michael Dominic."

A sudden chill ran down his spine. His brother's message, and now this discarded letter? He hastily picked it up, smoothed it out on the desk, and began to read. The note described the Guardian with awe, attributing its design to Leonardo da Vinci and its capabilities to something that bordered on the mystical.

The letter also hinted at Ricci's ambition to seize control of the Guardian. The cardinal clearly saw it as a tool for gaining power within the Church. But for Benito, a faded scholar with memories of exploring the night sky, it was an echo of a past he had left behind.

His thoughts wandered back to the early days of his chaplaincy, the excitement of shared exploration, the thrill of discovery alongside Europe's most skilled engineers and bravest astronauts. The Guardian represented not just a tool, but a link to a forgotten era of his own life, full of wonder and innovation. It was a challenge, a call to his dormant curiosity.

As he pocketed the paper, his mind raced. The knowledge he had now could potentially alter the course of history. Ari's message had hinted at an even deeper secret surrounding the Guardian.

Returning to his phone, he typed out a swift message to his brother: *We **need** to **talk**—but **not** by **phone**. Must research first*. He tapped the Send button, then extinguished the lamp, shrouding the office in darkness.

Benito stepped out of the room, the dim light from the hallway casting a long shadow behind him. The seeds of a plan began to sprout in his mind. The Guardian had become his new obsession, his path into a game of power and knowledge. But first, he needed to understand more.

IN THE DAYS THAT FOLLOWED, Benito Finelli became increasingly consumed by his quest. He pored over historical texts, decoding ancient documents, searching for any whisper of da Vinci's Celestial Guardian. When not buried in books, he shadowed Ricci closely, carefully constructing a façade of routine service while patiently waiting for any opportunity to glean more about the Guardian.

Benito's moment came sooner than expected.

One afternoon, Cardinal Ricci was away for the day, leaving Benito alone in the office. Benito seized his chance. He scoured Ricci's sanctum, his gaze eventually falling on an elegant sheet of Vatican stationery partially hidden beneath a stack of theological texts on the cardinal's desk.

He recognized the handwriting instantly—it was Ricci's, and it spoke of the Guardian again, in similar detail as was known, but not about its ability to influence the movement of celestial bodies. Up to now he hadn't known if Cardinal Ricci was aware of that fact—and this did nothing to confirm or deny it—though it was likely Ricci was developing his own plans for establishing authority over such power.

The Church's control of such a device could shift global power dynamics in ways that Benito hadn't dared imagine.

Over the next few days, the young priest insinuated himself further into Ricci's confidence, and by mentioning his astronomical expertise, the cardinal eventually began to ask Benito questions related to the Guardian. He then proved himself indispensable in the cardinal's mission to gain control of the Guardian, although Ricci remained cryptic about the subject overall. Benito's astronomical acumen gave the cardinal a unique understanding of the Guardian's potential and, over time, he was able to subtly guide Ricci toward a more aggressive pursuit of the device.

Yet, Benito kept the fact that he already knew the deeper power of the Guardian and its implications to himself. For now, his place was in the shadows, playing the faithful assistant while he plotted his next move.

The stage was set, the players unknowingly bound in a high-stakes game of cosmic proportions, and Benito Finelli was ready to manipulate it all to his advantage.

CHAPTER
TWENTY

The Vatican canteen buzzed with midday life, a respite from the demanding schedule of religious service and spiritual devotion. Priests, nuns, Swiss Guards, and Vatican staff all mixed together, enjoying the brief moment of community and connection that the lunch hours offered.

In one corner, sitting across from each other at a small wooden table, were Ian Duffy and Sister Teri. Their usual friendly banter was tinged with an undertone of curiosity as they watched Father Michael and Hana chatting intimately from across the room.

"Those two are quite close, aren't they?" Teri observed, her eyes never leaving the pair. She knew them both well—she had worked alongside Michael for years in the Archives, and she had developed a respect for Hana's intellect and dedication during her brief visits to the Vatican and in their past adventures.

Ian, sipping on his coffee, nodded. "They've been through a lot together. Saved each other's lives more times than I can count. It's hard not to grow close after something like that."

Teri agreed but remained silent for a moment. "Ian," she began cautiously, "what do you make of Pope Ignatius's recent ruling about priests marrying?"

Ian glanced at her, the edges of his mouth curving into a knowing smile. He had been wondering when this topic might come up. "It's a big change, that's for sure. A lot of folks are still trying to get their heads around it."

"I wonder," Teri continued, "if Michael has given it much thought."

Ian looked back at Michael and Hana. They were deep in conversation, Michael's usual earnest demeanor softened by Hana's presence. "I can't speak for him, of course," he said, "but I reckon he's too focused on this Guardian business to think about much else."

But as he watched them, Ian couldn't deny the possibility. There was a connection between them, something deeper than friendship. And with Pope Ignatius's ruling, that connection could evolve into something more, something that would have been unthinkable just a few months earlier.

Ian looked back at Teri, his eyes sparkling with a mix of amusement and curiosity. "What do you think, Teri? Should we start planning their wedding?"

The young nun laughed, the sound a welcome break from the canteen's clamor. "Let's not get ahead of ourselves, Ian. But I must admit, it would be a beautiful thing to see."

Their laughter joined the hum of the communal room, a small pocket of joy amid the rising tide of uncertainty. For now, at least, they could find comfort in these shared moments, a reminder that even in the face of impending doom—as Michael had recently shared with Ian in confidence —there were still reasons to smile.

Just as their laughter subsided, a server arrived, setting a plate of *penne alla arrabbiata* in front of Teri and a panino stuffed with prosciutto and mozzarella before Ian.

"They do make a lovely couple, don't they?" The server, a young, cheerful Italian girl, chimed in, not needing to clarify who she was referring to.

Ian shared a knowing glance with Teri before responding, "I suppose they do, yes."

The server gave them a nod, her eyes twinkling with mischief before she moved on to the next table.

"Everyone seems to have noticed," Ian said, a hint of amusement in his voice. He speared a piece of mozzarella with his fork, watching as it stretched and then snapped. "But Michael's devotion is to the Church," he pointed out, his tone more serious now. "And Hana's first love is her work."

Sister Teri considered this for a moment. "Perhaps," she conceded. "But hearts have a way of making their own rules, don't they?"

Ian chuckled, taking a bite of his panino. "Indeed they do, Sister. Indeed they do."

THE CANTEEN HAD BEGUN to empty, the afternoon light streaming through the tall windows and casting long, golden shafts onto the terracotta tiles. The usually bustling space was now quieter, the murmur of the remaining diners fading into a comfortable hush. At a corner table, Michael Dominic and Hana Sinclair sat across from each other, their half-empty plates of fusilli, green with pesto, growing cold.

Michael pushed the corkscrew-shaped pasta around his plate, a distant look in his eyes. His mind was elsewhere, consumed by worries about the future. He felt the edges of his independence fraying under the looming prospect of Cardinal Ricci's authority. His position as prefect of the Archives, once a shield that offered him the freedom to navigate his own course, now felt like a sword hanging over his head.

"I feel like a bird who's about to have his wings clipped, Hana," Michael confessed, his voice barely more than a whisper. He glanced up from his plate, his gaze locking with hers. There was a vulnerability in his eyes that tugged at her heart. "I've long had the privilege of autonomy under Pope Ignatius's reign. But with Ricci... I don't know if I can operate under someone's thumb."

Hana watched him for a moment, her heart aching for him. She reached across the table, her hand covering his. The touch was gentle, a silent promise of her support.

"Change is difficult, Michael," she said softly, her thumb rubbing small circles on the back of his hand. "But remember, you're not alone. You've got allies who will stand by you, come what may."

His gaze softened at her words, a small smile pulling at the corner of his lips. "You've got such a knack for making mountains seem like molehills."

"Perhaps that's why we make such a good team," she replied, her smile matching his. "Together, we'll face whatever comes our way."

In the quiet solitude of the canteen, they sat, hands clasped and hearts connected. The world outside carried on, but for a moment, they found solace and strength in each other's company amid the uncertainty.

Michael gave Hana's hand a gentle squeeze before letting go, picking up his fork and starting to toy with his pasta again. After a moment, he put the fork down and looked at her with a serious expression. "There's another matter that we need to address," he said. "The Guardian... its potential power... it *could* alter the trajectory of that asteroid."

Hana's eyebrows shot up in surprise. "You're talking about actually using it? Changing celestial paths? But we haven't found that missing page or information, if it even exists, to know the complete formula."

He nodded. "I believe we're reaching the point where we'll have no choice. We've spent days trying to uncover it without success. Even without the full formula, we need to start the process. The question is, who should manage its operation? It's not a matter to be taken lightly. In the wrong hands, the Guardian could be dangerous. And we certainly can't do it."

"I agree," Hana replied thoughtfully. "But given its required dependency on a nuclear reactor, wouldn't we need the cooperation of the government where the reactor is located? I mean, we'd probably be talking about the Leibstadt Nuclear Power Plant in Switzerland, I suppose, right?"

"Yes, Dr. Neri told me that's the most likely candidate, since it's the youngest and most powerful of that country's four operating reactors. Years ago, after the Chernobyl disaster, Italy shut down all its nuclear plants," Michael confirmed. "But we'd have to keep this highly secret, for obvious reasons. And it's not just the Swiss government we need to worry about. If word gets out about the Guardian's capabilities, every government will want to stake a claim, not to mention their military leaders, who will see this as *the* ultimate weapon. And who knows what other kinds of bad actors will want a piece of that."

Hana nodded, her mind spinning with the implications. "It's a political and ethical minefield. We're dealing with powerful technology, sovereignty, international cooperation… not to mention the potential for misuse. As you said before, we really have to tread carefully here."

"But we don't have the luxury of time," Michael added, running his hands through his hair in frustration. "That asteroid isn't going to wait for us to sort out our political dilemmas."

"Maybe it's time to bring in more allies, Michael," Hana suggested. "People with power and authority. We can't carry this burden alone. We need to think strategically about who we can trust and how to navigate this."

Michael sighed deeply, feeling the weight of the world on his shoulders. Yet, looking at Hana, he felt a glimmer of hope. "You're right. But whoever is chosen to carry out this mission, the Celestial Guardian must remain under the control of the Vatican. I don't think any other person or entity can be trusted with power this all-consuming.

"So, yes, it's time to make some tough decisions."

Hana's brows furrowed. "We also need counsel, Michael. Sensible, ethical counsel. This device isn't just a potential savior; it's also a potential weapon of war."

"I couldn't agree more," Michael responded. His gaze turned pensive as he scanned the room. "We need people who can guide us, offer balanced advice on how best to control the Guardian."

Hana leaned forward, her elbows on the table, her mug of coffee cupped between her hands. "All right, so, who do we need for this... 'celestial' endeavor?"

"Well, firstly, we'll need an astrophysicist. It's all about moving an asteroid, right? Who better to understand the mechanics of space?"

Hana nodded, rubbing her forehead. "I know a guy, Dr. Richard Lindberg from the University of Tor Vergata. I interviewed him once about the potential for asteroid mining. He seemed eccentric, but his knowledge of celestial mechanics struck me as astounding."

Michael considered this. "Eccentric could work for us. All right, next we'll need an energy expert. We have to harness the power of a nuclear reactor, after all."

Hana's brows knit together. "The ESA should have someone... Ah! Dr. Neri mentioned a woman once. Dr. Marianne Schuler. Brilliant energy physicist. Bit standoffish, apparently, but she knows her stuff."

"Standoffish could keep the group focused. Okay, I like that," Michael said, making a note on his pad. "Finally, I think we might need a Leonardo da Vinci scholar. Someone who can get inside the man's head, understand his designs."

Hana grinned. "I have the perfect person for that. Professor Enzo Bellini. I met him during a journalism conference in Florence. He's an art historian who has spent his entire career studying da Vinci. His insights could be invaluable."

Michael leaned back, a satisfied smile on his face. "So we have Lindberg, Schuler, and Bellini. Sounds like a good start. Let's bring them in and see if they're willing to join this crazy endeavor."

Their gazes met, an understanding passing between them. This was the beginning of something monumental. They could only hope their chosen collaborators would be willing to leap into the unknown with them.

As they listed these names, a sense of hope kindled within them. It was a formidable task that lay ahead, but they knew they weren't alone. With trusted advisors, they would navigate these turbulent waters, ensuring that the Guardian was handled ethically, sensibly, and for the benefit of all humanity.

CHAPTER
TWENTY-ONE

C ardinal Lorenzo Ricci had received the news he had been anxiously awaiting: Pope Clement had granted his request. The Celestial Guardian, a device of profound importance, would now fall under the dominion of the Congregation for Artifacts. Despite the monumental victory, Ricci maintained a stoic façade, but privately, a triumphant thrill coursed through him.

Without wasting any time, he made his way to the Secret Archives, the fortress of historical and religious significance nestled deep within the heart of Vatican City. Here, a world of ancient secrets lay, untouched and unspoiled, their power and significance lost in time. But Ricci had one particular artifact in mind, one that held the promise of reshaping not just the Church, but the world itself.

As Ricci's office had phoned earlier announcing the cardinal's visit, Father Michael Dominic met him at the Archives' entrance. His eyes were filled with a mix of emotions—disapproval, frustration, and a hint of resignation. His voice, usually calm and controlled, trembled slightly as he greeted the man.

"Cardinal Ricci," Michael acknowledged, stepping aside to allow Ricci to pass. "I must express my disagreement with this decision. The Celestial Guardian is a delicate and powerful device. It's not just a piece of history; it's a potential harbinger of future events. I don't believe we can entrust it to just anyone."

Ricci paused, turning his gaze to meet Michael's. His response was measured, an assertive reassurance cloaked in respectful deference. "I understand your concerns, Father Dominic, and I respect your dedication to the Church and her artifacts—but I am not 'just anyone,' as you say. Rest assured, the Guardian will be handled with the utmost care and respect."

Continuing onward, Ricci navigated the vast corridors of the Archives, Michael reluctantly leading the way. They arrived at a secured chamber, the final resting place of the Celestial Guardian. A wrought iron gate guarded the entrance, its austere design an imposing contrast to the architectural grandeur that marked the rest of the Archives.

Michael hesitated, then with a resigned sigh, retrieved a set of ancient keys from within his cassock. The key turned in the lock with an echoing click, the gate creaking open. Inside, atop a pedestal of intricately carved marble, lay the Guardian. Its various gears and dials glinted in the dim light, reminiscent of a time when human understanding of the cosmos was less absolute and more mystical.

Ricci approached it with a sense of awe. His eyes traced the cool metal surface, dancing across the precise, delicate workmanship of Leonardo da Vinci. Beside the machine, encased in a glass cabinet, lay a blueprint of sorts, a testament to da Vinci's brilliance and ingenuity.

Turning to Michael, Ricci extended his hand. "The blueprint, if you please, Father?"

With a deep frown etched on his face, Michael reluctantly

handed over the document, his fingers lingering on the parchment. "I beseech you, Cardinal, to consider the implications of this power. The Guardian was crafted by a genius but left unfinished for a reason."

Ricci nodded, accepting the diagram. "I assure you, Father Dominic, the Church is not ignorant of its potential risks. And that is precisely why it now must be under our control. For the greater good of the Church, of course."

As Ricci departed with the Guardian and the blueprint, Michael was left standing in the silent chamber, a foreboding unease settling in his chest. The Celestial Guardian was no longer a silent artifact in the Secret Archives; it was now a tool in the hands of an ambitious cardinal. And as he stared at the now vacant pedestal, Michael couldn't help but wonder— had he just handed over a key to salvation, or a device of destruction?

~

WHEN MICHAEL CALLED her with the news, Hana was stunned. It wasn't as if she hadn't considered the possibility of someone stepping in at some point to assert their authority over such a profoundly important device, but the thought of a rival Vatican faction hadn't occurred to her. Something like that would never have happened under Pope Ignatius's watch, she reasoned. But this was a new regime, and not one Michael had quite settled into yet.

"The only saving grace," he said with a smile in his voice, "is that he may not discover the invisible ink identifying the more powerful capabilities of the Guardian. Which means, Ricci doesn't have access to Leonardo's specific modus operandi using infrared light. At least not yet. And we've taken careful notes and reproductions of what we found on it, so all is not lost there."

"But Michael," Hana protested, "if Ricci gets even the slightest hint of the truth, it won't take him long to piece everything together. We can't underestimate him."

There was silence on the other end of the line for a few beats. "Yes," Michael finally said, his voice far away. "That is a risk we have to consider. But for now, we have to use this time wisely."

Hana was pacing the length of her apartment now, her heart pounding. "And what if he does figure it out? He could potentially use it for... well, for *what* I don't know. Power? Control? The consequences could be catastrophic."

"We can't let that happen," Michael assured her. "Remember, we have yet to find the continuation page or pages in the Archives, if there *is* more to be found. Maybe, as the process unfolds, da Vinci left us more clues, more safeguards. We don't have much to go on when the device is used in actual practice. We need to remember, or assume, that it was only theoretical even in his time."

Hana sighed, pinching the bridge of her nose at the onset of a headache. She trusted Michael, but the stakes were higher than they had ever been before. "Good point," she said quietly. "Okay, but we need to move fast. And we need to be ready for anything."

As she hung up the phone, Hana felt the weight of their task settle heavily on her shoulders. She looked out the window at the stars twinkling innocently in the night sky, pondering the role they played in this age-old game of power and secrecy. She steeled herself for the difficult journey ahead, ready to do whatever it took to protect the Celestial Guardian's secret.

CHAPTER
TWENTY-TWO

The dim, cramped apartment in Rome smelled of old newspaper and overcooked coffee. Ari Finelli, his tall frame folded into a worn-out armchair, fiddled with a paperclip as he peered at his older brother across the room. Benito, who had traded a scientist's lab coat for a priest's cassock years earlier, was nervously pacing the small space.

"We need a plan, Benito," Ari began, his voice steady. "This Guardian... you said it's in the Congregation's vault?"

Benito nodded, wringing his hands in his cassock. "Yes, the cardinal got it from Father Dominic and it's now stored in our vault, to which I have access. But Ari, stealing from the Vatican... it's a sacrilege!"

Ari sighed, rubbing his forehead. "We're not stealing a relic, Benito. We're liberating a scientific marvel from those who would keep it hidden away. It's an astronomical device, not a holy artifact."

"Regardless, the consequences of getting caught..." Benito trailed off, his face pale.

"Oh, we won't get caught," Ari reassured him reflexively. "Think about it: the money we could get for this could change our lives. We could finally live free of all these... constraints."

Benito was silent for a while, lost in thought. He had joined the Church to seek answers, to find some meaning in the universe's grand design. But he had grown disillusioned over time with the politics and the secrecy and the gossip rampant throughout Vatican City. And now, this opportunity seemed like a ticket out.

Finally, he looked up at Ari. "Okay. Let's say we do this. How would we even find a buyer?"

Ari smiled, a gleam in his eye. "The black market for such artifacts is larger than you might think. There are plenty of private collectors, scientists, and especially governments who would pay top dollar for a device like this. We just need to find the right intermediary."

"But the vault," Benito said, his forehead creased in worry. "It's not just a simple lock and key. There's a coded access system needing biometric identification."

"You leave that to me," Ari said, leaning back in the chair. "I've been dealing with more complex systems at the ESA for years. You just need to get me inside the building, and I'll take care of the rest."

Benito nodded slowly, his heart pounding. He looked at his brother, the scientist, the renegade, and couldn't help but feel a spark of hope. It was risky, but the rewards could indeed be staggering, changing their lives forever.

"All right," Benito said, his voice barely above a whisper. "Let's do it."

Ari smiled, reaching over to clasp his brother's hand. This was it. They were in this together, ready to gamble everything for a chance at a different life. They were the Finelli brothers, against the world.

INSIDE A DIMLY LIT, wood-paneled room deep within the bowels of the National Security Agency's Fort Meade complex, a long mahogany table shimmered beneath the soft lights overhead. Seated around it were the top brass of the NSA and a few senior officials from the Central Intelligence Agency, a handful of serious-faced individuals with badges that bore clearance levels most wouldn't even dream existed.

At the head of the table sat CIA Director Bryce Caldwell, a stern man in his mid-sixties, a career intelligence officer with a reputation for ruthlessness when national interests were at stake. Displayed on a massive LED screen were satellite images of the Vatican and various aerial shots of the ESA facility.

"Here's the situation," Caldwell began, his voice cutting through the air like a knife. "A device, designed centuries ago by one of history's greatest minds, rightfully predicted an incoming asteroid event, something our scientists had yet to discover. That would be amazing, but apparently it is also capable of shifting the trajectory of an asteroid, and it is under the control of a foreign entity. This isn't just about averting a cosmic threat; it's about who holds the keys to an unparalleled weapon."

A woman on his right, NSA Deputy Director Lisa Monroe, leaned forward, her auburn hair tied in a tight bun, revealing piercing green eyes. "This Guardian, if our intel is accurate, represents a technological development that would put even our most advanced defense systems to shame. It's not just a tool to divert asteroids; it's potentially a weapon that could, in theory, redirect most any roving celestial body to any point on Earth. Imagine the strategic implications of that."

CIA Deputy Chief Angela Weber, a formidable figure known for her analytical acumen, interjected. "The implications are manifold. Beyond the immediate threat of the asteroid, if this Guardian does what it's rumored to do, it's not just a game-changer; it's a world-changer. Redirecting celestial bodies at will? The defense, or rather the weaponization potential, is both staggering and terrifying."

General Harrington, the Pentagon's military liaison to the NSA, added, "In essence, we're looking at the potential to weaponize space in ways we hadn't even imagined. This isn't just about protecting our nation; it's about maintaining a balance of power on Earth—but with the balance in our favor."

Director Caldwell nodded gravely. "Exactly. Our national security is paramount, and while global cooperation is preferred in times of shared threats, we can't risk a power like this Celestial Guardian falling into adversarial hands or being used against us. Which is why we need the CIA's expertise on this. We need to acquire that device swiftly and discreetly. We have the intelligence and resources, but we'll need your operatives' finesse and field experience."

Weber, leaning back, responded with measured confidence, "Consider it done. We have operatives in Rome experienced in extracting assets from high-security locations. But we'll need a detailed blueprint of the Vatican's security apparatus."

Another CIA official, an operations director named Mitchell, spoke up. "With the combined intel from both our agencies, I believe we can execute this operation with precision."

Monroe, from the NSA, looked around the table. "Given the magnitude of the situation, we need to act fast. This remains strictly 'need-to-know.' Every move should be shadowed in silence."

With the gravity of the mission evident on every face, Director Caldwell concluded, "We proceed with Operation

Nightfall, then. We covertly acquire the Guardian and any associated documents. No traces, no witnesses. The Vatican's security is tight, but we've dealt with tougher. We'll need the best team on this. Time is of the essence, people. Let's ensure the Guardian is in safe hands. Our hands."

CHAPTER
TWENTY-THREE

Each flickering screen and illuminated control panel in the Operations Center of NASA's Planetary Defense Coordination Office splashed cold, electronic light onto the faces of a sea of analysts and officers. Headquartered in Washington, D.C., the room buzzed with life, a pulsating engine of tension and anticipation. It was a chaos of orchestrated precision, a ballet of strategic coordination set to the drumbeat of a thousand keystrokes and hushed conversations.

Suddenly, the sharp voice of a young officer, new to the department but with an uncanny knack for her field, cut through the hum of focused activity. "Commander, we have a Level 5 detection on screen!" she exclaimed, her wide eyes frozen onto the data streams cascading down her workstation monitor.

Commander Karen Matthews, a veteran with silver-streaked hair and eyes that had seen more in decades than most would in a lifetime, broke away from a hushed consultation with her deputy. With a brisk gait that commanded respect, she navigated across the floor and stopped at the young officer's station. Her seasoned eyes scanned the screen, taking in the blips and flashes of data.

"Show me," she instructed, her voice as sharp as a whip.

The officer obediently brought up the screen that now held their collective fates, her fingers dancing across the keyboard. The display refocused, homing in on a specific sector of space. There, highlighted and blinking ominously, was the anomaly—a glowing blip that made Matthews's blood run cold.

"This is, what… an asteroid?" she asked, her words lacing the hush-filled room. Her voice remained steady, holding the creeping sense of dread at bay, steadying the nerves of those around her.

"Yes, ma'am," the officer responded, her voice strained. "Its size, velocity, and trajectory all match the characteristics of an asteroid. Preliminary measurements suggest a diameter of approximately six kilometers."

The atmosphere seemed to tighten in the room, as if the words had sucked the very oxygen from the air. An asteroid of that magnitude was a planet-killer. Fear, like a cold fog, swept through the room, chilling the hearts of even the most seasoned officers. A lump of unspoken foreboding lodged in Commander Matthews's throat. But she swallowed it down, her spine steeling. There was no room for fear; there was only room for action.

"Have we named it yet?" she asked, her gaze unflinchingly set on the screen.

The officer shook her head. "No, ma'am. You have that honor."

In the stark silence of the room, Matthews took a moment. Her eyes bore into the image of the impending doom. Though tradition allowed discoverers to name such celestial bodies after themselves, she didn't want any personal nomenclature associated with this particular beast.

Thus, her decision made, she spoke. "Well, until the International Astronomical Union assigns its official numerical designation, let's call it... TerraStygian," she declared, "for Dark Earth." It had a grave, somber ring to it, much like the asteroid itself.

"Now, plot its trajectory," she commanded, her figure casting a long shadow over the hushed operators.

Another officer, fingers poised above the keyboard, quickly followed the order. A line, sinister in its certainty, sprouted from TerraStygian. It cut a foreboding arc through the inky blackness of space, tracing a path of destruction toward an all-too-familiar blue dot. Earth.

"Commander, we have a projected impact with Earth in ninety-four days," the officer reported, his voice barely louder than the rustle of a leaf in a tempest. "Exact trajectory is uncertain at this point as the asteroid seems to be tumbling, providing a less than accurate prediction. At present it seems to be heading for the Atlantic Ocean but, to be honest, it doesn't matter. The size of such an impact anywhere on Earth will be devastating to the entire planet."

An oppressive silence descended on the room, a thunderous quiet that roared louder than any words. Every gaze was locked on the screen, the glowing trajectory a beacon of their shared doom. But then, as if an invisible switch had been flipped, the room came alive. The paralysis of fear was replaced by the kinetic energy of action. The Operations Center was transformed into a hive of determined activity. Officers and analysts scrambled, making calls, firing off alerts, and preparing to face the unthinkable. Every person, every cog in the machinery, moved with a newfound sense of urgency into preordained protocols and operational procedures conceived for just such an event.

The clock was ticking, and they had a planet to save.

CHAPTER
TWENTY-FOUR

I t was late afternoon when Michael and Hana reached Sapienza University. Rome was bathed in its timeless, warm ocher glow, the city's historic buildings casting long shadows on the cobblestone streets. They made their way through the campus where Professor Enzo Bellini had his office.

As they approached the Renaissance-era building, Hana turned to Michael, a look of determination on her face. "Let's hope Professor Bellini is as intrigued by da Vinci's Guardian as we are."

"How could he not be?" Michael responded.

The corridors were quiet, with most students and faculty already gone for the day. They found the professor's office at the end of a long hallway, a brass plate with his name marking the door. Michael rapped sharply on the old oak, the sound echoing down the corridor.

"Enter," came a voice from inside.

They pushed open the door to find a room that was more library than office. Shelves lined with ancient books, sketches, and dusty sculptures crowded the room. At the center of this chaotic but fascinating space sat Professor Bellini, a grizzled man in his sixties, engrossed in a manuscript.

He looked up as they entered, his eyes reflecting a flicker of curiosity. "*Buonasera*, my friends. Please, do have a seat. To what do I owe this unexpected visit?"

Michael took a deep breath before he began. He leaned forward in his chair, resting his elbows on his knees, and locked his gaze with Professor Bellini. He started by talking about the mysterious manuscript he had discovered in the Secret Archives, and how it had led them to one of da Vinci's long-rumored inventions. As he spoke, he watched the professor's face carefully, gauging his reaction. Initially, Bellini's countenance reflected skepticism, his brows knitting together as he listened.

But Michael didn't falter. He dove deeper into the subject, explaining how the parchment hinted at a device of apocalyptic proportions. A device conceived by the ingenious mind of Leonardo da Vinci, that could theoretically shift celestial bodies. Bellini's eyebrows shot up at this, and slowly, his skepticism was replaced by a growing fascination.

Hana watched this transformation, an anxious knot in her stomach slowly unfurling. She picked up where Michael left off, explaining the specifics of the Celestial Guardian.

"The Guardian," Professor Bellini interrupted, his voice barely a whisper as he leaned back in his chair. The room fell silent except for the soft rustle of ancient parchment. His gaze seemed to focus on something far away, as if he were visualizing the device. "You say da Vinci's mythical creation truly exists? And its purpose... to influence the course of an asteroid?"

Hana nodded, her heart pounding. "Yes, Professor. That's what we believe. And we think da Vinci designed the Guardian, if given the required amount of energy, to direct it in a way that it could exert just such an influence. But we need someone who understands his work, his way of thinking. We need your expertise to decode this."

Professor Bellini stayed silent, his fingers tapping on a weathered manuscript in front of him. His eyes seemed lost in thought, a myriad of emotions passing through them. The room was filled with an almost tangible tension as they waited for his response. The silence was punctuated by the distant tolling of the university bell, subtly marking the passage of time.

Finally, the professor broke the silence. He looked up at them, his eyes firm with resolve, a spark of excitement twinkling within. "Intriguing. Truly intriguing. To be part of a quest that could validate and breathe life into da Vinci's genius... It aligns perfectly with my life's work, my passion. Very well, I will join you in this unprecedented endeavor."

Relief washed over Hana and Michael. Their first hurdle crossed, the first collaborator on board, they were one step closer to unlocking the secrets of the Celestial Guardian.

As the sun dipped below the Roman skyline, casting an amber glow across the city, Michael and Hana found themselves seated in a rustic trattoria tucked away among the twisting streets of Trastevere. Their dinner companion was Dr. Marianne Schuler, a highly regarded energy physicist whose work had frequently taken her into the realm of the unconventional.

Dr. Schuler was a striking woman, her sharp features made sharper by the candlelight, her piercing hazel eyes reflecting the flickering glow. The hum of lively Italian conversation formed a pleasant background for their meeting, while the aromas of roasted garlic and fresh, hand-crushed herbs wafted tantalizingly from the kitchen.

With a note of gravity in his voice, Michael began their improbable tale. He spoke of a centuries-old mystery, an ancient design born from the ingenious mind of Leonardo da Vinci. The Celestial Guardian, a device of formidable power and incomprehensible potential, had been the focus of their recent endeavors, if given the power a nuclear reactor could provide.

Schuler's usually calm voice rose with slight incredulity as she began. "This Guardian," she said, her eyes flicking between Michael and Hana, "are you seriously suggesting that it's engineered to control such significant amounts of energy? That it has the power to deflect the course of an asteroid hurtling through space? Forgive me, but I find that highly improbable."

Hana met the scientist's gaze with a steadfast affirmation. Her eyes glowed with the intensity of their mission. "Yes, Dr. Schuler. The Guardian is exactly that powerful. And its predictions have been authenticated by the ESA itself. But it's your unique knowledge and experience that we need to unlock its full potential, to bring this piece of history to life."

The conversation hit an abrupt pause. Silence seeped into their corner of the bustling trattoria, making it seem as though they were the only three people left in the world. Schuler's attention was drawn to the solitary candle placed between them on the table. Its wavering flame, casting long shadows that danced on the surface of the rustic wooden table, seemed as mystifying as the proposition laid in front of her. The outlandish nature of the task appeared to hang in the air, a challenge that was undeniably enticing despite—or perhaps because of—its veer into the realm of the fantastical.

As Schuler's eyes remained transfixed on the dancing flame, Michael cut through the silence. His voice, firm and unyielding, mapped out the urgency of their mission. He laid out the details of the approaching asteroid, painting a bleak picture of the cataclysm that could ensue if its path remained unaltered.

As the priest's impassioned speech came to a close, Schuler's gaze finally moved away from the hypnotic dance of the flame. Her eyes met those of Michael and Hana, their combined conviction reflected back at her. It was a proposal unlike any she had ever faced—an invitation to take a leap into the uncharted territories of scientific exploration. Her career, after all, was built on defying convention, on pushing the envelope of established norms. And this—this might just be the most profound challenge she had ever been offered.

"Well," she started, her gaze focused on the middle distance as she sorted through the complexities. "Firstly, we must understand that a nuclear reactor operates on the principles of nuclear fission, producing tremendous heat which is then converted into electricity. Now, our task is to devise a mechanism to channel this energy into the Guardian."

She looked at them, her eyes alight with the challenge. "Imagine a heat exchanger system, of sorts, that takes the thermal energy and converts it into a form that can be utilized by the Guardian. That's the crux of our first challenge."

Hana chimed in, "But wouldn't harnessing that energy be dangerous?"

A nod from Schuler affirmed Hana's concern. "Precisely. Safety procedures are of utmost importance. We must implement fail-safes, redundancies... subjecting it to forces it was never originally designed to withstand.

"And then," she continued, "comes calibration. The energy from a reactor is enormous. We have to fine-tune the system to ensure that the Guardian neither overloads nor underutilizes the energy provided."

She took a deep breath, letting the weight of her words settle. "This, of course, is all hypothetical. But if we're going to attempt this, we must cover all bases, anticipate all outcomes."

The atmosphere in the room was charged with apprehension and excitement. "It's a daunting task," Schuler finished, looking at her two companions, "But not impossible. And certainly worth attempting."

With a final moment of contemplation, Dr. Schuler leaned back in her chair, a slow smile creeping onto her face. The light of intrigue in her eyes mirrored the curiosity she saw in Hana and Michael. "I must admit, this is… captivating," she confessed, her voice echoing the fascination in her eyes. "Regardless of whether it leads to an unprecedented discovery or a scientific dead end, it promises to be extraordinarily compelling. Count me in."

Michael and Hana experienced a wave of relief. Their journey was far from over; in fact, it was just beginning. But with Dr. Marianne Schuler on board, they were a step closer to confronting the imminent threat. They had a shot at saving the world.

THE NEXT DAY, the sun was a brilliant disk hanging in the crisp morning sky as Hana and Michael made their way through the historic campus of Rome's University of Tor Vergata. Surrounded by stately buildings that embodied decades of academic pursuit, they navigated their path toward the astrophysics department, where their next potential collaborator was found.

Dr. Richard Lindberg, an esteemed astrophysicist known for his groundbreaking work on celestial mechanics, was a character straight out of an academic fantasy. His office, a spacious room lined with shelves crammed with well-thumbed books and scattered piles of paper, was as eccentric as its occupant. A parrot named Kepler, with feathers as vibrant as the rings of Saturn, was perched on a wooden stand, occasionally squawking out phrases in a cacophony of sounds.

Dr. Lindberg himself was seated behind a grand desk, his white hair standing at odd angles, giving him an Einstein-esque appearance. His eyes sparkled with curiosity as they entered, reflecting a mind that, despite its age, was still as active and eager as that of a young scholar.

Hana started the conversation, reintroducing herself from their previous encounter—an interview about asteroid mining—some years earlier. Lindberg's face cracked into a warm smile of recognition. "Ms. Sinclair," he said, his voice a gravelly echo bouncing off the book-laden walls. "I remember your piece. It was enlightening."

With the ice broken, Michael and Hana began to lay out their story—the discovery of the Celestial Guardian, the threat of the asteroid, and their desperate quest to alter its path. As the tale unfolded, Lindberg listened, his initial look of perplexity gradually replaced with an expression of growing fascination. Even Kepler seemed to tune into the conversation, its head cocking from side to side with avian interest.

When they finished, Lindberg leaned back in his chair, casting a long look at his visitors. His mouth opened, closed, and then opened again. "Are you serious?" he finally asked, his voice trembling with incredulity. "You're talking about a device—an ancient device designed by Leonardo da Vinci, no less—with the ability to alter the trajectory of celestial bodies?"

"That's correct," Michael replied, holding Lindberg's gaze. "And we believe that your expertise in celestial mechanics is vital for understanding how to use this device effectively."

Lindberg was silent for a long moment, his brows

furrowing as he pondered their proposition. Then, slowly, a smile began to spread across his face. It was the kind of smile one wears when presented with a challenge that isn't just intellectually stimulating, but potentially groundbreaking.

"A challenge of astronomical proportions," Lindberg mused, his eyes twinkling with anticipation. "This sounds... exciting. Very well, Ms. Sinclair, Father Dominic, I am on board. Let's see what Leonardo's Celestial Guardian can truly do."

TWENTY-FIVE

The conference room at NASA's Planetary Defense Coordination Office was thick with tension. Charts and projected paths of TerraStygian were plastered across the walls, screens displaying simulations of its trajectory. At the head of the long mahogany table, Commander Karen Matthews sifted through her notes, her fingers tapping a rhythm betraying her own anxiety.

"The key is to keep this discreet and professional," she began, her tone firm. "We inform without inciting panic. And most importantly, we ensure our global partners are on the same page." Her eyes met those of her senior communications officer, Alex Reyes.

Reyes nodded, pulling up a draft of the press release on the large screen at the front of the room. "This is what we have so far, Commander," he said.

Everyone leaned in to read:

NASA's Planetary Defense Coordination Office – Official Statement

Re: (4679) TerraStygian Celestial Body

NASA's PLANETARY Defense Coordination Office, in its ongoing commitment to monitor celestial entities, has recently detected a celestial body, which has been designated "(4679) 2024 PY2 TerraStygian." Our latest observations place this object on a near-Earth trajectory. This discovery underscores the value of persistent surveillance of our cosmic neighborhood and our dedication to ensuring the safety of our planet.

At present, a multidisciplinary team of astronomers, astrophysicists, and other experts are engaged in a thorough evaluation of TerraStygian's path, composition, and potential implications. While preliminary assessments indicate a near-Earth trajectory, we are employing advanced modeling techniques and simulations to project more precise path determinations and ascertain any potential risks. It is our goal to not only understand the trajectory but to also develop any necessary preparatory and defensive measures that may be required.

Recognizing the importance of global collaboration in these endeavors, we are actively partnering with international space and defense agencies. Through this international collaboration, we are pooling expertise, technology, and resources. Such a cooperative approach maximizes our capabilities to devise effective strategies for defense and preparedness. By doing so, we reaffirm our dedication to ensuring the safety and well-being of communities around the globe.

We understand the weight of our responsibility and the concerns that information of this nature can raise. Therefore, we implore all partner agencies and relevant institutions to maintain the utmost discretion and professionalism when addressing or disseminating information about TerraStygian. In times like these, accurate, measured, and unified communication becomes vital. It is imperative that the information relayed to the public is consistent, transparent, and does not incite unnecessary alarm.

As the situation progresses and our understanding of TerraStygian evolves, we pledge to keep all stakeholders updated with timely and factual information. We appreciate the trust placed in our office and remain unwavering in our commitment to the protection of Earth and its inhabitants.

COMMANDER MATTHEWS READ the release twice, then looked up at Reyes. "Add, 'Further updates will be provided as our understanding of the situation evolves,'" she suggested.

Reyes made the addition swiftly. "Done."

"Send this to our counterparts at ESA, Roscosmos, JAXA, Indian Space Research Organisation, China National Space Administration, and the other major space agencies immediately," Matthews instructed. "Make it clear that we're here to collaborate and share information, not compete."

A murmur of agreement passed through the room.

With a heavy breath, Commander Matthews closed her notes. "All right, team, it's in our hands now. Let's get to work."

TWENTY-SIX

The morning sunlight streamed into the conference room at the European Space Agency's Near-Earth Object Coordination Center in Frascati, not far from Rome. It was a broad room, all steel and glass, filled with an air of palpable urgency. The world outside buzzed with the news from NASA's recent press release, naming the impending threat "TerraStygian."

A large, round table stood at the center of the room, encircled by seven individuals, a most unlikely assembly of minds, each distinguished in their roles and expertise and now unified by a single, monumental mission. Besides Michael and Hana, the group comprised Professor Enzo Bellini, the Leonardo da Vinci scholar; Dr. Marianne Schuler, the energy physicist; Dr. Richard Lindberg, the astrophysicist; and Drs. Sofia Neri and Lars Henriksson, mission analysts from the ESA.

Amid the weight of the news and the gravity of their task, it was Hana who broke the silence, setting the stage for the imminent discussion. "With TerraStygian threatening our world, we're here not just to decipher Leonardo's masterpiece, but to wield it as our savior. So, the question stands: how do we do that?" She then turned, gesturing toward Bellini, inviting him to initiate the conversation.

Professor Bellini appeared to be the embodiment of an academic titan—aged but sharp as a tack. The lines on his face crinkled as he adjusted his glasses, the morning sunlight catching in the lenses. His fingers, old but steady, skimmed over a copy of da Vinci's sketch of the Guardian on the table before him. He cleared his throat, commanding the attention of the room as he began to articulate his understanding of the device.

"My extensive analysis of da Vinci's designs suggests a rather ingenious principle at work in the Guardian: that of harmonic resonance," he started, his Italian accent coating the scientific terminology with an alluring charm.

Bellini continued, using his hands to animate his explanation. "You see, every celestial body, including asteroids, has its own natural frequency—much like the unique note produced by each individual key on a piano. These frequencies are a result of the body's mass, composition, and physical structure."

He gestured toward the sketch, tracing the intricate design with a finger. "Leonardo's Celestial Guardian, it seems, was designed to create and emit frequencies. Not just any frequency, mind you, but one specifically tailored to match, and influence, the natural frequency of a particular celestial body—in our case, this threatening asteroid."

The professor sat back, allowing his words to settle before he dove into the crux of the matter. "With a significant energy source, and I mean truly significant, the Guardian should theoretically be capable of sending out a powerful resonant frequency. This frequency would travel through space, and upon reaching the asteroid, would 'vibrate' with it."

Bellini's eyes sparkled with a mix of scholarly excitement

and the gravity of their task. "This harmonic resonance, if powerful enough, would start to subtly influence the asteroid's path. It's rather like nudging a pendulum with tiny, persistent pushes until it swings wider and wider."

He spread his hands wide, indicating the potential trajectory change. "With a steady application of these 'nudges,' we could potentially divert TerraStygian off its collision course with Earth."

Dr. Marianne Schuler, the energy physicist renowned for her groundbreaking work in nuclear energy conversion, sat poised, her analytical mind already probing the challenge at hand. Her posture was erect, shoulders squared, as she leaned forward across the conference table. Her fingers were interlaced on the polished wood, the only outward sign of her focused determination. Her gaze was piercing, cutting through the heart of the matter with its unwavering intensity.

"From an energy perspective," she began, her voice steady and clear, "we're not talking about a trivial amount of power. We're considering an energy requirement that, quite frankly, is mind-boggling."

Dr. Schuler didn't mince words. Her stark honesty hung in the air, painting a clear picture of the magnitude of their undertaking. But in the next moment, she moved on to the solution, her voice filled with the determination that had marked her successful career.

"Our most feasible option is to connect the Guardian with a nuclear reactor," she stated. "Nuclear energy is the only source we have that can generate the immense power we need for such a major operation. You're all familiar with how a nuclear reactor works, correct?"

Seeing several unconvincing nods, she elaborated. "All right, let me try to break this down," she began, her voice steady.

"The core process involved is nuclear fission, where heavy

atoms—usually uranium or plutonium—are split, releasing vast amounts of energy in the form of heat. This heat is then typically used to create steam, which in turn drives a turbine to produce electricity.

"In the case of the Celestial Guardian, the nuclear reactor wouldn't directly power the Guardian. Rather, it would generate the power needed to run a complex system that aligns with the Guardian's instructions. This power-hungry system might include superconducting magnets, large-scale laser arrays, or other exotic machinery. I've been calling this the 'Gravity Resonance Emitter,' or GRE."

Schuler stood and moved over to a large whiteboard, where she began drawing a rudimentary diagram of the system. "Think of the GRE as a sophisticated machine that translates the Guardian's instructions into a form of energy pulses, ones that can interact with the gravitational field of a celestial body like the asteroid."

She glanced around the room. All eyes were shifting intently between her and the whiteboard.

"Now, creating these energy pulses requires enormous amounts of power, hence the nuclear reactor. Once the Guardian calculates the precise pattern of energy pulses required to nudge the asteroid off course, these instructions are sent to the GRE."

Dr. Schuler traced the line from the Guardian to the GRE on her diagram. "The nuclear reactor then powers the GRE, converting the electricity into the energy pulses. The GRE emits these pulses according to the Guardian's instructions."

She capped the marker and turned back to face everyone. "So, in essence, the Guardian is like the brains of the operation, while the nuclear reactor and the GRE act as the muscle, generating and directing these energy pulses in sync with the Guardian's instructions, subtly interacting with the asteroid's gravity and thus influencing its path."

Hana, who had been diligently jotting down notes, looked up, her brow furrowed in thought. "So essentially," she ventured, "we're talking about a translation device, right? Something that can convert one form of energy into another."

Dr. Schuler nodded, a faint smile playing on her lips at Hana's succinct summary. "Exactly," she confirmed. "A translation device capable of handling the immense power of a nuclear reactor and making it 'speak' the language of the Guardian. It's a colossal task, but it's within the realm of our combined expertise."

Schuler's statement echoed in the conference room, a reminder of the uncharted territory they were venturing into. But despite the daunting task, there was a spark of excitement, a collective thrill of being part of something bigger than themselves—a mission to save their home planet.

A deep, contemplative silence followed Dr. Schuler's words. Then, Dr. Richard Lindberg, the astrophysicist whose extensive research on celestial mechanics had brought him significant acclaim, entered the conversation. A tall man with a tousled mop of gray hair and an almost childlike enthusiasm for his work, his lanky frame was hunched over in thought.

"The harmonic resonance idea is genius," he said, complimenting Professor Bellini's deduction, "and while the power requirement is indeed enormous," he added, nodding toward Dr. Schuler, "the intricacy of this operation lies not just in power or resonance. It's also a matter of cosmic precision."

His words brought a new depth to the discussion. The twinkling blue eyes beneath his bushy eyebrows hinted at the vast knowledge and experience they held. Lindberg had a knack for simplifying complex concepts without losing their essence—a talent that shone in his teaching and research.

"I have the expertise to determine the asteroid's natural

frequency," he said, his voice steady and confident. "I can also help calculate the exact magnitude of the shift required to ensure the asteroid's trajectory misses Earth."

A thoughtful frown creased his brow as he continued. "My main concern, however, is about timing. This operation isn't as simple as pressing a button and immediately seeing results. We must consider the asteroid's current speed, its distance from Earth, and the time it will take for the energy wave to travel from the Guardian to the asteroid."

He glanced around the room, his gaze serious. "If our calculations are even slightly off—if the energy wave arrives too early or too late—the asteroid may not shift in the way we want. In fact, we could inadvertently make the situation worse."

His words brought a stark realization of the precision they would need to achieve, a precision that went beyond engineering and entered the realm of cosmic choreography. It was a daunting task, but it was one they were uniquely equipped to handle. Lindberg's candid input added another layer to their strategy, underscoring the meticulous planning and timing their mission required.

Dr. Neri, the ESA mission analyst, nodded in agreement. "We'll coordinate with you, Dr. Lindberg, using our near-Earth object tracking data to refine those calculations. Once we have the precise timing, we can program it into the Guardian."

Dr. Henriksson, the other ESA scientist, focused on the logistics. "Transporting the Guardian may be a challenge, given its potential volatility. We need to ensure it's safely moved and properly installed at the Leibstadt reactor site in Switzerland."

Michael Dominic, mostly silent till now, looked around at the group, clearly concerned. "While we're focusing on this path, we must be aware of the other international agencies, especially following NASA's press release. One assumes they will be seeking their own solutions to divert TerraStygian. Our endeavor, shrouded in secrecy as it is, could lead to potential conflicts. They don't know about the Guardian and if they did, they might see it as an unprecedented, even dangerous, way of addressing the problem. How do we handle that?"

Dr. Neri responded, "You're right, Father Michael. ESA has connections with many of these agencies, and they'll expect us to share significant developments. We'll need a well-structured communication plan, without revealing our unique approach."

Bellini added, "Leonardo's Guardian is not just a tool, but a work of scientific genius. Its significance could be lost or, worse, misused if revealed prematurely."

Hana weighed in. "Not to mention the implications of releasing the news that Leonardo da Vinci, centuries ago, created a device potentially capable of shifting an asteroid's trajectory. It would send shockwaves throughout the academic and scientific communities, not to mention capture the interest of militaries everywhere."

Dr. Lindberg mused aloud, "And if others knew about the Guardian and our plans, they might either try to stop us, thinking it too risky, or attempt to take control of the operation for themselves."

Dr. Henriksson chimed in, "We have to be one step ahead. We must ensure the Guardian remains under the Vatican's protection, even after we achieve our mission. At the same time, it's crucial to maintain an open channel with these agencies, ensuring they see us as collaborators, not competitors. Speaking of which, Father Michael, would it be possible for you to bring the Guardian to our next meeting so we can see this marvel for ourselves?" The others' eyes gleamed with anticipation as all heads turned toward the priest.

Absorbing the feedback and the request, Michael nodded. "Yes, I think that would be possible. The device is currently in the custody of another congregation in the Vatican, but I'm sure I'll be able to acquire it for such a gathering as this.

"So," he continued, "secrecy in our operations, but diplomacy in our communications. We're using a technology that, in the wrong hands, could be a weapon of unbridled power. Ensuring the Guardian's safety and its secret status is paramount."

The room once again fell silent, each person digesting the enormity of the task at hand. They were venturing into uncharted territory, but the commitment and unity around the table were undeniable. They were prepared to unravel the secrets of the Celestial Guardian and save the world, all while navigating the complex web of international diplomacy and intrigue.

CHAPTER
TWENTY-SEVEN

The Vatican's grandeur took on a different visage in the midnight hour, its sprawling architecture casting long shadows under the pale moonlight. While the streets outside the walls echoed with the faint sounds of a city that never truly sleeps, within its heart, the Vatican lay wrapped in a quiet sanctity.

The Finelli brothers moved with an unspoken synchronization, honed from years of shared adventures together. The weight of their endeavor hung heavy between them, for attempting a theft within the Vatican was no ordinary venture.

Father Benito, having been a part of the Church and of this congregation in particular, knew the place intimately. It was this knowledge, coupled with Ari's meticulous planning, that had brought them to a little-known entryway near the back of the Vatican Library.

With deft hands, Ari made easy work of picking the ancient gate lock, illuminated only by the dim glow of his wrist-mounted light. The door yielded silently, revealing the dim interior, and the brothers made their way deeper into the bowels of Cardinal Ricci's Congregation for Artifacts.

Marble floors, reflecting the soft glow from wall-mounted lamps, seemed to guide their way inside as they wandered through a living tapestry of human history. Intricately carved statues of saints and martyrs peered down at them from alcoves, bearing silent witness to their clandestine mission.

Lining the halls were ornate wooden display cases, the treasures within shielded by thick glass. Benito's trained eye recognized fragments from the Dead Sea Scrolls, Byzantine relics, and even what was rumored to be a shard of the True Cross. A golden chalice glittered in the dim light, its age making the gold seem more burnished than shiny. Paintings, too, hung on the walls, depicting ancient religious scenes, their colors still vivid despite the centuries.

But as entrancing as these artifacts always were, at that moment none held the allure of the Celestial Guardian.

Reaching its chamber, the weight of their intentions bore heavily on Benito. Stopping in his tracks, he made the sign of the cross. His voice was a soft, guilt-ridden murmur. "Forgive me, Father, for I am about to sin." His fingers lingered on his chest, the finality of their mission pressing down on him.

Ari, with his usual stoic demeanor, didn't break stride. "Repent later. Move now," he whispered back. He had always been the grounded one, a counterbalance to his brother's more spiritual inclinations.

As they stood before the chamber, it became clear that Cardinal Ricci had taken extra precautions, unknown to Benito until just now. A state-of-the-art electronic lock, starkly out of place amid the archaic splendor, stood between them and their goal. Its neon blue light blinked intermittently, like a mocking beacon. Benito wouldn't risk using his normal biometric access for obvious reasons.

He watched, his heart rate quickening, as his brother

delved into his bag. Ari produced a compact device, no larger than a deck of cards, with various ports and a small LED screen. Swiftly, he connected it to the lock, initiating an override sequence.

For a few heart-stopping moments, nothing happened. The screen displayed a series of codes, changing rapidly as the device attempted to decipher the lock's encryption.

Then, the sweet sound of success—a gentle beep—and the lock's light turned green. With a soft click, centuries of secrecy were about to be unveiled.

Inside, the Celestial Guardian sat atop a marble pedestal, bathed in a soft light. The device, with its ornate cogs and glyphs, was both beautiful and mysterious.

Ari's voice broke Benito's trance, "We need to hurry. This is our narrowest window."

But as Benito approached to aid Ari, a distant echo reached their ears—a sound that shouldn't be there.

Footsteps.

Ari's hands froze over the Guardian, and the brothers locked eyes. The steps grew louder, approaching rapidly. Time seemed to slow as the weight of their predicament settled in. Someone was coming. The sanctity of the night was about to be shattered, and there was no place to hide.

MOMENTS EARLIER, Father Michael Dominic and Swiss Guard Karl Dengler navigated the mazy corridors of the Apostolic Palace, their footsteps echoing off the ancient stone walls. The urgency of their mission had set a serious tone, but assuming Cardinal Ricci's staff would be gone that late at night, they planned accordingly.

As they approached the private gallery of the Congregation for Artifacts, Michael's instincts kicked in. The

slight creaking of a door, the soft murmur of voices—
something was amiss.

He signaled for Karl to halt, his hand reaching out to
steady him. Peeking around the corner, his eyes widened at
the sight of Father Benito Finelli and another man, Guardian
in hand, caught red-handed.

"Benito, what are you two doing here?" Michael's voice
rang out, filled with suspicion. Then, with a look of dawning
recognition, he turned to Ari. "Don't you work at the ESA? I
remember you coming into the conference room during my
meetings there."

Father Benito's face turned pale, his eyes darting between
his brother and Michael. Ari, ever the calm one, took a step
forward, his face betraying nothing.

"Yes, Father Michael, I'm an ESA engineer," Ari began, his
voice smooth and reassuring, "and that's where I learned
about the Guardian's importance. We came to ensure it's put
to good use."

"You expect us to believe that?" Karl snapped, his eyes
narrowed.

Father Benito, seeming to find his voice, chimed in, "It's
the truth, Michael. This is my brother, Ari. We're all on the
same side here."

Michael looked from Benito to Ari, his mind racing. He
knew Benito; they had studied together at Loyola, shared
beliefs and dreams. Could he trust him now, under these
strange circumstances?

"*We* were coming to take the Guardian to the ESA,"
Michael finally said, his voice cautious, his next words
intentional. "They have the means to utilize it to save the
world from TerraStygian."

Ari's eyes flickered at the mention of the asteroid's name.
A momentary lapse, but Michael caught it.

"So. You know about TerraStygian," Michael stated, not as a question but a realization.

"Yes," Ari admitted, "we heard the news from NASA's internal release. The Guardian could be the key." He prayed that Michael wouldn't press him for how he had come upon the knowledge.

Michael studied the brothers, sensing that there was more to the story. But time was of the essence, and he couldn't afford to dig deeper now.

"Then we should work together," he finally said, his voice firm. "We'll take the Guardian to ESA tomorrow, and we'll do it as a united front. That way if Cardinal Ricci learns of it, at least his top aide will have been involved. And after I share it with the scientists there, we'll return it back here—where it will remain. Agreed?"

Ari and Benito exchanged a quick glance, a silent communication passing between them.

"Agreed," Ari said. With a blank look on his face, Benito swallowed, then nodded.

The four men left the chamber, the Guardian safely secured in Michael's care. The tension remained, but a fragile alliance had been formed.

But Karl was bothered. "You know, Michael, I don't know those two at all, but my first instinct is not to trust either one. Especially the younger guy, that Ari."

"I'm inclined to agree, Karl. But for the moment, we'll give them the benefit of the doubt. Let them show their hand and things may change."

As they made their way to their quarters, Michael couldn't shake the nagging feeling that the Finellis had an ulterior motive. Their willingness to cooperate had come too easily. But with the world's fate hanging in the balance, he had no choice but to depend on them, at least for now.

CHAPTER
TWENTY-EIGHT

The conference room at the European Space Agency's Near-Earth Object Coordination Center was filled with some of the brightest minds in their respective fields, each one brought together for an unprecedented mission. The room buzzed with excitement and anticipation as Michael and Hana carefully brought in the Celestial Guardian, hidden beneath a heavy, nondescript cloth.

The six individuals sat in eager attention: Professor Enzo Bellini, Dr. Marianne Schuler, Dr. Richard Lindberg, Dr. Sofia Neri and Dr. Lars Henriksson, and a newly introduced member, Dr. Samantha Harris, who was slated to serve as Mission Commander at the Leibstadt Nuclear Reactor facility.

Hana, feeling the weight of the room's expectation, began. "Ladies and gentlemen, what we are about to show you is the result of a journey that has crossed centuries. It's not just an artifact; it's a beacon of human ingenuity, a masterpiece crafted by Leonardo da Vinci himself." She looked at Michael, who nodded.

With a dramatic flourish, Michael pulled the cloth away, revealing the intricately designed Celestial Guardian, its rich bronze and walnut finish gleaming under the fluorescent lights. The room immediately filled with gasps and murmurs as eyes widened and jaws dropped.

Bellini was the first to speak, his voice trembling with awe. "It's... magnificent. To think that Leonardo's intellect extended this far. The design, the modern craftsmanship—it's beyond anything I could have imagined."

Dr. Schuler leaned forward, her eyes examining the Guardian with a physicist's curiosity. "I can see the potential here, the complexity. We're going to have a unique challenge harnessing its energy, but it's a challenge I'm excited to take on."

Dr. Lindberg's eyes sparkled with a keen interest as he absorbed the Guardian's layout. "The possibilities for calculating celestial movements... this is revolutionary. We're not just looking at history; we're holding the future in our hands."

Dr. Neri and Dr. Henriksson exchanged glances, their expressions reflecting a mix of amazement and determination. Neri spoke. "This could change everything for space research. We'll need to study this closely, understand its mechanics and how we can adapt it for our needs."

Dr. Harris, the person responsible for marrying the Guardian with modern nuclear technology, remained silent, her gaze locked onto the machine. Finally, she looked up, her face serious and determined. "It's a marvel, no doubt. But we have an immense task ahead of us. This is not just a piece of art; it's a tool, and we need to learn how to wield it. Time is not on our side."

Her words brought a sobering reality back into the room. They weren't just scholars and scientists admiring a masterpiece; they were a team on a mission to save the world.

Michael, sensing the shift in the room, stepped forward. "We have the blueprint, the knowledge, and the best minds to make this work. Together, we'll unlock the secrets of the Celestial Guardian and use it to avert a catastrophe. Let's get to work."

A newfound resolve settled over the room. The team, each person now fully aware of their role, nodded in agreement. The mission had truly begun, and the Celestial Guardian was no longer a relic of the past, but a key to the future.

LATER THAT AFTERNOON, Michael and Hana returned to the spot in the Archives where the priest had originally discovered the parchment for da Vinci's Celestial Guardian, the forgotten corner of the Archive filled with ancient texts and artifacts, each with its history and secrets. Michael's heart sank as he took in the sheer volume of materials. They had been searching this area off and on for days after first realizing something was missing in the coded instructions of the manuscript. And had found nothing. Now, they had no time left to remain in the dark. It was imperative they find it. Yet finding the missing part was going to be like chasing a ghost in the fog.

They began their search anew, pulling out drawers, opening heavy volumes, and sifting through layers of dust and time. Hours turned into what felt like days, each new discovery leading to disappointment. The silence of the Archives was only broken by the shuffling of papers and the creaking of ancient shelves.

Hana could see the frustration building in Michael's eyes. "Don't lose hope," she whispered, placing her hand on his shoulder. "We'll find it."

Just as the last rays of sunlight were giving way to the shadows of evening, Michael's hand trembled as he pulled out a hidden compartment in one of the less conspicuous shelves.

"Hana," he breathed, his voice barely a whisper. "I think I've found something."

Inside the compartment not far from where he had discovered the original document was a delicate parchment, folded neatly. As he unfolded it, his fingers quivering, he saw that the words written in Leonardo's hand, now visible, continued precisely where the first manuscript had stopped.

They looked at each other, eyes wide with realization. This was it, the missing piece of the puzzle. The information that could make all the difference in their monumental task.

Michael and Hana stared at the second part of Leonardo's Celestial Guardian manuscript, their hands trembling with anticipation. The parchment, yellowed by time and hidden away for centuries, was covered in da Vinci's unmistakable mirrored handwriting.

They continued unfolding the parchment, revealing more of the intricate diagrams and secret writings that had defined their understanding of the Celestial Guardian. Michael's eyes widened as he deciphered a section that described a fail-safe mechanism, something he had only hoped would exist.

"This is incredible," he said, his voice barely above a whisper. "Leonardo even designed a remote deactivation system. He foresaw the possibility that the Guardian could fall into the wrong hands."

Hana leaned in closer, her eyes scanning the text. "It seems he used a specific harmonic resonance frequency as a key to initiate the fail-safe. But how does it work?"

Michael's mind was racing as he absorbed the information. The fail-safe involved a carefully calibrated series of vibrations, each designed to interact with the Guardian's core mechanism. By emitting these vibrations from a distance, it was possible to disrupt the Guardian's function, rendering it inoperative.

"It's like a musical code," he explained, excitement building in his voice. "A symphony of frequencies that, when played in a specific order, can lock or unlock the Guardian's capabilities. It's a remote control, a way to safeguard the device's power."

Hana was captivated, her mind working to grasp the complex science and artistry behind the concept. "It's genius. A combination of physics, mathematics, and musical theory. Only Leonardo could conceive something so elegant and yet so practical."

They spent an additional hour poring over the manuscript, unraveling the intricacies of the fail-safe mechanism. There were drawings of unique instruments, designed by Leonardo himself, capable of producing the exact frequencies needed. The manuscript also described a sequence of calculations that would need to be made, taking into account the distance, atmospheric conditions, and even the time of year.

As they delved deeper into the text, they also discovered a list of materials and instructions for creating the fail-safe's remote control, all using technologies available during Leonardo's time. It was a mechanism to ensure the safe use and deployment of the Guardian. Without it, the Guardian, like all human devices, could be turned to evil purposes.

Finally, they looked up from the manuscript, knowing the path ahead was clear, but the stakes had never been higher. The Celestial Guardian wasn't just a tool; it was a weapon, one that could save the world or destroy it.

"We have to build this fail-safe," Michael said, conviction in his voice. "We have to make sure that the Guardian can never be used for harmful purposes."

Hana nodded, her eyes gleaming with resolve. "We have

the knowledge, we have the will, and we have the right people on the team. We'll make this work."

They left the Archives that night, the weight of their discovery heavy on their shoulders but the path ahead clear. They weren't just custodians of Leonardo's legacy; they were the stewards of the world's future. The Celestial Guardian was more than a machine; it was a symbol of hope, ingenuity, and the unbreakable bond between the past, present, and future. And they would do everything in their power to honor and protect it.

CHAPTER
TWENTY-NINE

TerraStygian, a colossal mass of rock and metal with a terrifying diameter of six kilometers, traversed the silent void of space. From the perspective of the universe, it was but a tiny speck, one of countless bodies weaving their way through the vast cosmic tapestry. Yet for the inhabitants of a small blue planet, it was a harbinger of doom, an existential threat that could very well defy all efforts to divert it.

The asteroid's surface, scarred and pitted from a million collisions, sparkled with a dark luster as it caught the distant rays of the sun. Its journey was one not of intention or design but of sheer gravitational fate.

As it careened through the asteroid belt, other space rocks loomed in its path. Smaller bodies were drawn toward it, trapped by its gravitational pull, only to be shattered upon impact, their fragments spiraling away into the darkness.

In one near-miss encounter, a sizable chunk of rock collided with TerraStygian's edge. The impact was colossal, the soundless explosion sending a shockwave through the asteroid's body. It seemed, for a moment, as if the trajectory might shift, as if its relentless march toward Earth might be altered.

But the forces at play were too immense, the momentum too great. TerraStygian continued on its path, the destruction merely a ripple in its surface, a brief and inconsequential pause in its cosmic journey.

It passed close to Mars, the red planet's glow a dull ember in the darkness. Its valleys and mountains, once thought to harbor life, now lay barren and cold, a silent witness to the asteroid's relentless approach.

The suspense of its journey was one felt only by those on Earth, who watched, calculated, and feared. To the universe, it was a dance of physics and time, a convergence of paths that had been set in motion eons ago.

As it moved ever closer, Earth's blue-and-white visage grew in the distance, a beacon calling TerraStygian toward it. Humanity's attempts to divert it seemed insignificant, almost futile against the backdrop of cosmic indifference.

The silence of space enveloped the scene, a quiet that spoke of both the beauty and the terror of the cosmos. TerraStygian's approach wasn't malicious or targeted. It was simply a fact of the universe, a reminder of the fragility and randomness of existence.

The trajectory was set, the course unaltered. The countdown to impact continued, a ticking clock that resonated in the minds of those who knew, a silent drumbeat echoing through the emptiness of space.

Earth awaited, and TerraStygian, indifferent and unstoppable, continued its approach.

CHAPTER
THIRTY

In an unassuming building near the outskirts of Rome, a clandestine operation was unfolding. Under the dim, focused glow of overhead lights, Father Michael Dominic surveyed the room filled with a select team of engineers, craftsmen, and scientists. Many were the very minds that had built the Celestial Guardian, and now they were gathered for a purpose equally profound but far more secretive.

At the center of the room lay a table filled with ancient manuscripts, modern blueprints, and an array of materials ranging from fine Italian bronze to cutting-edge microprocessors.

Professor Enzo Bellini, his eyes narrowed in concentration, was poring over Leonardo's hidden writings, translating lines that held the secrets to the fail-safe mechanism. His hands moved carefully over the parchment, his voice a mere whisper as he discussed his findings with Dr. Maria Galasso, a physicist responsible for the technological integration.

A few meters away, the clang of metal rang through the air as Maestro Antonio Ferrara, a master blacksmith, shaped the bronze components. The glow from the forge played across his weathered face, casting an ethereal light as he worked, melding the ancient with the modern.

Engineer Clara Lupino was engrossed in her task, soldering and calibrating, ensuring that the delicate balance of art and technology was maintained. Her hands were steady, her gaze unerring, as she breathed life into what would soon become the "Aegis Buffer."

Michael was focused on the dual significance of their task. The Guardian had the potential to save the world or unleash unimaginable chaos. The Buffer was their insurance, their safeguard against human folly.

He approached Bellini, who looked up with a weary but determined smile. "The last of it's been translated now, Professor," the priest said. "The Aegis Buffer can send a coded signal to decommission the Guardian from a distance. We've refined da Vinci's original plans to include deployment of the Vatican's own satellite, using our secure broadband connection to control the Guardian's active status remotely, without direct use of a nuclear reactor. But it requires a perfect calibration."

Bellini was astonished. "The Vatican has its own satellite?" he asked.

"It does," Michael replied, "and I was as surprised as you are when I learned of it myself. It's called *Oculus Petri*—Latin for 'Peter's Eye'—and it serves several functions for the Church. It provides navigation and mapping used covertly to ensure the safety of the pope and other high-ranking officials during international travels. It's used for information gathering for historical and archeological purposes, especially focused on discovering lost Christian artifacts or ancient biblical sites. And it provides secure communications between Vatican officials and various dioceses, ensuring privacy and integrity in sensitive matters."

Bellini nodded, impressed. Then he glanced at the Buffer as it took shape. It was more than a machine, he reasoned; it was a symbol of both wisdom and caution. It represented a bridge between eras, a testament to the timelessness of human curiosity and ingenuity.

Days passed quickly as they labored. The Aegis Buffer was tested, adjusted, and retested until it functioned flawlessly in trials using computer models.

Finally, as Michael held the completed Buffer in his hands, a profound sense of accomplishment settled over the room. They had done it. They had created a safeguard against the unknown, a protector of the very fabric of their world.

Everyone fell into a respectful silence, each person contemplating the enormity of what they had achieved. In their hands lay the power to control the Celestial Guardian, a power that could save or destroy, depending on who wielded it.

They had created a capable defense, but in doing so, they had also uncovered a haunting truth: the real danger wasn't the Guardian itself but the hearts and minds of those who might seek to misuse it.

As they filed out of the room, leaving the Aegis Buffer in secure storage, the weight of their responsibility lingered, a silent promise to guard not just a device but the ideals and integrity it represented.

CHAPTER
THIRTY-ONE

As they sat across from each other having lunch in the Swiss Guards' dining hall, Karl and Lukas savored their favorite meal, specially prepared that day by the kitchen's French chef—Swiss *Älplermagronen*, a hearty gratin of potatoes, Gruyère cheese, macaroni, cream, chopped bacon, and caramelized onions, with the traditional side of stewed applesauce—when their conversation turned to the asteroid.

"Father Michael said the European Space Agency is leading the project, in secret, of course," Karl explained, "and they plan to test da Vinci's Celestial Guardian some time in the next few days. I've never seen him so focused, and with good reason."

Lukas looked up from his plate, his fork hovering in mid-air. "Celestial Guardian? That sounds like something out of a sci-fi movie. Are you pulling my leg?"

Karl chuckled and shook his head. "I swear on my mother's grave, I'm not making this up. Father Michael is working with scientists, engineers, even historians. They're all huddled up in labs and archives trying to make sense of da Vinci's blueprints."

"Blueprints? From da Vinci?" Lukas finally put his fork down, realizing this wasn't a casual lunchtime tale. "Wait, you mean to say that this project is based on something Leonardo da Vinci created?"

"Exactly. Supposedly, the Guardian can divert an asteroid from its trajectory, hence saving us from a catastrophic event. They've assembled a team to understand and implement the mechanics."

Lukas shook his head in disbelief. "This is surreal. Father Michael is wrapped up in this, you say?"

Karl nodded, taking a sip of his water. "He's crucial to the project. Not in the scientific way, but more as a moral compass, an authority figure. The team respects him, and his knowledge of history and theology is helping them navigate some ethical minefields. He even found the manuscript in the Vatican Archives that started all this."

"That's remarkable," Lukas commented, "and terrifying at the same time. An asteroid?"

Karl sighed. "Yes, terrifying is one word for it. It's still classified, which is the only reason I haven't mentioned it before now, but if the Guardian's test fails, we're talking about potential global calamity. So, you can imagine why Father Michael is so focused. And the reason for my sharing it with you now, *liebchen*. In case anything happens…"

Lukas picked up his fork again as he looked into his partner's eyes, but his appetite had diminished somewhat. "This is a heavy burden for anyone, let alone a solitary priest."

"It's the sort of thing you hope stays in the realm of science fiction," Karl said, wiping his mouth with a napkin, "but here we are."

Both guards fell silent for a moment, contemplating the enormity of what was unfolding behind the Vatican walls.

Finally, Lukas broke the silence. "We Swiss Guards are trained for many situations, but an asteroid wasn't on the list."

Karl chuckled. "Maybe they'll add it to the curriculum after this."

With that, the two men resumed eating, but the weight of the conversation lingered, as heavy as the Gruyère in their *Älplermagronen*.

THIRTY-TWO

T he hum of machinery filled the air as Michael walked into the lab where the Celestial Guardian was being calibrated for its final test. Bellini was at his workstation, engrossed in a sea of calculations. Drs. Schuler and Neri were engrossed in a conversation by the 3D printer, and Dr. Samantha Harris was in a hushed discussion with Richard Lindberg near the Guardian prototype. Hana sat at the back of the lab monitoring project analysis reports, glancing up from time to time evaluating Michael. Clearly, there was something on her mind.

Michael approached Professor Bellini. "How are the final adjustments coming along, Enzo?"

The old man looked up, his eyes slightly red. "We're almost there, Father. A few more tweaks, and we should be ready for the last test."

At that moment, Dr. Harris broke away from her conversation with Lindberg and announced, "Team, the final test for the Guardian will be run tonight."

As the clock ticked away in the makeshift Vatican lab where the Celestial Guardian was housed, the atmosphere was electric with urgency. Each test, each calculation, brought them one step closer to diverting the incoming asteroid. The Guardian had to be precise; the margin for error was almost nonexistent.

Father Michael Dominic, the one around whom all this revolved, was a figure of quiet intensity. He was the calm in the storm, the rock upon which his team depended. But even rocks can erode, and Michael felt himself crumbling.

~

WITH THE PRESSURE having eased up a bit, Michael moved to the back of the lab, his attention now wholly consumed by the woman sitting before him. Hana's eyes searched his as she said, "Michael, there's something important we need to talk about.

"I've been doing a lot of thinking," she continued, hesitantly. "And despite what we discussed earlier, this whole situation with Earth facing a potential extinction-level event... well, I've been wondering more about... us."

Michael felt his heart swell. But alongside it rose a pang of guilt, sharp and unyielding. "Us," he repeated softly, almost afraid to give the word the weight it demanded.

Michael felt as if he were on the edge of two different worlds, teetering precariously between them. One world was filled with the sacred duties of his priesthood, the weight of the Guardian project, and the lives of millions hanging in the balance. The other world was smaller but no less significant— a world where he could explore a life with Hana, where the warmth of a single touch could eclipse even the gravest of responsibilities.

"Um... Michael?" Dr. Harris suddenly exclaimed from across the room. "We've got a problem with the Guardian's targeting system. We're out of alignment. If we don't fix it now, the whole mission could be compromised."

The words hit him like a sledgehammer, and suddenly, the back of the room felt stiflingly small. He looked up at Hana, his eyes full of a conflict that needed no explanation.

"I have to go," he said, nearly choking on the words.

Her eyes widened, but she nodded understandingly. "Go. We'll talk later."

Realizing the urgency, Michael immediately called Dr. Henriksson, the team's lead programmer and physicist at the Leibstadt nuclear station. "Lars, we've got a red alert on the Guardian's latest output. You need to look at this. Now."

Henriksson hurried over to a computer monitor, his eyes quickly narrowing as he assessed the data on the screen. "Ah, I see it," he muttered, fingers flying over the keyboard as he delved into lines of code and complex gravitational equations. "A deviation here could throw the entire mission off track. We need to correct this right now."

As Henriksson worked frantically to rectify the error, Michael felt his leadership being put to the test in a different way. Though he didn't possess the technical expertise to fix the problem himself, he recognized his role as the glue holding the team together, especially in moments of crisis.

"Okay, everyone," Michael announced, his eyes meeting each of his team members. "I want contingency plans ready in case we need to buy more time. Drs. Bellini and Lindberg, please explore alternative gravitational models. Drs. Schuler and Neri, can you double-check our most recent propulsion data? And Dr. Harris, would you liaise with the reactor team to ensure we have the power we need for any last-minute adjustments?"

As Henriksson continued his frantic coding in Switzerland, Michael took a moment to step back, observing his team swinging into action with efficient purpose. Though he couldn't manipulate the complex algorithms that powered the Guardian, he knew that his authority and ability to maintain focus were crucial.

In that moment, despite the chaos, despite the gaping unknowns of space and human emotion, Michael felt a sense of clarity. Perhaps this was his real gift—a gift not of technical prowess, but of human connection and leadership. And as he pondered this, the weight of his responsibilities seemed just a little bit lighter.

For the next several hours, the team labored intensively. Sweat, stress, and profound fear hung thick in the air, but gradually, they corrected the error.

OVER BREAKFAST THE NEXT MORNING, both Hana and Michael were unusually quiet, as if lost in thought. Lingering from last night's conversation was Hana's use of the word "us." It floated in the air, tangible and electrifying. It was a word he'd silently turned over in his mind during late nights in the lab, during casual conversations that always seemed to persist a little longer than necessary, and during those moments when their eyes met and held, speaking volumes that words could not capture.

For so long, Michael had accepted the limitations of his life as a priest, a life of service that often meant personal sacrifice. But the Church's new policy had shifted something fundamental, dislodging a piece of the wall he'd carefully built around his own desires. And now, faced with the astonishing reality of "us," that wall was crumbling faster than he'd ever thought possible.

The joy that filled him was unfamiliar, a euphoria that came from imagining a life where his love for the Church and his love for a woman were not mutually exclusive. But as quickly as that joy swelled within him, it was cut through by a sharp, almost visceral pang of guilt. Was he betraying his mission, his team, and the countless lives that depended on their success? Was he putting his own emotional satisfaction above the needs of the many? At the moment it felt as if he were standing on the precipice of a steep cliff, and the word "us" was a strong, almost irresistible, wind at his back.

THIRTY-THREE

T he cobblestones beneath St. Anne's Gate, having born witness to centuries of history, now served as the stage for a highly classified mission by a foreign government. Under the pitch-dark veil of a moonless night, three men, garbed in the ecclesiastical robes of priests, approached the threshold of the Vatican. Beneath the sanctified disguise, their bodies bore the hardened testament of years of special ops service to the U.S. Central Intelligence Agency—the ripple of trained muscles, the glint of concealed weapons—as the Gold Team carried out their assigned mission: Operation Nightfall.

On the surface, they blended seamlessly into the fabric of the holy city, their demeanors radiating calm solemnity. Their Vatican City credentials, works of impeccable forgery crafted by the NSA's elite documentation team, bore the seal of the Papal Office. Even the Swiss Guard, as trained and vigilant as they were, were fooled by the unfailing artistry of the deception.

With their identities unquestioned, the trio ventured into the Byzantine heart of the Vatican. Sacred silence echoed off the grand arches and frescoes, every gilded detail and venerated sculpture a testament to faith.

The men moved with the precision of a Swiss clock, their path winding through numerous rooms and galleries, past centuries-old works of art that held the gaze of countless pilgrims and tourists in daylight hours. The beauty of the place, however, was lost on the men; their focus was singular —find the device's secure development lab in the Vatican Archives' Belvedere wing, execute the mission, then exfiltrate.

This might have been a much more challenging effort had they not had the unknowing assistance of one Ari Finelli, whose own continued eavesdropping of Drs. Neri and Henriksson's private conversations at the ESA during development were themselves still being intercepted by the NSA. With that information, and the weighty resources of the American intelligence apparatus, the CIA operatives had little trouble locating the lab. The men had simply been told the Guardian was an artifact of immeasurable value, believed to reveal divine patterns in the celestial bodies. As if it mattered to them.

As they walked, their boots tread a rhythmic testament to their mission against the marble floor. The hallowed halls, usually echoing with holy chants, now reflected the clandestine whispers of the intruders. Their path was a labyrinth through history and faith, a path chosen for a singular purpose: to steal the Celestial Guardian before dawn broke over the holy city.

The smallest of the men, though "small" was a relative term, carried a large, black briefcase. It was unadorned and nondescript—a simple tool, yet it held a purpose of practical importance. The man's hands, scarred by years of service, gripped the handle firmly, his knuckles white under the strain of furtive tensions.

As they rounded a corner, they came across a group of

cardinals, their crimson robes a stark contrast to the austere marble backdrop of the Vatican hallway. The three operatives kept their heads lowered, relying on their disguises to blend in. They murmured soft greetings, their deep voices emitting practiced Italian. The cardinals returned the greetings, eyes brimming with curiosity but respectful of their assumed station.

One of the cardinals, an old man with sharp eyes, lingered on the departing figures. He noticed something amiss, something out of place—all three men were wearing black combat boots. The sound of hard leather on the marble floor echoed in his mind. It was unusual, even sacrilegious for priests to be so attired within the sacred confines of the Vatican.

His gaze hardened, but he said nothing. Doubts bloomed within him, but he silenced them. He was a man of faith, not suspicion, and he wouldn't let this break his focus on the evening's liturgical duties. But the image of the three priests and their boots remained etched in his mind.

"Brother John," the tallest of the three whispered, using their codenames. "Confirm again the exact location."

The man referred to as Brother John tapped an inconspicuous earpiece, receiving the coordinates from their off-site handler. "Fifth door on the right after we turn the corner. High-security access, biometric scan required."

The third man, Brother Paul, grinned. "Good thing we've got those covered."

The operatives reached the door, discreetly pulling out a device that looked like a modified PDA, equipped with a small screen and various cables. Brother John connected it to the door's control panel while Brother Peter took out a set of contact lenses and a thin, synthetic film shaped like a finger. They had been meticulously created from data hacked from the Vatican's own biometric databases.

With bated breath, they watched as Brother John's device bypassed the multiple layers of security encryption. The door clicked, then hissed open, granting them access to the room that held the Celestial Guardian. A rush of cold, conditioned air greeted them as they stepped inside, their eyes immediately locking onto the metallic casing of the Guardian. Without wasting a second, Brother Paul unzipped the case revealing a foam bed accommodated to fit the Guardian. For ultimate security, the case was fashioned after a Faraday bag, custom-lined with a metallic material capable of dispersing electromagnetic radiation across its surface forming a protective shield around the device. This prevented the device from sending or receiving any wireless signals, including cellular, Wi-Fi, Bluetooth, GPS, RFID, NFC, and others, in the event it might have been equipped with such capabilities. Men in their business took no chances.

"As of now, gentlemen, Operation Nightfall is a go," Brother Peter whispered, pressing another button on his earpiece. "We have the package."

With extreme care, the tallest operative lifted the celestial device, placing it gently into its new holder. Spying a series of actual modern blueprints lying near the device, they took those too, folding them carefully and tucking them into one of the case's inside pockets.

Closing the briefcase with a soft click, the men retraced their steps. Their footfalls echoed through the now quiet halls, passing resplendent artifacts and murmuring saints. They moved with renewed urgency, their mission completed but their escape far from guaranteed.

Finally, the Gold Team exited the Vatican from an entirely different gate, the Arch of the Bells, just south of St. Peter's Basilica, disappearing into the dark Roman night, the holy façade of the Vatican receding behind them. A sense of relief washed over them as they melted into the anonymity of the city's shadowy labyrinth, the Celestial Guardian secure in their possession. Unseen, the three priests who weren't priests vanished, leaving behind a Vatican under the unsuspecting watch of cardinals and guards, their presence a mere echo in the solemn corridors of power.

CHAPTER
THIRTY-FOUR

D r. Samantha Harris was the first to arrive the next morning, her swipe card and fingerprint granting her access to the high-security lab. She switched on the lights, expecting the gleam of the Celestial Guardian's metallic casing to greet her as it always did. Instead, she was met with an empty space on the workbench. She froze, her eyes widening in disbelief.

"No. No, no, *no!*" she muttered, rushing over to inspect the area, her eyes scanning for any signs of forced entry or disturbance. Most everything else was untouched: the sophisticated computer systems, the research notes, even the small quantum components that were yet to be integrated. Only the Guardian and its blueprints were missing.

As if on cue, the door swung open and Lindberg walked in, coffee in hand, only to freeze at the threshold.

"What happened? Where is it?" he stammered, the coffee cup dangerously close to tipping over.

"I don't know. I just got here," Samantha replied, her voice tinged with panic.

Within minutes, the lab was filled with the hurried

footsteps and confused voices of the rest of the team. Schuler, Neri, Hana, and finally, Father Michael Dominic. Each entered with the same moment of stunned silence as they processed the empty space where their last hope had been.

Michael stared at the void, his heart plummeting. "It's gone. But how? The security in this place is impenetrable!"

Hana clenched her fists. "Impenetrable for whom? We don't know who we're dealing with."

"It's an inside job," Lindberg declared, casting a suspicious glance around the room. "It has to be. No one else has access."

Schuler shook her head, disbelieving. "Do you realize what you're implying, Lindberg? That one of us—"

"I'm implying nothing more than the facts present," Lindberg cut in. "And the fact is, the Guardian is gone. Stolen from under our noses!"

Michael felt a knot of despair tighten in his chest. The room was thick with tension, suspicion turning allies into potential enemies within moments.

"We need to alert security," Neri spoke up, her voice tinged with fear.

"Security? The Vatican? And say what? Our secret celestial weapon is missing?" Michael retorted.

Samantha sighed, massaging the bridge of her nose. "We can't trust anyone. Not until we figure out how this happened."

Michael took a deep breath, fighting to keep his voice steady. "Right now, suspicion won't save the world. But we might have a chance to. We have to move forward, even in the face of betrayal."

The atmosphere in the lab was tense, a charged silence hanging heavy as the team gathered around the table. The absence of the Celestial Guardian was like a gaping wound, a silent testament to the disastrous turn of events.

"Is there nothing we can do?" Michael asked, his voice tinged with desperation. "Without the Guardian, we're helpless. All our work, all our planning—"

Hana looked at him, her eyes filled with a mixture of sorrow and something he couldn't quite decipher. "Michael, we failed. Whoever they were, they took everything. It's over."

Dr. Samantha Harris interrupted, pacing at the head of the table. "Actually, it may not be."

All eyes turned toward her. Lindberg, who had been quiet until now, looked up with interest.

"What are you suggesting, Samantha?" Michael asked, reading the veiled urgency in her eyes.

Dr. Harris glanced at Lindberg, who nodded almost imperceptibly. She took a deep breath. "During the development of the Celestial Guardian, we—Lindberg, Schuler, and I—anticipated the possibility of interference. The stakes were too high, the technology too potent."

Michael leaned in, hardly daring to hope. "What are you saying?"

Hana seemed to catch on first, her eyes widening. "You built another one, didn't you?!"

Dr. Harris nodded. "We called it Project Gemini, the twin backup to the Celestial Guardian."

Michael stood abruptly, his chair scraping against the floor. "Why wasn't I informed of this?"

Lindberg stood up, confronting Michael's incensed gaze with calm. "Father, we couldn't risk the knowledge of a backup falling into the wrong hands—especially not when those hands could potentially be among us."

It was a pointed statement, one that hung in the air with uncomfortable weight. Trust, it seemed, was a luxury none of them could afford.

Schuler piped in with, "We used separate servers, separate

workstations, even separate teams at times. Gemini is identical to the Guardian but kept in a remote secure facility. Even if they hacked our systems, they'd never find it."

Dr. Harris moved to her computer and tapped a series of keys. The wall screen flickered to life, showing a satellite image of a nondescript building. "Gemini is here. And it's ready."

Michael looked around the room, his eyes meeting each of theirs in turn—Hana's vibrant, Schuler's pragmatic, Neri's young but determined, Lindberg's steadfast, and finally Dr. Harris's, steely and resolute. In that moment, the weight of his responsibility—and their collective hope—settled firmly on his shoulders.

"We have a second chance then," Michael said softly, as much to himself as to the others. "Let's not waste it."

And so, in a lab filled with the brightest minds, under the vigilant watch of the Vatican, a secret hope was rekindled. Project Gemini, the shadow twin to their lost Guardian, became their last hope, their final gambit in a game where the stakes were nothing less than the fate of the world.

The room erupted into a flurry of activity, their newfound purpose reigniting the spark that had been so perilously close to extinguishing. But as they set forth on this renewed path, Michael couldn't shake the nagging question at the back of his mind: *Who among them could he truly trust?*

THIRTY-FIVE

I n the years leading up to this moment, NASA's NEOO center had operated largely out of the public eye, its mission shrouded in layers of national security concerns. It wasn't merely about observing celestial bodies; it was about preparing for a worst-case scenario. Just for such a mission, a spacecraft under the Double Asteroid Redirect Test (DART) program had been fast-tracked and kept on secret standby, equipped with a kinetic impactor designed to deflect asteroids off course. It was a hush-hush project, an insurance policy against the unthinkable, and that policy was about to be cashed in.

In a quiet, softly lit room filled with the radiant glow of computer screens, the tension was palpable. The men and women of NASA's Near-Earth Object Operations were huddled around their workstations, faces taut with concentration. The clock on the wall seemed to tick louder with each passing second, counting down to the moment of impact. Mission Control was a hive of last-minute checks and double-checks.

"Kinetic impactor is on target," said the flight director, her voice as steady as she could make it. "All systems are go for TerraStygian deflection. Counting down to impact in three… two… one…"

A collective breath was held for several long minutes as everyone waited for the data to confirm the kinetic impactor had struck the TerraStygian asteroid, a massive rock headed toward Earth. On a large screen at the front of the room, a live feed from the spacecraft showed the asteroid growing larger as it approached. The telemetry readouts were scrolling through green, all systems nominal.

"The impactor's onboard cameras are sending a visual," said the imaging specialist. The room's large screen flickered momentarily before displaying the crater-ridden surface of the asteroid, bathed in the cold light of space.

"Visual confirmed," the flight director acknowledged. "Stand by for impact confirmation."

Seconds stretched into an eternity. Team members exchanged tense glances, their thoughts a swirl of hope and dread. These were the longest seconds of their professional lives. The weight of humanity's future seemed to hang in the balance, teetering on the edge of this one pivotal moment.

The screen changed abruptly. A bright flash of light flooded the visual feed as the impactor met its target. A cheer started to form on the lips of the anxious observers, but it died just as quickly.

In the data analytics corner, an algorithm began crunching the new telemetry information. Numbers flickered on several monitors, graphs began auto-generating, and calculations ran at breakneck speed.

It was a few seconds before the telemetry expert's face turned ashen. His fingers hovered over the keyboard, seemingly paralyzed. Then, finally, he broke the silence.

"Flight Director, we have an anomaly," he announced, his voice tinged with disbelief.

The room froze. All eyes snapped to the main display screen where the asteroid's new projected trajectory was appearing. The line indicating its path should have already shifted subtly. It hadn't.

"On screen," she ordered, and a set of graphs and numbers popped up for everyone to see. The trajectory data didn't make sense. The asteroid's course had barely changed; the deflection was negligible.

"It looks like the impactor hit a softer section of the asteroid, almost like... quicksand. The energy was absorbed but the course alteration is minimal," the chief engineer explained, baffled.

Silence hung heavy in the room, broken only by the hum of machinery and the soft clattering of keys as analysts desperately scoured for data that might have suggested otherwise.

The flight director took a moment to absorb the weight of the situation. She then grabbed the red phone, reserved for dire circumstances, knowing that what she reported would travel up the chain to the highest echelons of government.

"As of now," she began, choosing her words carefully, "Operation DART is considered a failure. TerraStygian remains on a collision course with Earth. Recommend we initiate contingency protocols immediately."

The room was hushed, the reality sinking in. There was no escaping the facts; their best efforts to save the planet had failed. Every scientist, engineer, and technician in the room knew that it was back to the drawing board, but with a window that no longer offered the luxury of time.

The screen at the front of the room switched to a live feed of the asteroid in question. It was a silent, haunting image— this lifeless mass of rock tumbling through space, oblivious to the world it threatened.

"Notify the president," the flight director said solemnly.

"And get the international emergency response teams on the line. We need to explore every option, no matter how drastic."

In that moment, each person in the room felt the gravity of their failure but also the renewed urgency of their mission. They had trained for success but also for failure, and if humanity was to avert catastrophe, it would require something beyond what science and technology had so far been able to offer. With a collective nod, the NEOO team returned to their stations. There was much to do and, they now realized, terrifyingly little time in which to do it.

The asteroid continued on its course, indifferent to the flurry of human activity it had set into motion. And on Earth, the brightest minds convened in emergency meetings, racing against time now measured not in years, but in days and hours.

AGENT THOMAS BURKE sat in his sparse, utilitarian office at CIA headquarters in Langley, Virginia, his gaze lost in the maze of information displayed on his computer screen. The room was silent except for the faint hum of electronic equipment, a stark contrast to the tumult of thoughts churning in his mind. Burke, a seasoned agent, had become increasingly disillusioned with the agency's methods and priorities. His frustration stemmed from a deep moral conflict; as a conservative Catholic, he often found himself grappling with missions that contradicted his religious beliefs.

The ringing of his secure phone line curbed his introspection. Burke picked up the receiver, recognizing the number instantly. It was Ari Finelli, an analyst at the European Space Agency and an old friend from their college days. Their friendship had been forged in the crucible of shared faith and intellectual pursuits.

"Thomas, it's Ari," came the familiar voice, tinged with urgency. "I have something important to discuss. It's about something called the Celestial Guardian."

Burke's interest piqued. He had heard rumors about the device, a mysterious artifact of immense significance to the Church and, recently, to the intelligence community.

"What about it, Ari?" Burke asked, his tone shifting to one of professional curiosity.

"It's been stolen. Taken from a secret Vatican location by three men disguised as priests, as reported by a cardinal who witnessed three suspicious men in the area," Ari explained. "And we believe the CIA might be involved."

The CIA's involvement in such a sacrilegious act was unthinkable to him. "Why would the agency be interested in a religious artifact?" Burke inquired, trying to keep his voice steady.

"The Guardian isn't a religious symbol; it's believed to have extraordinary powers, potentially linked to ancient knowledge and technology. Its significance goes well beyond religion."

Burke felt a growing sense of unease.

"I need your help, Thomas," Ari said earnestly. "The Church needs someone on the inside. Someone to disrupt the CIA's activities concerning this device if it comes to that. Can you be that person?"

Burke was silent for a moment, weighing the gravity of Ari's request. Assisting Ari meant betraying the agency, becoming a mole. But his faith, which had always been his guiding light, seemed to point toward helping the Church.

"Of course I'll do it," Burke finally said, a sense of resolve firming in his voice. "I'll gather information and do what I can to protect the Guardian."

"Be careful, Thomas," Ari warned. "This is bigger than we can imagine. Stand by for further instructions. I'll be in touch soon."

After ending the call, Burke leaned back in his chair, his mind racing with the implications of his decision. He had just committed to a dangerous path that blurred the lines between faith and duty, between allegiance to his country and to his religion.

In the couple of days that followed, Burke carefully navigated the treacherous waters of espionage within the CIA, gathering information while waiting for Ari's next call. He knew that the path ahead would be fraught with danger, but for Thomas Burke, the fight for a cause he believed in—the protection of the Celestial Guardian, an artifact important to his beloved Church—was a battle worth risking everything for.

CHAPTER
THIRTY-SIX

Nestled amid the verdant valleys of northern Switzerland, the Leibstadt Nuclear Power Plant stood as a testament to human ingenuity. The sprawling complex, stark against the gentle pastoral landscape, was perched on a vantage point that overlooked the undulating flow of the Rhine River. The river's shimmering surface reflected the morning sun, providing a distinct contrast to the industrial façade of the plant. Not far away, the German border traced an invisible line, marking the beginning of another country, another culture.

Today, the control room of the plant, typically bustling with the relentless rhythm of a modern nuclear facility, the usual sounds—the low hum of computers, the *click-clack* of keys, the occasional murmur of voices—had given way to a reverent silence.

Dominating the room sat the second Celestial Guardian, an enigma birthed from the mind of Leonardo da Vinci, bathed in an azure glow, casting an otherworldly radiance that painted every corner of the sterile room.

Engineers, clad in their uniforms of white lab coats and

safety glasses, huddled around this relic of the past with a mix of awe and anticipation. These men and women, accustomed to the precision of modern technology, found themselves grappling with the genius of an age long past.

The silence of the room was punctuated by the occasional murmur of conversations, hushed out of respect for the daunting task ahead.

Above their heads, a massive screen displayed a killer asteroid, code-named TerraStygian, steadily inching closer to Earth on a collision course. A scientist broke the silence. "The Guardian is operational, Dr. Harris."

Project Lead Samantha Harris nodded, her focus unwavering from the complex contraption before her. The Guardian, with its intricate web of gears, orbs, levers, and lenses, was a marvel that defied its age, an artifact crafted on parchment centuries ahead of its time.

The nuclear reactor of the Leibstadt plant, the youngest and most powerful of four such facilities in Switzerland, had been secretly repurposed for the task at hand. It was to provide the necessary energy to power the device. da Vinci's machine, though designed at a time when electricity had yet to be discovered, contained an intricate network of channels that seemingly anticipated some form of energy transfer.

After weeks of intensive work, the engineering team had managed to connect the reactor to the Guardian, enabling the flow of nuclear energy into the ancient machine's veins. The team's renewed energy was almost tangible, sending a faint hum of vitality through the operations center.

The control room was abuzz with activity, a striking contrast to the heavy silence that had filled the room a few moments earlier. Michael, Hana, and Enzo Bellini stood huddled around a table spread with blueprints, Bellini scribbling hasty calculations onto his clipboard. His eyes, a pale blue magnified by his thick spectacles, were darting from one page to another. His expertise in thermodynamics was crucial in the final hour.

Off to the side, Lindberg, a tall figure whose normally wild gray hair was now neatly combed back, sat before a row of monitors. His role as the celestial mechanics analyst had him cross-checking readouts, ensuring that the energy flow to the Guardian was regulated and consistent. Next to him, Dr. Schuler confidently toggled the switches under her purview. She also monitored the coolant systems, a critical job given the immense heat produced by the Guardian in operation.

Drs. Neri and Henriksson had found their positions by the massive windows overlooking the reactor. Lars Henriksson, with an imposing beard, was intently monitoring a set of seismographs, looking for any indication of structural instability that might result from the energy surge. Dr. Neri, a slender woman with distinctive features, seemed to be in deep conversation with Schuler, discussing potential countermeasures in case of an emergency. As the site's crisis response coordinator, her job was to anticipate and manage any possible exigencies.

In the center of the room, Dr. Samantha Harris stood with an air of calm determination. She observed her team members, each engrossed in their work, a sense of nervous excitement hovering in the air. A glance at the digital clock on the wall informed her that the time had come. She cleared her throat, her voice resonating across the room, announcing, "It's time."

As she began to operate the Guardian, manipulating the levers and gears as though playing an organ, the room filled with the low, resonant hum of the device. The glow intensified, as an interconnected display of vectors and gravitational computations streamed across the screen. The Guardian had begun its silent dialogue with the network of global satellites as the eyes of the world turned toward the asteroid.

As Dr. Harris manipulated the Guardian's ancient controls, the air in the control room seemed to thicken with anticipation. With each movement of the levers, the Guardian vibrated in harmony, exuding a deep, sonorous hum that echoed across the room. This was the sound of the Guardian launching itself into its main task, transmitting a sequence of potent, low-frequency waves, each precisely calibrated for the task at hand.

Each pulse was the product of raw nuclear power, harnessed from the depths of the Leibstadt reactor and channeled through the Gravity Resonance Emitter and on to the ancient conduits of the Guardian. These waves, although invisible to the human eye, carried a resonance so profound that they passed unhindered through the layers of the earth's crust, the vast expanse of its oceans, and the swirling mists of its atmosphere.

Once free from the confines of Earth, these waves journeyed at unfathomable speeds across the cosmos, leaving the pale blue dot far behind. They darted across the dark interstellar expanse, leaving a silent echo in their wake, until they reached their final destination: TerraStygian, the rogue asteroid hurtling ominously toward Earth.

The initial contact of these energy pulses with the asteroid was subtle. The waves, acting like unseen cosmic hands, began to interact with the asteroid, finding resonance with its natural frequencies. A monstrous rock formation born in the fiery crucibles of the universe, the asteroid wasn't an immovable object in the face of these harmonized energy waves. It responded, as any cosmic body would, to the forces acting upon it, however delicate they might be.

Each pulse of energy from the Guardian nudged the asteroid, causing a minute alteration in its trajectory. To the untrained eye, these changes were imperceptible, the asteroid appearing to maintain its course, steadfast and unyielding. Yet with each successive wave, each finely tuned oscillation, the path of TerraStygian was being recalibrated, the impending catastrophe gently deflected.

As the minutes morphed into hours, the effect of these constant adjustments began to coalesce. The trajectory, once set on a deadly rendezvous with Earth, was now visibly deviating. Each pulse was turning potential disaster into a narrow miss, transforming a planet-killer into a harmless celestial traveler grazing past Earth.

In the heart of the reactor's observatory, a grand, austere room hummed with nervous anticipation. Dimly lit by the low glow of computer screens and projection equipment, the place echoed with an uneasy silence. The team, composed of brilliant astrophysicists, mathematicians, and computer scientists from all around the world, was united by a common purpose. Their gazes were locked on the massive display dominating one wall of the room, filled with a complex array of mathematical algorithms, astronomical graphs, and a rapidly updating simulation of an asteroid's trajectory.

As they watched, the graphical representation of the doom-bringing asteroid began to show a marked change. The formerly terrifying line, a sword of Damocles hanging over the head of humanity, had begun to waver and drift away from Earth. It was as if the ominous harbinger of destruction was being pulled away by some unseen force. The doomsday scenario, once threatening to reduce the bustling world to an icy, silent graveyard, was fading away. The promise of a new day, of a future untouched by apocalyptic calamity, began to take its place.

An air of tentative hope began to permeate the room, laden with an unspoken question that bounced off the stark, white walls and high ceiling. Could they dare to believe that they, a small group of scientists working against a ticking cosmic clock, had successfully averted the apocalypse?

The moment of truth arrived. A collective gasp, as tense as the drawn string of a longbow, filled the room. The display updated in real-time, bringing a decisive verdict. The asteroid was no longer a threat. Its trajectory had shifted away from Earth, now simply a passerby in the vast emptiness of space rather than a harbinger of doom. The room erupted into cheers, a cacophony of relieved shouts and whoops of triumph echoing through the cavernous space.

Yet amid this raucous celebration, Dr. Harris remained focused. A seasoned astrophysicist and the project's leader, she stood motionless, her eyes locked onto the hum of the Guardian. A soft, almost maternal smile of relief gradually spread across her face, her steely eyes now glimmering with triumph and a tinge of disbelief.

She knew the truth behind their savior. The Celestial Guardian wasn't simply a creation of modern science. It was the embodiment of an idea penned in the lost sketches of Leonardo da Vinci, the genius of the Renaissance. It was the distillation of his ancient wisdom into tangible technology, an instrument capable of altering destiny itself.

It was a silent victory, won not on the battlefield with guns and bombs, but within the quiet confines of a nuclear control room, with the power of thought, knowledge, and an unwavering belief in the ability to change the future.

Beyond this initial success, however, no one could have predicted what the future was about to bring Michael and his team.

CHAPTER
THIRTY-SEVEN

I nside NASA's Near-Earth Object Observation center, the mood was electric. The wall of monitors displayed a myriad of data, but all eyes were on the central screen showcasing TerraStygian's trajectory.

Dr. Eleanor Wallace, the deputy director of NEOO, paced around the room, unable to sit. She was a formidable scientist, a force of nature who had devoted her career to studying celestial bodies that could potentially pose a threat to Earth. But the data coming in now was unlike anything she or her team had ever seen.

"Someone please explain this to me," she said tersely, pointing at the screen. "This object was on a fixed trajectory just hours ago. A deadly one. Now it's moving as if it's avoiding us. What is going on?"

Doug Thompson, the lead data analyst, hesitated before speaking. "The trajectory alterations don't match any natural phenomenon we know of, Dr. Wallace. Gravitational slingshots, solar winds, cosmic collisions—none of those would result in this pattern."

Jason Hernandez, an astrophysicist, jumped in. "I ran the

numbers again and again. A random space object like an asteroid doesn't just change course like this, not without an external force."

Wallace leaned over a console, scrutinizing the data. She looked up and locked eyes with Alice Collins, the project's communication lead. "Get me the director. Now."

As Collins scrambled to establish the video link with their superior, Wallace felt a knot tighten in her stomach. *Could it really be...?*

The screen flickered to life, displaying the stern face of Director Alan Bennett. "This had better be important, Eleanor."

"It's TerraStygian, sir. Its trajectory has changed. And not in any way that makes sense."

Bennett looked at the data Wallace motioned to project onto his screen. After a few moments' analysis, he asked, "Is this accurate?"

"As far as we can tell, yes. We're seeing a deliberate alteration in its path."

"Deliberate? You're not suggesting—"

"I don't know what to suggest, Alan," Wallace said tersely, cutting him off. "But we have to consider every possibility. Including that TerraStygian might be... controlled."

"Controlled? As in, by someone? Or should I say, something?"

Director Alan Bennett's eyes narrowed. "Controlled? Eleanor, you do realize the gravity of what you're suggesting?"

"I'm fully aware, Alan," Wallace responded. "Which is why I'm bringing it to your attention. We have to consider every angle—however unlikely—including the possibility of deliberate interference with TerraStygian's trajectory."

Before Bennett could further question the notion, Alice Collins chimed in. "Excuse me, Dr. Wallace, Director Bennett, we've just received an urgent message from the Vatican. They say it's related to TerraStygian."

"The Vatican?" Bennett raised an eyebrow. "Why would they be involved in this?"

"I don't know, but we can't afford to dismiss any potential leads," Wallace said. "Fine, patch them through," she instructed.

The screen transitioned to a Catholic priest and a woman, standing amid the scholarly backdrop of the Vatican Secret Archives.

"Good evening, Dr. Wallace," the priest began. "My name is Father Michael Dominic, and this is my colleague, Hana Sinclair. We have been closely following your research in concert with the ESA and have information for you that will shed light on TerraStygian's altered trajectory, which you must at least be curious about."

Wallace, puzzled but intrigued, nodded for him to continue.

Michael explained about their da Vinci discovery and manufacture of the original Celestial Guardian device; of its having been stolen by unknown forces; of its proven capabilities of not only predicting asteroidal provocations with Earth but its ability to control the trajectories of such orbiting bodies.

"Proven?!" Wallace exclaimed. "So it was *you* who caused TerraStygian to deviate from its potential collision with Earth? How can that possibly *be*? Does the Vatican even possess such powerful technology?"

"For the moment, I'd prefer our processes in that regard remain confidential, perhaps permanently. At least until we learn who stole our original device and what their purposes were for doing so. It was a very talented tactical team that carried out the theft, as it happens. It's not easy to gain access to the inner sanctums of the Vatican, and yet three men disguised as priests seem to have done just that. Which compels me to ask: are you aware of any such activity, or where the device might be now?" Michael looked earnestly, almost accusingly, into the eyes of Dr. Eleanor Wallace, whose face turned crimson as she struggled to avoid direct eye contact with the priest.

"I'm afraid I have nothing to report to you, Father Dominic," she said, adroitly sidestepping knowledge of the matter or admission of her government's involvement. "But if we learn more, I shall certainly advise you at once. Thank you for sharing your information with us. We'll be in touch."

With that, she motioned to the technician to disengage the video link.

WALLACE LOOKED around the room at her team, each member engrossed in their screens, still trying to decode TerraStygian's erratic behavior and by what means the Vatican may have been involved—*if* they were to believe the priest. "Stay vigilant, everyone. Keep probing, but remember, we don't know who or what we're dealing with. The Vatican's involvement, if legitimate, suggests a layer of complexity we haven't encountered before."

Just as she was about to return to her own analysis, Alice Collins, her face pale, beckoned her over. "Dr. Wallace, you need to see this. It's… it's from our internal security feed."

Wallace moved swiftly to Collins's desk and looked at the screen. What she saw took her breath away.

On the monitor was a live video feed from one of the facility's high-security labs. A figure, face obscured by a hood and wearing what appeared to be a lab coat, was tampering with the main server that housed TerraStygian's tracking data. The feed flickered momentarily, and when it returned, the figure was gone.

Wallace turned sharply to face her team. "Security breach! Lock down the facility, now!"

Alarms began to blare throughout the NEOO center. Security protocols were initiated, sealing off the room as Wallace looked at the now-empty lab on the screen.

Director Alan Bennett's face reappeared on the video link. "Eleanor, what the hell is going on down there?"

"Sir, it appears we've had a security breach. Someone was just in one of our secure labs, tampering with TerraStygian's data. I've initiated a lockdown."

Bennett's eyes widened. "Do you think there's a connection between this breach and the object's altered trajectory?"

"I don't know, but we have to consider the possibility," Wallace replied. "We could have a mole, someone operating from the inside."

Bennett's face hardened. "Find them, Eleanor. We don't have much time. Every second we lose makes it harder to understand what's going on with that damned asteroid."

Wallace nodded, feeling the pressure build. "We're on it, sir."

As the screen went dark, Wallace's eyes met those of her team members. Each face mirrored her own tension and uncertainty. But it was Doug Thompson who voiced the question they were all thinking: "If someone on the inside is responsible for this, what exactly are they trying to achieve? And how far are they willing to go to do it?"

As if in answer to his question, all the screens displaying TerraStygian's data suddenly went black. Then a single line of text appeared, sending a shiver down everyone's spine:

"You cannot stop what is coming."

CHAPTER
THIRTY-EIGHT

Two days later, inside a secure, nondescript government building in Langley, Virginia, a group of the nation's brightest minds gathered around a conference table. The room was stark and lit by clinical white lighting, but the atmosphere was anything but sterile; it was charged with a palpable sense of urgency and high stakes. The Celestial Guardian lay in its foam casing at the center of the table, almost like an artifact from a bygone era, surrounded by modern-day wizards in lab coats and suits.

NASA NEOO Director Alan Bennett stood at the head of the elongated conference table, his eyes sweeping across the room to meet those of the assembled team—scientists, analysts, and engineers, all experts in their fields. The room was thick with tension, the kind that comes from an assembly of people who all know the weight of the task at hand but don't yet know how to lift it.

"All right, listen up," he reiterated, pacing a bit to let his words marinate. "By now, you've all been briefed about the Celestial Guardian. This isn't just a piece of advanced tech that we've gotten our hands on; it's something that we've never encountered before. It's said to be able to manipulate gravitational fields, altering orbits, and the like. This sounds like science fiction, which is likely why it wasn't ripped open for its secrets when we first grabbed it." He looked across the room where a couple of others, whose job it had been to research it, sat, their heads down. Not that he could blame them for putting it on the back burner, so to speak. After all, the efforts made by his team to divert the asteroid with a rocket-based bomb had taken precedence over some antiquity machine. Well, it did until their asteroid-buster project went *"poof."*

Bennett sighed and got back on track. "Anyway, if it's real, we're holding a potential game-changer. I'm talking about a technology that not only could avert a global catastrophe but could revolutionize our understanding of physics and space-time."

Director Bennett paused, letting his words sink in, then leaned forward onto the table. "And this isn't a theoretical exercise; we don't have the luxury of time. There's an asteroid, remember? One that, as of last report, has taken an inexplicable detour from its expected path. Which would be fine if we understood why. And if it can be diverted, who's to say it can't be reoriented to Earth again? Then, out of the blue, this priest from the Vatican contacts us, admitting to having interceded in the asteroid's trajectory using this type of device. Which means the Vatican either has a duplicate of this device of ours, or some other technology we're completely unfamiliar with. So, if this Guardian really can do what it's claimed to do, then we need to unlock its secrets ourselves, and we need to do it yesterday. And, unnecessarily complicating our mission at hand, it seems we have a mole of some sort in our midst, one with either a sick sense of humor or legitimately sending us an unsettling warning."

His eyes met those of each team member, one by one,

locking in for a moment before moving on. "What we do here could affect the course of human history. This is why you all were chosen. You're the best of the best, and if anyone can figure all this out, it's you."

The gravity of his words lingered for a beat, and Bennett could see the sense of resolve solidify in the eyes of his team. It was an unspoken contract; they would give this everything they had.

"So, let's get to work," Bennett finally said, breaking the silence. "I don't have to spell out what's riding on this. Lives, nations, possibly the future of our planet. Let's unlock this enigma and do what we do best: defy the odds."

With that, Director Bennett stepped back, allowing the team to swarm around the Celestial Guardian, a newfound urgency fueling their actions.

A tall woman with dark, pulled-back hair took the floor, her eyes examining the Guardian intently. "I'm Dr. Emily Farber, astrophysicist. We've looked into the initial scans, and it's intricate beyond belief. The gravitational field manipulations alone are decades ahead of current science. To fully understand it, we need to access its central processor."

A slim, earnest young man with rimless glasses piped up, introducing himself as Dr. Ben Cheng, mathematician and cryptographer. "Our initial inspection suggests the device is coded in a series of complex algorithms. We need to decipher them to understand its capabilities," he offered.

"As for me, I'll handle data analysis," said a younger man, Brian, tapping away on his laptop. "Once we get past the encryption, I'll validate the calculations and predictions it makes."

Nods of agreement circled the table. "Well, let's get this thing open then," Director Bennett ordered.

The group set to work, connecting the Celestial Guardian to an array of computers via a nest of wires. Dr. Farber began the process of trying to access the device's central processor while Dr. Cheng set up algorithms to decrypt any coding.

Hours ticked away. The room had turned into a hive of activity, filled with the hum of computers and murmurs of experts deep in concentration. Finally, a ping resounded from one of the computers. "I'm in," Farber announced.

Eyes widened; the room grew quiet. Cheng immediately began the decryption while Brian prepared to analyze the data.

A half hour passed before Dr. Cheng's face paled. "Uh, we have a problem," he said, nervously adjusting his glasses.

"What is it?" Bennett leaned in, his eyes narrowing.

"We got past the initial layers of encryption, but it seems like we're missing a component—a cryptographic key, perhaps, or a buffer of sorts. Without it, we can't access the core cessation algorithms, and by extension, can't instruct the device to cease or suspend operation and validate its predictions."

The room filled with a sense of dread. Director Bennett looked at the Celestial Guardian, then back at his team. "So you're telling me that we've got this supposed miracle machine right here, and we can't even turn it off?"

"Well, in a manner of speaking, yes," Cheng confirmed. "Without that fail-safe component, we're at a standstill. It would be too dangerous to simply initiate the device and let it process who knows what kind of instructions, especially without an off key. And from the looks of it, that key might not even be a physical piece of the device. It could be information, a sequence of numbers and letters, or something else entirely."

Director Bennett sighed, his eyes meeting each of the experts, several of them nodding in agreement. "Then we need to find that fail-safe key, and fast." Turning to an aide, he whispered, "Put the agency's Rome team on alert again.

There may yet be more for them to do. And prod their Vatican embed for any word of this so-called fail-safe buffer."

As the scientists returned to their stations, considering their next steps, the Celestial Guardian sat there, as enigmatic as ever—a puzzle missing its crucial piece, a riddle wrapped in layers of codes and cosmic complexities.

CHAPTER
THIRTY-NINE

In a secluded corner of the Vatican Gardens, Monsignor Chaz O'Reilly sat on a stone bench, surrounded by statues of saints who seemed to silently judge him from their marble pedestals. He held an encrypted satellite phone in his hand, his eyes lost in thought. The call he had just ended was with his CIA handler, and it had thrown his world further into a spiral of moral complexity.

Born and raised in Cambridge, Massachusetts, Chaz O'Reilly entered the Boston College Jesuit Seminary at a young age, demonstrating a deep intellectual curiosity and a marked facility for languages. His academic prowess caught the attention of his superiors, and after his ordination, he was sent to Rome to study canon law. But it was his next assignment, as a junior diplomat in the Vatican's Secretariat of State, that set the stage for his clandestine activities.

While serving in the diplomatic corps, Monsignor O'Reilly became proficient in information gathering and intelligence analysis. His job ostensibly involved ecclesiastical diplomacy, but he found himself at the intersection of global politics and Church affairs. He was then recruited by the CIA for his exceptional skills in linguistic analysis, knowledge of international law, and most importantly, his deep connections within the Vatican.

As the CIA's secret liaison, Monsignor O'Reilly had been involved in a range of activities: providing the CIA with critical information about geopolitical shifts and ideological trends within the Church that could affect U.S. interests; access to a wide range of individuals from different countries for help in identifying and recruiting new assets within the Vatican or in any country where the Church had a significant presence; identifying extremist elements that had tried to infiltrate the Church or use its global network for nefarious purposes; and, leveraging his theological acumen, he had been a consultant to the CIA on religiously motivated conflicts or crises, offering a nuanced perspective that standard intelligence may not have provided.

O'Reilly was aware of the moral and ethical tightrope he walked. He rationalized his actions by believing that he served a higher purpose—protecting not just American interests, but also the global influence of the Catholic Church. However, as the geopolitical landscape shifted and the Church faced internal challenges, he found himself questioning the dual loyalty that defined his existence.

His current duty as the prefect for the Pontifical Council for Social Communications provided him the perfect cover and access for his CIA activities, a role that required him to interact with a variety of departments and personnel, giving him both the access and the reason to be inquisitive. But even as he delved deeper into his dual roles, Monsignor O'Reilly couldn't shake off the feeling that he was becoming a pawn in a much larger game—a game that challenged the very core of his faith and loyalty.

. . .

Just as he was about to get up from the stone bench, he heard someone approaching. Turning around, he saw his old seminary friend Michael Dominic walking toward him.

"Chaz, you look like you've seen a ghost," Michael said, taking a seat next to him.

"Let's just say, my friend, that the line between saint and sinner is finer than we think." O'Reilly sighed.

Michael studied him closely. "You've always had a way of carrying the weight of the world on your shoulders. Even back in seminary, you were different—always so concerned with the politics of the Church, not just the theology."

O'Reilly chuckled. "Ah, the perils of being a part of the Vatican's diplomatic corps. And now, as prefect for the Pontifical Council for Social Communications, the politics *are* the theology."

Michael sighed with empathy. "Or perhaps they're a path to redemption, Chaz. Sometimes, we're placed in morally complex scenarios not to damn us, but to redeem us. To redeem others."

O'Reilly looked at Michael, finding some solace in his friend's words. But even as he nodded, the encrypted phone in his pocket vibrated, pulling him back into the complex world he navigated—a world where faith met geopolitics, and where salvation was an ever-receding horizon.

The phone vibrated again, this time with a sense of urgency that was impossible to ignore. Monsignor O'Reilly sighed, pulling the device from his pocket. The screen displayed a message that read: **Urgent Communique: Eyes Only**.

"Excuse me, Michael," O'Reilly said, rising from the bench. "Duty calls, and it seems to be rather insistent."

Michael nodded, a look of understanding mixed with concern crossing his face. "Of course, Chaz. We all have our crosses to bear…" Then, as he watched his friend walk away, he added under his breath, "… and our secrets."

O'Reilly retreated into the meandering pathways of the Vatican Gardens. He found a secluded alcove shielded by tall hedges and activated the secure line on his satellite phone. The voice that greeted him was clipped and laden with a sense of urgency.

"Cardinal, we have a situation. The HUMINT from Langley has been compromised. Immediate action required."

His CIA handler never referred to him by his monsignor title. It was always "Cardinal," a nickname that had stuck since his days as a young CIA recruit with aspirations that seemed as lofty as they were unattainable.

"What are our options?" O'Reilly asked, his voice tinged with a stress that he couldn't entirely mask.

"We need access to the Vatican's internal communiques regarding this Celestial Guardian device we recently acquired. Any information could be a lead. Can you facilitate, especially where this so-called 'Aegis Buffer' is involved?"

O'Reilly hesitated for a moment, the gravity of the request weighing on him. Providing such HUMINT—or Human Intelligence—information was risky and could put the Vatican's diplomatic relations on the line. But the implications of compromised intelligence could be disastrous on a global scale.

"I'll see what I can do and get back to you," he finally said, disconnecting the call before his handler could reply.

As O'Reilly made his way back to his office in the Apostolic Palace, he couldn't shake the unease that settled in the pit of his stomach. His double life was a high-wire act with stakes that reached far beyond his own soul. There were moments, like now, when the wire seemed to wobble perilously, leaving him questioning whether he could maintain his balance—or whether he should even try.

Returning to his office, O'Reilly bypassed his secretary and locked the door behind him. He activated the secure terminal that connected him with a highly classified CIA server. After authenticating his identity through multiple firewalls, he accessed a covert program designed to infiltrate secure communication lines. As he initiated the program that would give him access to the Vatican's correspondence with the European Space Agency and related entities, he paused and crossed himself.

"In nomine Patris, et Filii, et Spiritus Sancti," he murmured, aware that he was invoking the Holy Trinity for an act that was anything but holy.

O'Reilly's fingers lingered above the keyboard, hesitant. Then, with a deep, steadying breath, he pressed Enter. The terminal screen flickered to life with the words "Access Granted," and a complex mix of relief and anxiety swept through him. Here he was again, at the precipice of moral ambiguity, straddling the fine line between righteousness and duplicity in a life increasingly mired in such paradoxes.

As O'Reilly delved into the labyrinth of Vatican communiques, his eyes searched for clues, pieces of a complex puzzle that bore implications for both global security and the Church he devoutly served. It was then that he stumbled upon a startling revelation: Father Michael Dominic, a man he knew well, was overseeing the Celestial Guardian and the Aegis Buffer devices. The shock of this discovery reverberated through him. Michael, his friend and early confidant, entwined in this web of intrigue?

This new knowledge weighed heavily on O'Reilly. He now found himself in a delicate position, needing to tread with utmost caution. The Aegis Buffer, an artifact of apparently immense power and significance, lay within his grasp, yet Father Dominic's involvement complicated his mission. O'Reilly wrestled with the implications. Was he a beacon of hope in a troubled world, or just another piece on a grand chessboard, playing a game whose stakes were as immense as they were unfathomable?

The path ahead was fraught with uncertainty. Only time, and perhaps a higher judgment, would unveil the true nature of his role in this unfolding drama.

CHAPTER
FORTY

Cardinal Ricci sat in his opulent study, the glow from a solitary lamp casting long shadows across rows of antique Russian icons lining one of the walls. His eyes, narrowed and thoughtful, were fixed on the television screen, where a newscaster excitedly reported the unexpected change in trajectory of the TerraStygian asteroid. Suspicion filled Ricci's mind even as a perverse disappointment filled his heart that, without a catastrophe facing—or hitting—the masses, his chance at overflowing the Church's pews with new converts was now lost. However, the public rejoiced at this miraculous turn of events.

He had known, of course, that the Celestial Guardian could potentially alter such a course. But it was supposed to be under lock and key, hidden away from the world, including those in the Vatican's own corridors of power. *Could it have been used without my knowledge, or was this a completely natural event?* he speculated.

Rising abruptly, he made his way to the special chamber beneath the Vatican where the Guardian was secured. The dank passages, lined with centuries-old stone, echoed with his hurried steps. Upon reaching the chamber, his heart sank. The pedestal where the Celestial Guardian should have been was empty. A cold sweat broke out on his brow as he realized the implications of its absence.

Ricci was quick to suspect Father Michael Dominic, the young and idealistic prefect of the Secret Archives. Dominic had always been vocal about using the Church's resources for the greater good of humanity, and Ricci recalled he had clearly been disturbed at losing possession of the Guardian.

Wasting no time, Ricci summoned Father Michael to his office. When the priest arrived, he found the cardinal pacing like a caged animal, his face a mask of barely contained anger.

"*Where* is the Celestial Guardian, Father Dominic?" Ricci's voice was a dangerous whisper.

Michael, composed yet forthright, met the cardinal's gaze. "Your Eminence, the Guardian... we *had* to use it. The asteroid, TerraStygian, was a threat to all life on Earth. There was simply no choice. Surely you must understand this?"

Ricci slammed his fist on the desk. "No choice? You had no right! Do you understand the implications of what you've done? The Guardian was not meant for such... blatant intervention."

Michael stood his ground, his voice steady, though he was shocked at the man's misplaced priorities. "With all due respect, Eminence, I believe saving the planet aligns with our most sacred duties."

Ricci's eyes flashed with anger, but also something else—fear, perhaps, or regret. "You don't understand, Father. The Guardian... it was part of a larger plan. There are forces at work here beyond your comprehension."

Michael sensed the depth of the cardinal's agitation. "The Guardian has served its purpose. It has saved countless lives. Isn't that what matters most?"

Ricci turned away, looking out the window into the night. "You've meddled with forces you don't understand, Dominic. The consequences of this… they could be dire. Not just for us, but for the Church."

The air in the room grew heavy with unspoken fears and the burden of decisions made. Michael knew he had acted for the greater good, but the cardinal's words left him uneasy, wondering what unseen machinations he had unwittingly disrupted.

Michael stood silently for a moment, processing the cardinal's demands. He knew he couldn't reveal the full truth about the Celestial Guardian—that the original had been stolen, and the one used to avert the asteroid disaster was merely a backup. The implications were too grave and the potential for chaos within the Vatican's hierarchy too severe. Nodding slowly, he assured Cardinal Ricci of his compliance.

"I'll retrieve the Guardian and its blueprints, Eminence," he said, his voice calm despite the turmoil within.

As he made his way to the lab where the backup Guardian was stored, Michael's mind raced with the weight of his decisions. He knew that returning the device to Ricci would plunge them back into uncertainty, given the cardinal's opaque intentions.

Upon arriving at the lab, Michael was met by Karl and Lukas, stationed to ensure the security of such sensitive areas within the Vatican.

"Father Michael," Karl greeted him with a formal nod. "We heard about the asteroid. Remarkable work."

Michael offered a tight smile. "Thank you, Karl. But now I need to take the Guardian back to Cardinal Ricci."

Lukas raised an eyebrow. "Back to the cardinal? Is everything all right?"

"It's a long story," Michael replied, sidestepping the question. "Let's just say it's beyond just our hands now."

The guards exchanged a look, sensing the gravity of the situation. They followed Michael into the lab, where the backup Guardian lay secured in a nondescript case. Michael hesitated for a moment before picking it up, feeling its weight both physically and metaphorically.

As he considered the situation, an inner voice cautioned him not to turn over the more recently discovered and assembled Aegis Buffer, the Guardian's companion device about which Ricci had no knowledge. Michael wasn't sure what compelled him to keep the Buffer's existence secret, but he trusted his instincts. For now, that device would remain under his control.

As they walked back, Karl spoke up. "Michael, if there's anything we can do..."

The priest glanced at the two loyal guards. "Just keep this between us for now. There may be layers to this that go beyond our immediate understanding."

Lukas nodded, comprehending the need for discretion in the intricate web of Vatican politics and secrets.

The trio made their way to Cardinal Ricci's office. Michael knew that the return of the Guardian wouldn't be the end of this saga, but rather a new chapter in a story that was unfolding in unpredictable ways.

Upon reaching the cardinal's domain, Michael handed over the case containing the Guardian. Cardinal Ricci's eyes lingered on the device, a mix of relief and calculation crossing his features.

"Thank you, Father Dominic," Ricci said, his voice betraying none of his deeper thoughts. "You've done the right thing."

As Michael and the guards left the office, the weight of uncertainty hung heavily in the air. The future of the Celestial Guardian, and the secrets it held, remained shrouded in mystery and intrigue. Michael knew that the days ahead would demand wisdom and courage, as the delicate balance of power and knowledge continued to teeter on the edge of revelation and concealment.

CHAPTER
FORTY-ONE

I n the clandestine depths of a secure, nondescript room within the Vatican, Cardinal Lorenzo Ricci convened a meeting of minds not dissimilar to the scientists assembled by Father Michael Dominic for the same purpose several weeks earlier. The room, typically reserved for high-level ecclesiastical discussions, was now a gathering place for scientists, experts in artificial intelligence, imaging specialists, astrophysicists, and others. Among them were figures who normally worked in the shadowy peripheries of their fields, unaccustomed to the public eye or the hallowed halls of the Vatican.

At the head of the table, Cardinal Ricci unfolded the blueprints of the Celestial Guardian. The ancient, intricate designs sprawled across the paper, a testament to the genius of Leonardo da Vinci and the enigmatic technologies of a bygone era.

"Gentlemen, ladies," Ricci began, his voice resonating with a blend of authority and charisma. "I must first remind you of the extreme secrecy this project requires, as evidenced by the stringent nondisclosure agreements each of you has signed. We are here to embark on a project of unparalleled significance. Our goal is to create an event, a celestial phenomenon that will capture the hearts and imaginations of people across the globe."

The scientists exchanged intrigued glances. Such a task, though daunting, sparked a fire of intellectual curiosity, especially coming from the Vatican.

Dr. Elena Vargas, a renowned astrophysicist, was the first to speak. "Your Eminence, with all due respect, are we to understand that we're using this... Celestial Guardian, to project something into the night sky? Is such a thing even possible?"

Ricci nodded. "In a manner of speaking, yes, Dr. Vargas. But it's not mere projection so much as it is the physical rearrangement of celestial bodies far above the heavens. The Guardian is not merely a relic; it's a tool, one that harnesses principles we're only beginning to understand. Leonardo da Vinci was far ahead of his time, and we believe that with modern technology and your expertise, we can unlock its full potential."

Simon Baxter, a young prodigy in the field of artificial intelligence, leaned forward. "If we're to create a visible, global phenomenon, we need to consider the scale. We're talking about creating an image that can be seen from multiple vantage points around the world simultaneously. Or at least during each of the world's darkness periods."

The room buzzed with excitement as ideas began to flow. The team discussed everything from atmospheric projections to the use of satellites and advanced holographic technology. The challenge was not just technical; it was also about creating an image that would resonate with people of all cultures and beliefs.

As the hours passed, Ricci listened intently, guiding the conversation, ensuring the team stayed aligned with his vision. He knew that what they were planning transcended science; it was about touching the very soul of humanity.

Finally, after much debate and collaboration, the group converged on a plan. They would use a combination of satellite technology, advanced imaging, and the unique properties of the Celestial Guardian to lay out a powerful, unifying image into the night sky. The image would need to be simple yet profound, something that would evoke a sense of wonder and spiritual contemplation.

Dr. Vargas summed up the sentiment in the room. "What we're proposing is groundbreaking, Cardinal Ricci. But if we succeed, we'll have created something that goes beyond science, beyond religion. It will be a moment that unites the world in a shared experience of awe."

Ricci smiled, a sense of satisfaction filling him. "That is precisely the goal, Dr. Vargas. We will give the world a spectacle that will be remembered for generations, a sign of hope and unity in times of uncertainty."

As the meeting adjourned, the team left with a sense of purpose, energized by the challenge ahead. Ricci remained behind, gazing at the blueprints of the Celestial Guardian. The asteroid impact had been diverted and, for that, he knew he should be grateful. After all, it meant first, that the Guardian worked, and second, that any loss of life would have resulted in that many fewer potential converts. So, in a way, if he had to admit it, Father Dominic's interference had benefited him. Now he knew that what they were about to undertake would change the course of history and, in doing so, would solidify his legacy and that of the Church in the annals of time. The path ahead was fraught with unknowns, but Ricci was resolute. This was his mission, his divine gambit in the grand chessboard of faith and power.

~

THE ORNATE CHAMBER within the Vatican, usually a place of solace and prayer, was tonight the setting for a conversation of a far more sinister nature. Cardinal Ricci, his figure looming in the dim light, sat across from Ari Finelli, whose face bore the signs of a man caught between ambition and apprehension.

"Ari," Ricci began, his voice a low rumble, "thank your colleague at NEOO for sending our message. It's a fitting warning, don't you think? *'You cannot stop what is coming'*?"

Ari shifted uncomfortably. "Yes, Eminence, but I must confess, the risk involved... it's significant. My colleague at NASA's NEOO center, he's taking a huge gamble tampering with TerraStygian's data."

Ricci's eyes gleamed with a mix of fervor and cunning. "Sometimes, Ari, great endeavors require great risks. Our plan is not just about power or influence. It's about restoring the Church to its rightful place, guiding humanity through fear, if necessary."

Ari nodded, though his expression remained troubled. "And this asteroid, TerraStygian, its altered trajectory... was that a key part of our plan?"

"Actually, I had nothing to do with that. But it was a stroke of good luck provided by our Father Dominic and his people. Indeed," Ricci confirmed with a sly smile, "imagine the panic, the fear, when the world believes a celestial disaster is imminent. And then, who will they turn to for salvation? The Church, Ari. They will look to us, to the Bishop of Rome, and in their desperation, they will return to the fold."

Ari frowned, the ethical implications of their actions gnawing at him. "But what of the innocent lives at stake, the chaos we might cause?"

Ricci waved a dismissive hand. "Collateral damage in the grand scheme, Ari. History is littered with sacrifices made for the greater good. Our goal is a renaissance of faith, a world united under the Church's guidance. Sometimes, fear is the best catalyst for change."

Ari sat in silence, the weight of their conspiracy heavy upon him. He was a man of science, once driven by a quest for knowledge. But now, entangled with Ricci's machinations, he was a pawn in a game that threatened to spiral out of control.

The cardinal stood, his figure casting long shadows on the ancient walls. "Remember, Ari, we're not just men. We're shepherds of souls. And if we must use fear to herd our flock, so be it. The end will justify the means."

As Ricci exited the chamber, leaving Ari alone with his thoughts, the room felt colder, the sacred ambiance tainted by their unholy alliance. Outside, the Vatican slept, unaware of the storm brewing within its walls, a storm that could shake the very foundations of faith and reason.

Ari sat there, a solitary figure in the dim light, the enormity of their plan weighing heavily on his conscience. He had crossed a line from which there was no return, and the path ahead was fraught with peril and moral ambiguity. The message they had sent was clear, but the consequences were as dark and unpredictable as the void of space itself.

FORTY-TWO

I n the seclusion of his opulent study, Cardinal Ricci gazed upon the Celestial Guardian, its intricate design and ancient symbols reflecting the dim light of an amber-shaded desk lamp. His mind was alive with a plan both audacious and perilous, a scheme that would cement his influence not just within the Vatican, but around the world. And in that moment of global wonder, he would be the unseen hand, the architect of a new celestial narrative.

The Vatican's statement—a press release with no one's name or signature and referencing no particular dicastery or department, but meticulously crafted and imbued with a sense of profound mystery—simply read:

Under the canopy of night, a divine spectacle will unfold across the heavens. On this sacred date, as darkness embraces each corner of our world, we invite humanity to cast their gaze skyward. Await a celestial manifestation, a message of hope and unity, divinely ordained and revealed to all. Look to the heavens and wait, for in the tapestry of the night sky, a miracle will be inscribed for all to witness.

This message, with its bold prediction and spiritual

undertones, sparked a wildfire of media attention. News programs around the world dissected every word, pondering its implications and the likelihood of its fulfillment.

"Tonight, the world waits with bated breath for the Vatican's promised celestial event," declared a leading international news anchor, the press release displayed prominently beside him on screen. "The Vatican's announcement has been met with skepticism and wonder alike. Is this a genuine prophecy or mere theatrics from the Vatican?"

His co-anchor chimed in, holding up a copy of the release. "The statement is quite poetic, isn't it? *A miracle inscribed in the night sky.* If something does happen, it'll be unlike anything we've ever seen."

The panel of experts on the show voiced their opinions, ranging from outright disbelief to cautious curiosity. A theologian pondered the religious implications, while a scientist questioned the feasibility of any natural phenomenon fitting the description.

For its part, while acknowledging it appeared that the press release had indeed come from its office, the Vatican's official communications center professed to know nothing about the event, much less who sent out the press release. They could neither confirm nor deny its authenticity as a result but, erring on the embarrassing side of caution, suggested it might be a hoax by parties unknown. That, however, didn't stop the media from feasting on the startling news. There was no turning back now. As instructed, everyone waited.

~

As DARKNESS ENVELOPED each region of the earth in turn, people gathered in squares, parks, and rooftops all over the world. News of the coming miracle had gained swift momentum across social media, newspapers, and TV channels. An unexplainable celestial event was about to occur. Telescopes, binoculars, and cameras with high-zoom lenses were in abundance as humanity collectively looked up, waiting.

From the Vatican Observatory's satellite control room at Castel Gandolfo high in the Alban hills, Cardinal Lorenzo Ricci watched multiple screens showing both the celestial event's current progress and the various gatherings around the world. With a malevolent smile, he nodded at the technician beside him.

"Initiate the final sequence," he commanded.

The technician hesitated for a few seconds before pressing the key that would send the terminal commands to the Celestial Guardian, linked through a special encrypted channel to the Vatican's secret satellite, Oculus Petri.

High above the earth, in a hidden orbit controlled by the encrypted signals of the satellite, the Celestial Guardian's influence sprang to life. A fusion of Renaissance ingenuity and modern technology, the machine hummed softly, almost as if whispering ancient secrets to the vacuum of space. For a device that had its origins in the parchment sketches of Leonardo da Vinci, the Guardian demonstrated a level of computational finesse that could rival the most advanced supercomputers on Earth.

An onboard AI, modeled on algorithms so complex they seemed more like alchemy than science, began calculating vectors and forces. It accounted for gravitational pulls from Earth, the sun, and even far-off planets. The Guardian made thousands of micro-adjustments to its gravitational field projectors—ingenious devices that created localized changes in gravitational force to move celestial objects.

With the final sequence initiated by the encrypted

command from Earth and energized this time by the power of the sun, gravitational waves emanated from the Guardian like ripples in a cosmic pond. The targeted cluster of asteroids, some as big as city blocks, others no larger than pebbles, began to stir from their dormant orbits.

Many kilometers away, another subsystem of the Guardian activated. This was an array of small, highly reflective meteoroids stationed at strategic Lagrange points around the solar system. These reflective objects were mobilized to adjust their angles in real-time, coordinating with the Guardian's master plan.

As the asteroids began their slow, balletic movements, the meteoroids shifted to capture the sun's intense rays from the opposite side of the earth. Like a conductor coordinating an orchestra, the Guardian sent harmonic signals to the meteoroids. Their surfaces tilted with precision, focusing beams of sunlight into a concentrated point aimed at the cluster.

The celestial fragments came under the spell of dual forces: gravitational nudges altering their paths, and photons from the sun illuminating them. Each asteroid found its designated position in the sky, like a child finding its spot during a school assembly. The smaller pieces filled in the gaps, and together they started forming a discernible pattern —a visage both unmistakable and awe-inspiring.

The meteoroids made one last adjustment, subtly changing the angle to give the depth of eyes and the curve of a mouth. In space, no one could hear the Guardian hum in satisfaction as its work neared completion. But down on Earth, the silent echo of its orchestration resonated in the hearts of millions.

And thus, the celestial fragments achieved their final alignment, creating a heavenly face that looked down upon the earth. A face that would soon be etched into the collective memory of humanity, a supposed "miracle" that would instigate discussions, debates, and, for many, newfound devotion.

On Earth, gasps arose from the crowds as the first pinpricks of light appeared, brighter than any stars. They grew in intensity, their alignment forming a shape that was unmistakably a bearded human face. The angles of the meteoroids were adjusted minutely, the sunlight hitting the fragments just so.

And then it happened. The face in the sky seemed to open its eyes and smile, the radiant light making it appear as if it were crying tears of joy. The image was majestic, peaceful, and inexplicably clear against the backdrop of the stars.

People around the world stopped in their tracks, looking up in awe. Cameras captured the image, broadcasting it across every medium, a shared global experience of wonder and mysticism. "It's a miracle!" someone shouted, and the cry was taken up all around the world.

Tears flowed freely from people's eyes. They knelt on the ground, arms outstretched, overwhelmed by what they were witnessing. Prayers were murmured, hymns sung, as millions felt they were in the presence of something divine.

The celestial face remained for what felt like an eternity but was barely minutes. Slowly the eyes closed, and the fragments dispersed, becoming indistinct points of light before disappearing entirely.

Beaming with satisfaction, Cardinal Ricci leaned back in his chair, watching the world's reactions on his computer screens.

The pope, usually so composed, was caught on camera in a candid moment, looking awestruck and humbled. Other religious leaders around the globe were equally struck. And then there were the politicians, scientists, skeptics—faces marked by confusion, disbelief, or wonder.

"Phase One is complete," Ricci murmured to himself, contemplating the immense power he had just wielded. "Now for the world to hear God's new message."

As people all over the earth discussed what they had seen, Cardinal Ricci prepared for the next phase. It wasn't enough for people to see; they had to listen, and for that, he had other plans. Plans that would require the world to not only witness the divine but to follow it—or more precisely, him—as its sole interpreter on Earth.

FROM INSIDE THE walled expanse of the Vatican's Pigna Courtyard, Father Michael Dominic and Hana Sinclair stared up at the celestial spectacle in the otherwise dark sky over Rome, a sense of dread filling them. Already wary of Ricci's ambitions, Michael more than suspected the cardinal's involvement. The unprecedented event, so closely following the return of the Celestial Guardian, was more than mere coincidence.

"This isn't a divine miracle," Hana said, her voice tinged with anger. "This is the work of da Vinci's Guardian! Someone is using it to play God."

Michael looked at her, his eyes filled with a complex mixture of shock and determination. "This is Ricci's doing. And we have to stop him before it's too late."

The world may have been in awe, but for those who knew the secret behind the celestial event, a dangerous game had begun.

CHAPTER

FORTY-THREE

As the magnificent face in the sky faded into the night, Pope Clement XV stood at his window in the Apostolic Palace, deep in thought. The world had witnessed a miracle, or so it seemed. But the pope's mind was troubled, his thoughts turning to the conversation he'd had recently with Cardinal Ricci about an enigmatic device crafted by Leonardo da Vinci—the so-called Celestial Guardian. Could Ricci have used this device to engineer the night's spectacle?

The next morning, under the high vaulted ceilings of a grand room in the Apostolic Palace, Cardinal Ricci stood before Pope Clement. The pope's expression was stern, his eyes searching.

"Cardinal Ricci," the pope began, his voice echoing slightly in the spacious room, "last night's event has stirred the world. And I cannot help but recall our discussions about da Vinci's device. Tell me, did you use the Celestial Guardian to create this 'miracle'?"

Ricci's eyes flickered, but he maintained his composure.

"Holy Father, the Church has always been a beacon of hope and guidance. In these times of turmoil and doubt, people look to us for signs of divine presence, for reassurance that God has not forsaken them."

The pope's gaze hardened. "You're avoiding my question. Did you use the device to create this spectacle?"

"Your Holiness, we live in times of uncertainty and dwindling faith. Science and secularism erode the spiritual foundation upon which our Church stands. We needed something... unequivocal, a demonstration of divine presence, to rekindle the faith of the masses." Ricci paused, choosing his next words carefully.

"The Celestial Guardian, a marvel of divine inspiration through da Vinci's hands, was the key. By creating the face in the sky, we projected an undeniable sign of God's presence, a beacon of hope and unity. It was a call for the world to look toward the Church for guidance in these troubled times."

The pope listened intently, his expression softening slightly but still laced with concern. "And what of the truth, Lorenzo? The authenticity of our faith? Do the ends justify such means?"

Cardinal Ricci nodded respectfully. "I wrestled with these questions, Holy Father. But consider the outcome. Last night, billions looked to the heavens and saw a symbol of hope. Today, they look to us for answers, for leadership. We have a renewed opportunity to shepherd the faithful, to bring wandering souls back to the fold. In this act, I saw not deception, but a reinvigoration of faith through a modern-day miracle."

The Holy Father leaned back, his eyes reflecting the weight of centuries of papal responsibility. He understood the gravity of Ricci's actions, the delicate balance between faith and truth, and the immense power of belief. He also understood that, by strengthening the faith of the masses, this served to bring him all the more power as their pope. Yet it being done without his knowledge or permission was unacceptable.

"Your actions, though well-intentioned, tread a dangerous line. We must lead with truth and integrity, for they are the bedrock of our faith. We are shepherds of souls, not illusionists. I will need time to reflect on this and seek guidance from above. We must ensure that our path aligns with the true will of God."

Ricci bowed his head. "I acted for the greater good, Your Holiness, for the future of our Church. I pray that, in time, you will see the wisdom in this action."

As Ricci exited, the pope remained in his chair, gazing out the window at the Vatican grounds. The world had indeed been changed by last night's event, but at what cost, and to what end? These were questions that Pope Clement knew he, and the Church, would have to grapple with in the days to come.

IN THE DAYS THAT FOLLOWED, the world was abuzz with speculation and reverence. The Vatican was inundated with inquiries and pilgrims, seeking answers, guidance, and leadership in this new, miraculous era. Ricci watched, a shadowy figure in the background, as his influence grew.

But his plan had a crucial flaw—the assumption that he could control the narrative entirely. The image and message, while stirring faith in many, brought them to the feet of Pope Clement—Ricci was an unknown player. It also ignited debates and skepticism. Scientists and skeptics around the world sought to understand and explain the phenomenon, unwilling to accept a purely divine explanation.

The face in the sky, intended as a symbol of divine authority, became instead a symbol of the intricate dance between faith, power, and human ambition. Cardinal Ricci, once confident in his control of the narrative, now found himself navigating a path fraught with unforeseen challenges and adversaries, as the true impact of his "miracle" continued to unfold in unpredictable ways.

FORTY-FOUR

T he hallowed halls of the Vatican echoed with the soft footsteps of Monsignor Chaz O'Reilly as he made his way to Father Michael Dominic's office. Chaz's mind raced with a singular, daunting task—to learn the location of the Aegis Buffer, a secret so closely guarded that his knowledge of its existence had to remain hidden, even from his old friend.

Michael greeted Chaz with a warm smile, unaware of the hidden agenda behind the drop in. "Chaz, what a pleasant surprise. To what do I owe this unexpected visit?"

"Just passing by, Michael," Chaz replied casually, taking a seat opposite the priest. "I thought I'd catch up with an old friend, since we didn't have much time in the gardens the other day."

As they exchanged pleasantries, Chaz carefully steered the conversation toward the recent upheavals within the Church. "These are troubling times, aren't they? It seems the Church is under constant threat."

Michael nodded, his expression growing solemn. "Indeed,

the recent incidents have put us all on edge. The theft of sacred artifacts is particularly concerning."

Seizing the opportunity, Chaz ventured a subtle probe. "I can only imagine the type of relics that require your attention. It must be a heavy burden to bear."

Michael regarded Chaz thoughtfully. "The burden is significant, but the Church's legacy must be preserved."

Chaz nodded, feigning a contemplative look. "I sometimes marvel at what hidden wonders lie beneath these ancient walls. Artifacts that the world has forgotten..."

Michael's eyes narrowed slightly, a hint of caution in his voice. "The Vatican holds many secrets, Chaz. Secrets that are often best left untouched for the greater good."

Feeling the conversation edging toward dangerous waters, Chaz decided to retreat slightly. "Of course, you're right. The less we know, the better. The mere thought of such power... it's almost frightening."

Michael's gaze lingered on Chaz for a moment longer than usual. "That's true. Sometimes, ignorance is not just bliss; it's a necessity."

The meeting ended with Michael still warm but perceptibly more guarded. Chaz left the office with a sense of unease. He had treaded carefully, but Michael's final words left him wondering if he had aroused suspicion.

As Chaz walked back through the silent corridors, he realized the complexity of his task. Extracting information from Michael without revealing his own knowledge was akin to walking a tightrope. Michael's intuition and his commitment to protecting the Vatican's secrets made him a formidable guardian.

~

THE VATICAN'S Secret Archives sprawled beneath the city like an ancient, slumbering beast. Within its heart, Chaz O'Reilly, with the air of a man on a clandestine mission, navigated the dimly lit corridors. He was searching for the Aegis Buffer, an artifact that had to be hidden in the depths of these archives. The air was thick with the dust of centuries, and the faint scent of aging parchment lingered, a silent witness to the secrets housed within.

As he turned a corner, his heart skipped a beat. Ahead stood two Swiss Guards he knew as Sergeants Dengler and Bischoff, their presence an unexpected obstacle. They were stationed like statues, guarding an area deemed off-limits to most. Chaz's mind raced. He couldn't retreat now; too much was at stake.

With a deep breath, he approached, mustering a casual demeanor. "Good evening, gentlemen," he greeted them, his voice laced with a feigned nonchalance. "Quite the night for extra duties, isn't it?"

Karl, his expression unreadable, nodded curtly. "Good evening, Monsignor O'Reilly. It's rare to see someone from Social Communications here at this hour. Is there something specific you're looking for?"

Chaz, aware of Karl's probing gaze, met his eyes with a steady look. "Actually, yes," he replied, his brain weaving a convincing tale. "I'm on a bit of a diplomatic errand. There's an artifact I need to examine. A piece relevant to an upcoming international symposium. Strictly routine, you understand."

Lukas, silent until now, shifted slightly, his curiosity piqued. "An artifact, sir? Most of the items here are of historical and religious significance. I'm not sure how they'd relate to your council's work."

Chaz smiled, an expression of feigned ease. "Ah, but you see, the Vatican's influence is far-reaching. History, religion, art—they all intertwine with our modern communications.

It's a delicate dance of preserving the past while embracing the future. This particular artifact, well, let's just say it's a bridge between eras."

Karl, though still cautious, seemed to relax slightly. "I see. But regulations are strict, Monsignor. No one is allowed in these sections without proper authorization, especially after hours."

Chaz felt the weight of suspicion in Karl's words. He needed to tread carefully. "Of course, I understand completely," he said, his tone one of reassurance. "But given the sensitive nature of this task, discretion was advised. I assumed a quiet evening would be ideal for such a delicate matter. You understand the need for confidentiality in our line of work."

There was a pause, a moment where the balance tipped uncertainly. Chaz held his breath, his mind racing with contingencies should this encounter turn unfavorable.

Finally, Karl nodded. "Very well, Monsignor. But we must accompany you. Regulations, you understand."

Chaz exhaled silently, his relief masked by a gracious smile. "Of course, gentlemen. I wouldn't have it any other way."

As they ventured deeper into the archives, Chaz knew his lie had bought him time, but not trust. The eyes of the Swiss Guards were upon him, as watchful as the ancient walls that surrounded them. The search for the Aegis Buffer continued, now under the gaze of guardians whose duty was to protect the very secrets Chaz sought to uncover.

The trio moved deeper into the vaulted passageways, the air growing cooler and the silence more profound. The only sound was their footsteps and the distant, occasional creak of ancient wood. Chaz's mind was a whirlwind of thoughts. Not even sure what it looked like, he needed to find the Buffer, yet every step took him further into a web of deceit and danger.

Karl led the way, his hand grasping the shaft of his raised halberd, a reminder of the ancient power he wielded. Lukas followed, his eyes scanning the surroundings with the trained vigilance of a guard. Chaz walked between them, an interloper in a world of secrets and sanctity.

As they passed rows of ancient manuscripts and religious artifacts, Chaz's eyes darted around, searching for any clue, any sign that might indicate the location of the device. He knew his time was limited; his ruse could unravel at any moment.

"Remarkable, isn't it?" Chaz remarked, hoping to ease the tension. "Centuries of knowledge and history, all within these walls."

Karl nodded, his expression softening slightly. "It's a sacred trust," he said. "We are but temporary custodians of eternal wisdom. It's our duty to protect these treasures."

Chaz sensed an underlying reverence in Karl's words. It was more than just a job for these men; it was a calling.

They continued onward, the path narrowing and the air growing mustier. Chaz noticed a faint light emanating from an alcove ahead. His heart quickened. Could this be the place?

As they approached, Karl held up a hand, signaling them to stop. "This section is highly restricted," he said firmly. "Only a few are permitted access. I must ask for your specific authorization, Monsignor."

Chaz felt a surge of panic. He had no authorization, no proof to back his claim. He was trapped in his own lie.

Thinking quickly, he reached into his coat and pulled out a special Vatican access card, something issued by his prefecture granting him higher access to most areas in the Vatican. "Will this suffice? I have no problems anywhere else in all of Vatican City," he said with mock confidence, his voice steady. "I am assured it would serve for any necessary access."

Karl and Lukas exchanged glances. The access card, an authoritative Class A pass Karl had rarely seen before, seemed to carry weight. After a moment's hesitation, the guard nodded. "Very well. But we must report this visit to our superiors."

Chaz nodded, his relief hidden behind a mask of solemnity. "Of course. I would expect nothing less."

They stepped into the alcove, and Chaz's eyes scanned the room. Shelves lined with ancient texts and artifacts glimmered in the dim light. His gaze fell upon a small, unassuming metal case of new construction, its surface gleaming in the flickering light.

Could this be it? Could this unremarkable case hold the Aegis Buffer?

As he stepped forward, his heart pounding, Chaz knew that he was about to uncover a truth that might change everything. The secrets of the Vatican, the mysteries of the past, all converged in this moment, in this hidden corner of the world's most enigmatic archives. The truth lay within reach, but so did peril. The game of shadows and light continued, and Chaz was its reluctant player.

Standing before the unassuming metal case, he felt a surge of anticipation. He reached out, his fingers grazing the cool surface of the case. His heart was pounding, a loud echo in the silence of the alcove. Karl's and Lukas's eyes were upon him, their expressions a blend of curiosity and caution.

But as his fingers traced the contours of the case, a sense of doubt crept into his mind. Something felt off. The Aegis Buffer, a relic shrouded in mystery and legend, seemed unlikely to be housed in such a modern enclosure. The discrepancy gnawed at him.

With a subtle sigh, Chaz withdrew his hand and turned to

face the Swiss Guards. "Gentlemen, it seems I was mistaken," he said, his voice tinged with disappointment. "This isn't what I'm looking for. The artifact I need... it must be stored elsewhere. I'll need to verify the records again, perhaps consult with Father Dominic. He's quite knowledgeable about these matters."

Karl, still vigilant, nodded slowly. "We understand, Monsignor. But please ensure you have specific authorization next time. The archives are a sensitive area."

"Of course," Chaz replied, his tone respectful. "I appreciate your understanding and assistance tonight. I assure you, my next visit will be fully coordinated."

Lukas stepped forward, a polite but firm expression on his face. "We'll escort you back to the entrance. It's protocol, especially after hours."

As they walked back through the winding corridors, Chaz felt a mix of relief and frustration. He had come so close, yet the Buffer remained elusive. The walk back was quiet, each man lost in his own thoughts.

Exiting the Archives, Chaz breathed in the fresh air of the Roman night. The guards bid him a curt farewell, their duty fulfilled. He watched as the ancient doors closed behind him, sealing the secrets within once more.

As he walked away, his mind was already racing with new plans. He may need to consult with Michael Dominic again, devise a more foolproof strategy. The Aegis Buffer was within those walls, its secrets waiting to be uncovered. And Chaz was determined to find it, no matter the cost.

CHAPTER

FORTY-FIVE

I n the dim light of his personal office, Father Michael Dominic sat at his desk, his brow furrowed in concentration. The news from Karl had set off alarm bells in his mind. Monsignor O'Reilly's clandestine search in the Secret Archives the previous night was not a mere coincidence. It had to be a piece in a larger, more dangerous puzzle involving the Aegis Buffer and Cardinal Ricci's manipulative use of the Celestial Guardian.

Surrounding him were ancient manuscripts and modern technology, a juxtaposition that mirrored the complex world he navigated. At the heart of his desk lay the Aegis Buffer, its ancient design an enigma of power and mystery. Michael knew that securing it was paramount. He had moved it to his office, a place where he alone held the key, a sanctuary within the labyrinth of the Vatican.

His thoughts were interrupted by a soft knock at the door. Ian, his assistant and technology guru, entered, his expression a blend of curiosity and concern.

"Father Michael, are we ready to proceed?" Ian asked, his eyes glancing at the Buffer.

Michael nodded, his voice steady. "Yes, we must prepare the Buffer. If Ricci or anyone else attempts to misuse the Celestial Guardian again, we need to be ready to counteract it immediately."

Ian approached the desk, his hands deftly opening his laptop. "I've been studying da Vinci's instructions," he said, pointing to the intricate diagrams on the screen. "If we can route the Buffer through the Vatican's satellite, Oculus Petri, we can amplify its range and effectiveness."

Michael leaned in, his eyes tracing the complex schematics. The plan was audacious, threading a line between ancient wisdom and cutting-edge technology. "Do it," he said firmly. "But we must be cautious. We're treading uncharted waters."

Ian's fingers flew over the keyboard, his concentration absolute. The Buffer was connected to the laptop via a series of cables, an odd yet necessary union of epochs. The room was silent except for the soft clicking of keys and the low hum of the Buffer as it interfaced with the modern equipment.

As Ian worked, Michael watched, his mind racing with the potential consequences of their actions. The Aegis Buffer, once a hidden relic found only on parchment, was now a pivotal weapon in a shadowy battle of ethics and power. The responsibility weighed heavily on him.

Finally, Ian looked up, his face a mask of cautious optimism. "It's done. The Buffer is now synced with Oculus Petri. We can activate it remotely if and when necessary."

Michael nodded, a sense of grim resolve settling over him. "Let's hope we won't need to. But if Ricci or anyone else threatens the sanctity of the Church with deception, we'll be ready."

"Speaking of which," Ian asked, "what do you suppose Monsignor O'Reilly was looking for? Karl was clearly suspicious of his motives when he showed up in the Archives last night. Isn't that out of character for a man in his position?"

The look on Michael's face told Ian this wasn't a new thought for the priest; obviously he had been considering the same thing.

"If I didn't know better—and if I'm being honest, maybe I don't—I'd say Chaz is working on behalf of others. I can't imagine the Pontifical Council for Social Communications needing access to either the Celestial Guardian or the Aegis Buffer, and yet he seems curiously bent on having access to one or the other, if he even knows the difference. Given that the first Guardian was stolen by highly competent forces—and I wouldn't exclude the CIA or similar governmental agencies from bearing responsibility for that—'they' likely realize by now that the Aegis Buffer is the essential companion to the Guardian, and that's next on their shopping list."

"You make a good point, Michael. All the more reason to keep its location here secret."

The two men shared a look of understanding, a silent acknowledgment of the gravity of their task. They were guardians in their own right, protectors of truth in a world where truth was often obscured by shadows.

CHAPTER

FORTY-SIX

Under the cloak of twilight, Cardinal Ricci, shrouded in his crimson cassock, again stood in the secluded control room of the Vatican Observatory at Castel Gandolfo. His hands moved with a practiced grace over the controls of the Celestial Guardian. A sense of solemnity filled the air as he prepared to unveil another "miracle" to the world, a spectacle of faith and power designed to turn eyes toward Rome, specifically toward the Bishop of Rome.

As the cardinal adjusted the final settings, his eyes glinted with a mix of piety and ambition. This time, there would be no announcement, no forewarning. The surprise would amplify the impact, with shock and amazement cementing the belief in the divine intervention he orchestrated.

IN A COZY TRATTORIA NEAR ST. Anne's Gate, Michael Dominic and Hana Sinclair were deep in conversation over dinner. The quaint restaurant, with its rustic charm and aromatic scents of Italian cuisine, provided a brief respite from the intrigues and mysteries in which they were entangled.

As their conversation progressed, the sudden buzz of excitement outside caught their attention. Patrons and staff rushed to the windows, their expressions a mix of wonder and confusion. Michael and Hana exchanged a quick, knowing glance. Something was happening at the Vatican.

They left their meals untouched and hurried outside, joining the crowd gathering in the streets. People pointed toward the sky, where an ethereal light began to shimmer, casting an otherworldly glow over Rome.

"It's Ricci," Michael muttered, his voice tense. "He's doing it again."

Hana nodded, her journalistic instincts kicking in. "We need to stop him this time, Michael. But are we prepared?"

"Follow me," the priest urged as he reached for her hand.

Without another word, they dashed toward the Vatican. The streets were abuzz with excitement and confusion, a perfect cover for their swift but inconspicuous return.

INSIDE THE VATICAN, they navigated the familiar maze of corridors with haste, heading toward Michael's locked office, where the Aegis Buffer was set up.

Reaching the door, Michael quickly unlocked it, and they slipped inside. The Buffer, a deceptively simple-looking device, sat atop a side table, its surface etched with the intricate symbols of da Vinci's instructions.

Michael's hands were steady as he activated the Buffer, his knowledge of the ancient texts guiding him. Hana watched intently, her mind racing with potential headlines and the enormity of what they were about to do.

"The signal should disrupt Ricci's projection," Michael explained, his focus unwavering. "It's designed to interfere with the Celestial Guardian's frequencies."

Outside, the crowds marveled as the celestial display

slowly began taking shape, unaware of the battle of wills and technology unfolding within the Vatican walls in Rome and at Castel Gandolfo in the distant Alban hills. Beyond the moon, the sky above St. Peter's Basilica danced with lights, forming ethereal shapes and patterns, a mesmerizing spectacle.

Back in the chamber, the Buffer hummed to life, its core emitting a pulsating light. Michael adjusted a few dials, fine-tuning the disruption signal. Hana held her breath, the tension palpable.

Suddenly, the serene patterns in the sky began to flicker and warp. The crowds gasped and murmured, their awe turning to confusion. The lights twisted and contorted, losing their divine semblance.

Michael and Hana watched the Buffer do its work. The device vibrated with energy, its ancient technology a stark contrast to Ricci's modern machinations.

As the celestial spectacle above the Vatican dissolved into chaos, the message of faith and awe Cardinal Ricci intended to broadcast was lost. The heavens returned to their normal state, leaving the onlookers bewildered.

Michael and Hana exchanged a look of relief and determination. They had thwarted Ricci's plans, at least for now. But they knew this was just one battle in a larger war, a war where faith, power, and technology intersected in the shadows of the Vatican.

As they left the office—leaving the Buffer's autonomous engagement option activated should Ricci keep trying tonight —they knew their journey was far from over. The Vatican's secrets were deep, and the stakes were higher than ever. Their alliance, a priest and a journalist, was an unusual one, but it was proving to be a powerful force against the machinations at the Vatican Observatory on the grounds of Castel Gandolfo.

Outside, the crowds slowly dispersed, the night

reclaiming its quiet dominion over Rome. The miracle they had almost witnessed would be a topic of speculation and wonder, a mystery added to the many that surrounded the Vatican.

But for Michael and Hana, the mystery was a call to action, a reminder of their quest for truth in a world where nothing was as it seemed, and where the light of faith often cast the longest shadows.

CHAPTER
FORTY-SEVEN

The control room of the Vatican Observatory, usually a haven of celestial exploration and discovery, was filled with an air of tension and frustration. Cardinal Ricci stood before the console controlling the Celestial Guardian, his hands clenched into fists, his expression a mixture of shock and anger.

The Guardian sat inert, its usual hum of activity silenced.

Ricci jabbed at the console controls again, his movements becoming more frantic. He had orchestrated what was supposed to be a divine spectacle, a "miracle" that would reaffirm the power and relevance of the Church in the eyes of the world. But something had gone wrong, terribly wrong. The device, his tool for inspiring awe and reverence, had failed him.

"Why won't you work?" he muttered under his breath, his voice laced with frustration. The screens blinked with error messages and scrambled data, a chaotic symphony of failure.

He tried to initiate the routine once more, then again and again, his fingers moving with practiced precision. But the

Guardian remained unresponsive, its systems seemingly locked in a state of disruption.

Ricci's mind raced with possibilities. Sabotage? A technical malfunction? Or something else, something beyond his understanding? He couldn't accept that his plan, so carefully crafted, could be undone by mere technical deficiencies.

He slammed his fist on the console, the sound echoing through the room. "Useless!" he exclaimed. The Guardian, once a symbol of his ambition and cunning, now stood as a testament to his failure.

With a heavy sigh, Ricci turned away from the console, his thoughts dark and turbulent. He couldn't let this setback deter him. He needed to regroup, to find another way to assert his vision.

He motioned to a pair of attendants waiting in the shadows. "Take this back to the Vatican," he ordered, his voice cold and composed. "Store it in the vault. I will decide what to do with it later."

The attendants nodded, moving to the console to carefully disassemble the Guardian. Ricci watched them for a moment, his gaze lingering on the machine that had promised so much yet now delivered so little.

As he left the observatory, the night air of Castel Gandolfo greeted him, a stark contrast to the stifling atmosphere of the control room. The town lay spread out before him, its ancient streets a maze of shadow and light.

Ricci's mind was a whirlwind of thoughts and emotions: anger, frustration, but also determination. This was a setback, yes, but not the end. He would find another way, a different path to achieve his goals.

The Guardian, now silent and defeated, was carried away, its potential unfulfilled. Ricci knew that the road ahead would be challenging, but he was no stranger to obstacles. He would rise again, his resolve unbroken.

As the cardinal headed back to Rome, the Vatican Observatory stood silent and watchful adjacent to the Papal Palace, both centuries-old witnesses to the ambitions and failings of those who sought to use its mysteries for the Church as well as their own ends. The stars above, eternal and unchanging, shone down on the Alban hills, indifferent to the struggles and schemes of mortals below.

THE FOLLOWING MORNING, Cardinal Ricci summoned the Finelli brothers to his office in the Congregation for Artifacts. Ari and Benito sat opposite him, their expressions a mix of anticipation and wariness. They were accustomed to the cardinal's dramatics, but today there was a palpable tension in the air.

"I've been thinking about last night's operational failure, gentlemen," Ricci said slowly, "and it makes no sense. Our first demonstration was carried out flawlessly, as was Father Dominic's participation in the original TerraStygian affair. The technology has been proven, yet I get the feeling last night's collapse had been intentionally orchestrated to fail. There's no other logical explanation for it. Given each of your spheres of influence, can you think of how this might have occurred, and more importantly, by whom?"

Both men were silent as they turned their thoughts to the problem. Ari shifted in his seat, his mind racing. He remembered a recent conversation with his confidential contact at NASA's Near-Earth Object Operations center, a casual mention of the CIA's suspicion about Father Dominic possessing another device, crucial for the Celestial Guardian's control.

"Your Eminence, if I may... There's been talk. Rumors, really. The CIA suspects Father Dominic of having another device. Something... significant. It bears the name Aegis Buffer, but we know little else about it."

Ricci's eyes gleamed with a mix of curiosity and alarm.

"Another device? Are you certain?"

"It's just hearsay, but it fits, doesn't it? Perhaps Father Dominic used this... Buffer to sabotage your demonstration."

Benito, who had been silent until now, leaned forward.

"If Dominic does have this so-called Buffer, it could certainly explain the failure. He's always been a step ahead, always hiding something, it seems."

Ricci's fingers tapped on the desk, his mind working furiously.

"This could be a significant development. If Dominic indeed has such a device, it could be the key to everything. We need to find out more. And if it exists... we *must* acquire it —at any cost."

Ari and Benito exchanged a glance.

"I trust you understand the gravity of this situation," Ricci said. "I want you to investigate this matter discreetly. Use your resources, your contacts. Find out what this device is and how we can use it to our advantage."

The brothers nodded, a new sense of purpose igniting in their eyes. They stood, ready to embark on this new, mysterious endeavor.

"Remember, gentlemen, discretion is paramount. We cannot afford another failure."

As the Finelli brothers left Ricci's office, the cardinal's words echoed in their minds, setting the stage for a new chapter in this clandestine war of power and deception.

FORTY-EIGHT

T he next morning, Michael and Hana sat in the quiet confines of his office, lines of concern etched on both their faces. Cardinal Ricci was proving to be a more vexing problem than they had anticipated.

"It's pretty clear to me," Hana said, "that Ricci is unlikely to give up his newfound power, Michael. And since we can't always be ready when he opts to put on another demonstration using his 'God machine,' we need to look at this problem from other angles. ESA, NASA, or any competent space agency would be better equipped to handle future asteroid threats. We need to ensure this technology doesn't get misused again."

"I agree," the priest confessed. "But if we were to succeed in retrieving the Guardian from his vault again, he'd reflexively suspect me due to my involvement with the earlier TerraStygian incident. And we don't even know what arrangements he may have made with the Holy Father. What if they're in league with each other? We'd be going up against some mighty forces in that case. No, it can't be me this time. There must be another way."

Hana, ever the puzzle maven, put her mind to work. "We need someone beyond reproach who isn't well known and ideally is unrelated to you. Know anyone here who owes you a favor? Someone others won't suspect is connected to you?"

Michael thought for a moment. Then, his face reflecting the recollection of a memory, he told Hana about the recent visit of an old friend to the Secret Archives… a particular unauthorized visit, in fact.

Hearing the story, Hana had an idea.

The room grew quiet, the gravity of their plan settling in. The risk was immense, but the threat of leaving the Guardian under Ricci's control was far greater.

IN THE QUIET solitude of a small, nondescript café near the Vatican, Michael Dominic sat across from Chaz O'Reilly, his expression serious, his voice barely above a whisper. The café, with its subdued lighting and hushed atmosphere, was a perfect place for a conversation that needed to stay hidden from prying ears.

"Chaz," Michael began, his eyes locking with those of the man across from him, "I understand you've been looking for something… specific. Something you believe might be hidden within the Vatican."

Chaz, a man whose half-time profession had always skirted the edges of legality, leaned forward, his interest piqued. "Go on," he said, his voice cautious yet curious.

Michael took a deep breath, weighing his words carefully. "Karl, one of the Swiss Guards, mentioned your interest in a particular device. Something you thought might be in the Secret Archives."

Chaz's eyes narrowed. "And what of it? If you have information, I'm listening."

"There *is* a device, one of significant power and potential danger. It's not in the Archives, though," Michael disclosed, his voice low. "Cardinal Ricci has it... in his vault at the Congregation for Artifacts."

Chaz's expression shifted, a mix of surprise and intrigue. "Ricci? What's he doing with something like that?"

Michael hesitated, considering how much to reveal. "It's a tool, one that can be used for great good or great harm. Ricci has already demonstrated a willingness to use it unethically. We believe it should be retrieved and destroyed, or at least put in more responsible hands."

"And you think I can get it?" Chaz asked, skepticism lacing his tone.

"Yes. But it's not going to be easy."

Chaz leaned back, processing the information. "And why should I get involved in this? What's in it for you? And for me?"

Michael met his gaze squarely. "Well, if Ricci continues to wield this power, it could have catastrophic consequences. Not just for the Church, but for the world. This is about more than personal gain, Chaz. I'm willing to gamble that it being in anyone else's hands is better than being in Ricci's. It's about preventing a disaster. And as for your intentions with it, well, whatever you needed it for in the first place is better than this alternative. Obviously, I don't need any details beyond that."

There was a moment of silence as Chaz considered the lure of the proposition. His superiors in the intelligence community were adamant he find the device called the Aegis Buffer, and here it was—whatever "it" was—being handed to him on a silver platter.

Finally, he nodded slowly. "All right, I'm in. But I'll need help getting into Ricci's vault."

"I can arrange for two of the Swiss Guards to assist you,

discreetly," Michael offered. "Sergeants Karl Dengler and Lukas Bischoff are aware of the risks involved with Ricci's actions. And you can trust both of them."

Chaz finished his coffee and stood up, a determined look on his face. "Then let's do it. But I'll do it my way. I don't want any loose ends."

As they left the café, the streets of Rome lay quiet around them, oblivious to the plot unfolding in its shadows. Michael and Chaz, two unlikely allies, were now set on a path that would take them into the heart of the Vatican's secrets.

CHAPTER
FORTY-NINE

The night was still over Vatican City as Chaz O'Reilly, accompanied by Karl Dengler, made his way through the shadowed corridors of the Belvedere Palace toward the Congregation of Artifacts' area in the Vatican Museums. The atmosphere was thick with tension, each step measured and silent. Karl led the way, his knowledge of the Vatican's layout proving invaluable for shortcuts and a more secure route. Lukas, his fellow Swiss Guard, stood watch, a silent sentinel against any unexpected interruptions.

The Congregation of Artifacts was a fortress within a fortress, its vault housing relics and secrets that spanned centuries. As they approached, the imposing door of the vault loomed before them, a testament to the treasures it guarded.

Karl glanced at Chaz, nodding subtly. "This is it. Ricci's vault." His voice was a whisper, barely audible in the hushed corridor.

Chaz, a man who had faced many high-stakes situations, felt his pulse quicken. He looked at the vault door, its surface etched with religious iconography and secured with a state-of-the-art electronic lock system.

"Time to work," he muttered, pulling out a compact device designed by the NSA to bypass such security measures. His fingers moved with practiced ease, attaching the device to the lock's interface.

Karl watched intently, aware of the risk they were taking. Any mistake could trigger an alarm, bringing the entire Swiss Guard and Vatican gendarmerie down upon them.

Minutes passed like hours as Chaz worked on the lock. The device beeped softly, and then, with a final click, the door unlocked. Chaz exhaled slowly, a silent triumph in the face of immense pressure.

They entered the vault, their eyes adjusting to the soft, pale light. Inside, the vault was a cavern of history, lined with shelves that held artifacts of unimaginable value and historical relevance. In the center of the room, secured on a pedestal, was the device they sought, its sleek, modern construction a stark contrast to the ancient relics surrounding it.

Chaz moved toward it, his eyes scanning for any additional security measures. Beside the device lay a set of diagrams on parchment, their detailed schematics a blueprint for power and danger.

Karl kept watch at the door, his ears straining for any sound of discovery. Lukas, outside, was their last line of defense, ready to signal if anything went amiss.

Chaz carefully lifted the device, feeling its weight and the gravity of what it represented. He then rolled up the blueprints, securing them in a protective tube.

As they prepared to leave, a distant sound echoed through the corridors, the faint footsteps of a night patrol. Karl's eyes widened. "We need to move, now."

They exited the vault, Chaz carrying the backup Celestial

Guardian—believing it to be the Aegis Buffer—along with its blueprints. The door closed silently behind them, its lock re-engaging as if nothing had been disturbed.

They retraced their steps, moving with even greater urgency now. Each corner turned, every shadow passed, brought them closer to safety but also to the risk of discovery.

As they neared the exit, Lukas joined them, his expression tense. "We need to hurry. The patrol is changing course."

They quickened their pace, the weight of the theft heavy in their hands and on their consciences. Chaz disappeared into the Roman night, the device and its blueprints now in his possession. He had successfully infiltrated the heart of the Vatican and extracted its most dangerous secret. The night air was cool on his face, a stark contrast to the adrenaline that still coursed through his veins.

The game had changed, the balance of power shifted. And as everyone vanished into the darkness, Karl imagined Cardinal Ricci's fury at finding his precious device missing. And he smiled.

CHAPTER
FIFTY

Michael Dominic paced his office, phone pressed to his ear, speaking with his assistant, Ian Duffy. "Ian, the Aegis Buffer's security is paramount," he said, his voice low. "With so many parties seemingly interested in both devices, we need to take precautions with the only one we have left." As he discussed the details of its secret location, he heard a faint clicking on the line, a subtle distortion in the background.

"Did you hear that?" Michael asked, pausing mid-sentence. Ian, on the other end, heard nothing unusual. Michael's mind raced. *Was the line compromised? Who could be listening? Cardinal Ricci? Chaz O'Reilly? Or perhaps an intelligence agency?* His suspicion deepened.

"We should be cautious, Ian," Michael continued, carefully choosing his words, aware each one might be overheard. "I have another idea. But let's discuss this in person." The thought of the Buffer falling into the wrong hands was unthinkable. But the plan he was hatching just might work...

Ending the call, Michael reflected on the situation. The

Aegis Buffer was now at the center of a dangerous game. He wondered if the CIA was behind the eavesdropping, possibly relaying information to its operatives in Rome. The stakes were high, and Michael knew he had to act swiftly and discreetly. The fate of the Aegis Buffer and its unique powers hung precariously in the balance.

~

ONCE THE SPECIAL alert came in on his sat phone, Chaz O'Reilly wasted little time contacting his handler at the CIA's headquarters complex in Langley, Virginia.

"Cardinal, our friends at the NSA have picked up something you need to hear," the handler said. "Your priest Dominic still has the device we're seeking, and he's just revealed its secret location to someone in his office."

"But that's impossible! I just retrieved the device last night from its special vault in the Vatican!"

"Well, whatever you got may have been a decoy, but in any event we'll want to see it. Meanwhile, this so called Aegis Buffer is the missing link we need." He went on to explain the secret location in the Vatican where they had heard Michael tell Ian the Buffer was safely stored. "You need to acquire it, Cardinal, and soon. Will you need assistance?"

"Possibly, I can't be sure yet. I'm familiar with the location you mentioned, but that chamber is often guarded on a changing schedule, so planning the acquisition may be a challenge. Let me work out the details, and I'll let you know if I require your team's help. Cardinal out."

Thinking he had been duped by Father Dominic, O'Reilly's face flushed an angry shade of red, his fists clenched in barely contained rage.

~

FAMILIAR FACES CROWDED around the central workbench in the Vatican Archives' secure lab as Michael Dominic looked around the high table. These weren't the accomplished astrophysicists or ESA mission analysts, though. The people standing here were the original fabricators of both the Celestial Guardian and the Aegis Buffer before the scientific team had their way with both devices.

"Thank you all for coming on such short notice," Michael began, his tone measured. "We have a task of utmost importance and sensitivity. It requires your expert skills, discretion, and absolute loyalty."

The team listened intently, understanding the gravity of the situation. Michael continued, "We need to construct a... well, let's just say it's a special project. For now, its nature and purpose must remain confidential, even among ourselves."

One of the fabricators, a seasoned expert in intricate mechanisms, raised an eyebrow. "Can you give us more details yet, Father? Specifications, dimensions?"

Michael hesitated, aware of the need for circumspection. "Let's call it a device of significant historical and scientific value. Its design is complex, involving intricate mechanical and electronic components." He paused, choosing his words carefully. "Think of it as replicating a masterpiece, where precision is key. You'll learn more tomorrow."

The team nodded, understanding the challenge. "And the timeframe for completion?" asked the project manager.

"As soon as possible, without compromising quality. A few days at most," Michael answered. "Security and discretion are paramount. This project doesn't exist outside these walls."

The team exchanged glances, a silent agreement forming. They were used to working on unusual projects, but this one was clearly different. They felt a mixture of excitement and apprehension, aware that they may be stepping into uncharted territory.

As the meeting concluded, Michael added, "Remember, this stays between us. The success of this project depends not just on your skills, but on your silence."

With a promise to return early the following morning, the team dispersed, each member lost in thought about the mysterious task ahead. Michael watched them leave, a sense of unease mingling with his resolve.

CHAPTER
FIFTY-ONE

N early a week had passed during which Chaz O'Reilly planned his strategy to acquire the CIA's top priority asset being held in the depths of the Vatican Secret Archives: the elusive Aegis Buffer.

Having surreptitiously obtained the guard schedule for that particular vault area on his planned day of assault, he was fairly certain no Swiss Guards or Vatican gendarmes would stand in the way of his ambitions for that night's undertaking. Too much was at stake.

It was later that evening when Chaz was summoned to St. Anne's Gate to escort three colleagues purportedly visiting from the Pontifical Gregorian University not far from Vatican City, ostensibly for a meeting on security protocols for an upcoming summit of religious leaders led by the pope. Though Chaz hadn't met the men before, he well knew who they were. And as it happened, they weren't unfamiliar with the Vatican, having visited one dark night several weeks earlier.

Among themselves, they were known as Brother John, Brother Paul, and Brother Peter: the CIA's undercover Gold

Team, garbed in their assumed black clerical cassocks beneath which were certain tools for the night's mission—tools designed not to set off the metal detection security screeners at St. Anne's Gate.

On guard at the time were two Swiss Guards: Sergeants Dieter Koehl and Lukas Bischoff. After issuing visitor passes to the brothers and having Chaz O'Reilly sign in as their escort, Lukas returned to the gate's guard shack and made a phone call as he watched the four men enter the Belvedere Palace.

"Thanks for the heads up, Lukas," Michael said, the phone to his ear. "That means the clock starts now. Let Karl and the others know, keep an eye on Chaz's team, and we'll see you later, as planned." He placed the receiver in its cradle, his gaze vacant, his mind processing the lineup of tasks for the evening.

There was so much out of his control—a situation he rarely found himself in—but given the presumption that Chaz's quarry was the Aegis Buffer, Michael felt he was as prepared as he could be. And everything depended on split-second timing.

"I'm a little uncomfortable with your being here for this, Hana," Michael said, turning to her in his office. "Who knows what could go wrong, and the last thing I'd want is for anything to happen to you." The two had just returned to the Vatican after having dinner at a trattoria across from St. Peter's Basilica.

"Are you kidding? After all we've been through to prepare for this, you'll have to pry me away now."

"All right, let's get into position then. If I'm right, Chaz believes he knows where the Aegis Buffer is being kept, so that's where his team will be headed."

Getting up, Michael led Hana out of the office, down the long marble corridor to the Tower of the Winds, then down the stairs leading to the vast Gallery of Metallic Shelves, the main storage area of the Secret Archives west of the Cortile del Belvedere and beneath the Pigna Courtyard. At the southern end of the massive expanse was a heavy oak door leading to a warren of labs and other processing rooms of the Secret Archives, as well as a series of vaulted rooms in which were kept some of the Vatican's most profound treasures.

It was here, in Vault A2, where Michael had stored the Aegis Buffer, the location referenced during his phone conversation with Ian Duffy before he suspected his line might have been tapped.

And it was here where Michael's plan would take place.

HAVING BROKEN off from the rest of their team after entering the Belvedere Palace, Brother John and Brother Paul, their hands tucked beneath their cassocks, made their way to the Vatican Museums, a good distance from the vault area. They were seeking an ideal location for setting up a diversion, one designed to draw attention away from the Secret Archives area to thin out the ranks of security personnel once their main operation was in play. With the museum having closed some three hours earlier, at six o'clock, the halls and rooms were devoid of any personnel.

In the guise of a mobile phone—thanks to the brilliant technicians at the CIA's Directorate of Science and Technology—Brother John had activated a mid-range signal jammer, briefly causing static white noise distortions to any video camera signals they encountered along the way, thus masking their progress through the hallways and display rooms of the Vatican museums.

Conscious of bringing no harm to the Vatican's treasures, Chaz O'Reilly was insistent that the operatives not target any rooms in the museum containing porous or absorbent materials, such as the Gallery of Maps or the Gallery of Tapestries, meaning targeting mainly rooms containing statuary, urns, and other such solid objects.

So they chose the Gregorian Etruscan Museum on the upper floor of the Belvedere Casino. Sufficiently distant from the vault area, this section was dedicated to Roman antiquities and included works in bronze, glass, ivory, terracotta and ceramics from pre-Rome and former Etruscan cities—materials that would prove impervious to the nontoxic emissions of a smoke grenade.

From a utility belt beneath his cassock, Brother Paul withdrew two slim, specially designed smoke grenades, each composed of dense plastic and ceramics in place of any metal fittings, sufficient to pass through security metal detectors. These also had the advantage of having built-in timers, allowing him to set a predetermined time for detonation while they were clear of the area.

Setting the timers to discharge in about twenty minutes, at ten o'clock sharp, Brother Paul placed the two smoke grenades behind one of the larger Etruscan urns in the corner of main gallery, beneath one of the many fire and smoke detectors positioned throughout the room.

Then they made their way back down the stairs, through the Gallery of Metallic Shelves and headed back to the vault area to join their colleagues.

MEANWHILE, Chaz and Brother Peter were working on opening Vault A2's combination lock, a fairly routine matter using an advanced automatic lock decoder also provided by the CIA's DS&T unit.

At the stroke of ten, the smoke grenades discharged their duties as programmed, filling the Gregorian Etruscan Museum with thick white smoke, which in turn triggered the smoke sensors in the room. Instantly, fire alarms sounded even where Chaz and Brother Peter were located, three stories down and some distance south from the source of the commotion.

Time was of the essence now. They had mere minutes to get into the vault and take their prize before Vatican security realized they were dealing with a diversion of some kind rather than an actual fire.

The lock decoder was just one digit away from revealing the combination to the vault, but tensions were high among the two operatives, with sweat forming on their foreheads as they nervously waited for that final number.

At last it appeared. Disengaging the apparatus, Chaz punched in the six-digit code and the lock mechanism clicked, with a green light appearing on the keypad. Swinging open the steel door, he entered the vault and saw what appeared to be something akin to an astrolabe—a device bearing a disk with one edge marked in degrees, with components similar to retes and maters, various plates and odd markings; plus the fact that it was the only such device in the vault, with a parchment tucked into a cubby directly beneath the unit. *This must be it!*

He also noticed a black polypropylene Pelican cargo case sitting in the corner of the room. Grabbing and opening that, he smiled. Inside was a custom foam insert specially created with the shape of the Aegis Buffer cut into the center, with a top covering resembling an egg carton pattern for extra protection.

Chaz lifted the device up and carefully laid it into the preformed foam, placed the parchment on top, then closed the case, snapping the two metal fasteners shut.

He and Peter left the room and shut the door behind them. "John and Paul should be here any minute now. Then we're out of here."

Chaz O'Reilly took a deep breath and let it out. *The Aegis Buffer is mine!* he exulted—just as he heard the voice of Michael Dominic say, "Not so fast, Chaz. I'll take that now."

CHAPTER
FIFTY-TWO

S pinning around, Chaz and Brother Peter were shocked to see the priest and Hana now standing before them, having quietly emerged from a nearby room.

"We agree, Monsignor. Hand the device to Michael," Karl said, as he and Lukas suddenly appeared from behind the two thieves, who were now trapped. Both guards were holding their SIG Sauer P220 service pistols, now aimed at the intruders.

Mere moments later, however, Brothers John and Paul quietly emerged from the double doors behind Karl and Lukas and, unarmed, pressed the bent knuckle of their first finger hard against the back of each of the Swiss Guards, emulating the feel of a gun barrel. Surprised, both guards raised their arms slightly.

"And we'll take those weapons, if you don't mind, gentlemen," John said confidently, reaching around to liberate Karl's pistol as Brother Paul did the same with Lukas's. "Now, go join your friends."

Turning around, Karl was both embarrassed and furious to see they had been duped, that the two fake priests standing before them had no other weapons at all—other than the Swiss Guards' own guns.

"Sorry about that," John said with a sardonic smile. "We had to improvise by conjuring a little illusion. No hard feelings?"

"Exactly what do you suppose the purpose of that device is, Chaz?" Michael asked. "Do you even know how it works?"

"I'm sure we'll be able to find experts capable of figuring those things out, Michael," he replied. "For now, that's above my pay grade.

"All right," Chaz continued, "let's make sure you're all secured so we can get on with our business." Using the same deciphered combination as before, Brother Peter reopened Vault A2 and ushered Michael, Hana, Karl, and Lukas inside. Then he closed the door with an audible *click*.

Leaving the area, they were alert to what was certainly an increased state of security, given their smoky diversion. As before, they headed toward the lesser-trafficked Arch of the Bells exit just south of St. Peter's Basilica. Encountering two guards there, Monsignor Chaz O'Reilly mustered his most authoritative manner, presenting the guards with his higher access credentials, then escorted his colleagues out the gate after being allowed to exit. Once the gate shut behind him, they all breathed a sigh of relief. Walking with confident, measured steps, they headed toward their getaway van two blocks south of the basilica.

INSIDE VAULT A2, Michael smiled at the others. "So far, so good," he said. He noticed unusual reactions to his comment on the faces around him.

"Easy for you to say, Father Michael," Lukas complained morosely. "You won't have to account for our lost weapons."

"Not to worry, Lukas. We'll handle that along with their stealing the Aegis Buffer, and Chaz O'Reilly will be deemed persona non grata in the Church after this."

"My question is, how do we get out of here?" Hana asked. "Are we locked in?"

"No, we can easily get out," Michael replied, opening the door from the inside. "I just wanted to give Chaz a little time to get away from the Vatican, while letting him think he got away with it."

"*Think* he got away with it?!" Hana exclaimed. "He *did* get away with it!"

"Well… not really," Michael said as he gave the others a sly look. "I suspected something like this might happen, given Chaz's odd behavior lately and the fact that I'm sure my telephone had been bugged. So I had our fabrication team come up with a fake Buffer with a self-destruct mechanism built into it."

Reaching into his pocket, Michael pulled out a compact control unit with a series of buttons on it and an extendable antenna. Pulling it out to its full length, his finger hovered over the largest of the buttons…

IN THE DIMLY LIT INTERIOR OF the getaway van, Chaz and his team secured the Pelican case in the cargo area. The air was charged with a sense of victory; they had just achieved the unthinkable—stealing an unspeakably powerful device from the guarded depths of the Vatican.

Chaz sat back, a mix of satisfaction and anticipation playing across his features. He was already envisioning the implications of their success, the power and leverage the Buffer might grant them with the agency. The van navigated the ancient streets of Rome, the team riding high on a wave of exhilaration.

Without warning, the celebratory atmosphere was shattered by an abrupt, shrill beep emanating from the cargo case. It escalated into a frantic alarm, slicing through the air. Confusion reigned for a split second before a muffled explosion rocked the van. The operatives were thrown off balance, the case jerking violently.

In a daze, Chaz was the first to react after the explosion. He lunged for the case, his movements fueled by a blend of dread and disbelief. Flipping it open, he was greeted by a plume of acrid smoke. Where the Aegis Buffer once sat, there was now only a mass of charred components and twisted wreckage. The coveted device—the irreplaceable Aegis Buffer —had self-destructed, and along with it, the parchment presumably describing its design and operation.

Chaz's face twisted into an expression of utter disbelief, morphing into a seething anger. His mind raced, trying to comprehend the loss of such an invaluable artifact. "*Michael...*" he uttered in a low growl, his voice laced with a mix of rage and incredulity. He had been so focused on outwitting the Vatican's security that he hadn't considered the possibility of the Buffer being rigged to self-destruct.

The operatives looked on, their faces etched with shock and uncertainty. They had witnessed the obliteration of a priceless piece of history, an artifact whose significance went beyond their comprehension.

"This... this was no accident," Chaz said, his voice hardening. "This was a fail-safe, a final act of defiance from the Vatican. They would rather destroy the Buffer than let it fall into our hands."

A tense silence enveloped the van. The realization that they had triggered the destruction of the Aegis Buffer was overwhelming. The magnitude of what they had lost—and what they had inadvertently caused—began to sink in.

Chaz slammed the case shut, the sound reverberating in the cramped space. He leaned back, his eyes dark with thought. The victory they had tasted moments ago had turned to ash, leaving a bitter aftertaste of failure and disbelief.

"The Vatican... they were prepared to sacrifice the Buffer," Chaz muttered, grappling with the enormity of what had transpired. "Michael knew we were coming, and he chose to destroy it rather than let it be used by others."

The younger operative, still grappling with the reality of their actions, spoke up hesitantly. "Cardinal, what does this mean for us? If the Buffer is gone, then—"

Chaz cut him off sharply, his mind racing with the implications. "It means the game has changed. We thought we were stealing a chess piece, but we were merely pawns in a larger strategy. Michael and his Vatican cohorts have shown they'll go to any lengths to protect their secrets."

His voice was a mix of anger and grudging respect. This unexpected turn of events had shifted his perspective of the Vatican and Father Michael Dominic. The priest had made a bold, sacrificial move, elevating him in Chaz's eyes from a mere guardian to a formidable strategist.

The van continued its journey through the streets of Rome, but the mood had irrevocably darkened. Thoughts of celebration were replaced by a somber reckoning. Chaz's thoughts were already on the future, plotting a course through this new, unpredictable landscape.

But it was clear his future excluded life in Rome, even his role in the Church, as he had known it. He only hoped the CIA still had a place for him.

CHAPTER
FIFTY-THREE

In the deep recesses of the Secret Archives lab beneath the Vatican's Pigna Courtyard, Michael and Hana gathered with their trusted team members to debrief the latest operation: Karl, Lukas, Ian, and the entire fabrication crew. The air was tinged with both relief and tension. Michael, standing at the head of the table, commended everyone for constructing the fake Aegis Buffer —one that had no function other than to serve as a decoy while the rest of his plan was executed—or otherwise safeguarding the genuine Buffer from being stolen. Ian's ability to create serviceable reproductions of da Vinci's blueprint parchments for the device was just the faux icing on the cake. Their strategic misdirection had worked, but O'Reilly's escape was a bitter pill to swallow.

Around the table, curiosity sparked. "Where's the real Aegis Buffer, then?" one team member ventured. Michael's enigmatic smile was the only response, a silent affirmation of the unspoken rule: the less they knew, the safer the operation. Understanding dawned on each face, a collective realization that some secrets were best kept even from themselves. Their role was clear; they were guardians of a truth too vital to risk. And, should some worldly or illicit power use one of the two Celestial Guardians as a warning of their power, then the Buffer would be available to mitigate that effort.

As the team dispersed, leaving Michael and Hana alone, the weight of their recent trials hung in the air. Hana reached for her coat, ready to step back into the shadows of their clandestine life, but Michael's voice halted her. There was a vulnerability in his eyes she hadn't seen before.

His words heavy with unspoken emotion, he confessed about his struggles with commitment, rooted in a childhood shadowed by the mostly lifelong absence of a father. Love was a labyrinth to him, but in its center, undeniably, was his love for her. He asked for patience, a chance to navigate his inner turmoil.

Hana listened, her heart echoing his sincerity. She saw in him a man of profound commitment, not bound by conventional labels but by a deeper, more primal bond. That was the essence of their connection, beyond vows or ceremonies.

As they stood in the quiet aftermath of confessions, Hana stepped closer, her decision clear. She needed no legal or spiritual validation. Their love, tested and true, was their anchor. And with a smile that spoke volumes, she sealed their understanding with a passionate kiss, a promise of a future written in the stars they both guarded.

EPILOGUE

Staffed continuously and equipped with state-of-the-art communications and data processing systems, the National Military Command Center, or NMCC, functions as the nerve center for military operations and national security coordination, providing a constant link between the President of the United States, the Secretary of Defense, and senior military leaders. Due to its critical role in national defense and security, its exact location and layout within the Pentagon are closely guarded secrets.

Currently tasked with carrying out its most highly classified operation in recent memory, several key center personnel had converged around Fat Albert, the primary workstation assigned to Operation Hawking and the one now possessing the launch codes for the convergence of asteroids on key structures in Novaya Zemlya. This targeted Russian archipelago sat in the Arctic Ocean and had been used for nuclear testing, including the 1961 detonation of the Tsar Bomba, the most powerful nuclear weapon ever tested.

∾

THE AIR in the NMCC was thick with tension, a palpable sense of imminent, world-altering decision-making hanging over the room like a heavy fog. Hushed conversations ceased abruptly as the room's oversized digital clock ticked down to the critical moment. Eyes flickered between the clock and the large, imposing screen dominating the front wall, displaying a live feed of the Novaya Zemlya archipelago, an isolated blip in the vast, icy expanse of the Arctic Ocean.

At the center of it all sat the sophisticated, high-security workstation dubbed Fat Albert, humming quietly amid the storm of silent anticipation. Its screens glowed with a myriad of data, projections, and trajectories related to Operation Hawking—the United States' bold, controversial plan to demonstrate its new celestial might.

The operation was simple yet audacious: to remotely direct a controlled asteroid toward a deserted area in Novaya Zemlya, showcasing the Celestial Guardian's capability to commandeer cosmic forces. It was a display intended more for its psychological impact than physical destruction, a message of deterrence wrapped in a demonstration of unparalleled technological prowess.

Major General Griff Carter, a stern figure with decades of military strategy etched into his weathered face, stepped forward. His hand hovered over the red button on Fat Albert's console, the final step in a series of carefully calculated commands. Beside him, a team of the nation's top astrophysicists and military strategists held their collective breath, their careers and, perhaps, the fate of international diplomacy balancing precariously on the edge of this moment.

"General, are we absolutely certain the impact zone is clear?" whispered an advisor, his voice barely audible.

Carter didn't take his eyes off the screen. "Satellite and recon confirm zero activity. We proceed."

In a distant, classified location, a team of operatives monitored the target asteroid, previously nudged into a calculated trajectory. Now, under the Celestial Guardian's influence, it was a mere pawn in a grand geopolitical chess game.

The general's finger descended slowly, a deliberate motion that seemed to draw out for an eternity. With a soft click, the command was sent, echoing silently through the high-security channels of the Pentagon.

On the screen, the live satellite feed showed a serene, snowy landscape, untouched and unaware of the cosmic force hurtling toward it. For a few heartbeats, nothing happened. Then, as if on cue, a bright streak appeared in the sky above Novaya Zemlya, growing larger and more menacing by the second.

In the command center, not a single person moved. They were transfixed, watching as the asteroid entered the atmosphere, its fiery descent a stark contrast against the cold, blue-white backdrop of the Arctic.

This was more than a test of technology; it was a statement, a line drawn in the celestial sand.

The message was sent. The power of the Celestial Guardian was no longer a secret but an open warning to all other countries of one nation's power. The United States had just changed the rules of geopolitical engagement, and the world would never be the same again.

~

FICTION, FACT, OR FUSION?

Many readers have asked me to distinguish fact from fiction in my books. Generally, I like to take factual events and historical figures and build on them in creative ways—but much of what I do write is historically accurate. In this section, I'll review some of the chapters where questions may arise, with hopes it may help those wondering where reality meets creative writing.

PROLOGUE

Although, to the best of my knowledge, Leonardo did not invent a Celestial Guardian, the two events mentioned—the conjunction of Mars, Saturn, and Venus in 1504 and the appearance of the Comet C/1506 Y1—were both actual events during his lifetime.

The concept of asteroids as we understand it today didn't exist during the time Leonardo lived (1452-1519). The scientific understanding of the solar system was vastly different during the Renaissance. The first asteroid, Ceres, wasn't discovered until 1801, nearly three centuries after da Vinci's death. Thus, while da Vinci was a man far ahead of his time in many respects, it's unlikely that he would have understood or predicted the impact of an asteroid in the way that we understand it today. However, he could have theoretically observed and recorded unusual celestial events and their potential terrestrial impacts, as was common with other scholars of the period.

CHAPTER 5

In 1809, shortly after annexing the Papal States as the property of France and arresting Pope Pius VII, Napoleon claimed title to the Vatican Archives and directed that they be shipped to Paris, where it seemed only natural that the world's greatest library and art collections should reside. Officials of the French National Archives were thus dispatched to Rome, where they packed up everything they could find into some three thousand cases, which were then escorted back to Paris in hundreds of fortified wagons drawn by teams of oxen and mules.

Following Napoleon's abdication in 1814, a decree was issued for the repatriation of all books, parchments, and other treasures taken from Rome. But it soon became evident that in the interim much of the collection had been pilfered or was otherwise unaccounted for. Indeed, of the three thousand cases originally seized from the Vatican alone, no more than seven hundred found their way back to Italy. It was later learned that one of the obstacles in effecting restitution was the vast expense necessary to pack and transport the shipments. And in one of history's most lamentable decisions, papal commissioners—conveniently influenced heavily by the chief French archivist—judged that great masses of documents were of insufficient interest or value to warrant the expense of their return all the way back to Rome, and so they were either retained by the French Library, or sold off by weight for use in making cardboard and as wrapping paper for fish and meats in the butcher shops of Paris.

CHAPTER 7

In the event of such a devastating threat as an asteroid impacting Earth, as described, the catastrophic fallout revealed here is realistic, based on information taken from official sources whose job it is to plan for such things. Just think of the cataclysmic Chicxulub impactor on the Yucatan peninsula sixty-six million years ago, the one that killed off the dinosaurs and other mass extinctions. Estimates of that asteroid's size vary, but it is generally thought to have been about ten to fifteen kilometers (six to nine miles) in diameter.

CHAPTER 23

The honor of naming asteroids falls primarily to the discoverers of these celestial objects. The process is overseen by the International Astronomical Union (IAU), which is the global authority for naming celestial bodies and their surface features.

Here is an overview of how the process typically works:

1. Discovery and Provisional Naming: When an asteroid is first discovered, it is given a provisional name by the discoverer. This provisional name usually includes the year of discovery and an alphanumeric code indicating the order of discovery within that year.

2. Observation Period: After its initial discovery, the asteroid is observed for several years to precisely determine its orbit. This is crucial because the IAU requires a confirmed, stable orbit before an official name can be assigned.

3. Suggestion of a Name: Once the asteroid's orbit is confirmed, the discoverer has the privilege to suggest a name for the asteroid. This name could be inspired by mythology, history, cultural figures, or even personal names, subject to certain rules and conventions set by the IAU.

4. IAU's Approval: The suggested name is then submitted to the IAU, specifically to its Small Bodies Nomenclature (CSBN) committee. The CSBN reviews the proposal to ensure it adheres to the IAU's naming conventions. These conventions include guidelines like avoiding offensive names, overly commercial names, or names too similar to existing celestial bodies.

5. Official Naming and Publication: Once the CSBN approves the name, it becomes the asteroid's official designation. The name is then published in the Minor Planet Circulars, making it internationally recognized.

It's worth noting that while the right to name an asteroid is traditionally given to its discoverer, in some cases, the discoverer may involve the public or specific communities in the naming process, especially in the case of particularly significant or interesting discoveries. However, the final submission and approval always go through the IAU's established process.

CHAPTER 30

Alas, the Vatican's "Peter's Eye" satellite is the product of "Gary's Imagination." To the best of my knowledge, the Church doesn't have its own satellite. Yet. If they did, I do think Oculus Petri would be a fitting name for it.

The Vatican does have access to satellite services through agreements with other countries or commercial providers for telecommunications, broadcasting, and other purposes. The Vatican's radio station, Vatican Radio, uses satellite technology to broadcast its programming around the world, as one example.

EPILOGUE

Novaya Zemlya, a Russian archipelago in the Arctic Ocean, was used by the USSR in the 1960s for nuclear testing, including detonation of the most powerful nuclear weapon ever tested, known as Tsar Bomba during the Soviet Union era.

AUTHOR'S NOTE

Dealing with issues of theology, religious beliefs, and the fictional treatment of historical biblical events can be a daunting affair.

I would ask all readers to view this story for what it is—a work of pure fiction, adapted from the seeds of many oral traditions and the historical record, at least as we know it today.

Apart from telling an engaging story, I have no agenda here, and respect those of all beliefs, from Agnosticism to Zoroastrianism and everything in between.

* * *

Thank you for reading *The Celestial Guardian*. I hope you enjoyed it and, if you haven't already, I suggest you pick up the story in the earlier books of The Magdalene Chronicles series—*The Magdalene Deception*, *The Magdalene Reliquary*, and *The Magdalene Veil*—and look forward to forthcoming books featuring the same characters and a few new ones in the continuing Vatican Secret Archive Thrillers series.

When you have a moment, may I ask that you leave a review on Amazon, Goodreads, Facebook, and perhaps elsewhere you find convenient? Reviews are crucial to a book's success, and I hope for The Magdalene Chronicles and the Vatican Secret Archive Thrillers series to have a long and entertaining life.

You can easily leave your review on Amazon by going to https://garymcavoy.link/wyhYRS. And thank you!

If you would like to reach out for any reason, you can email me at gary@garymcavoy.com. If you'd like to learn more about me and my other books, visit my website at www. garymcavoy.com, where you can also sign up for my private mailing list.

With kind regards,

Gary
McAvoy